DEADLY SECRETS

DEADLY SECRETS

PENNY ZELLER

Dedicated to Becky. Thank you for being the best sister ever.
I thank God every day for you.

"Even though I walk through the valley of the shadow of death, I will fear no evil, for you are with me; your rod and your staff, they comfort me."
~ Psalm 23:4

PROLOGUE

Betrayal had consequences.

He drove his truck to a spot in the forested area far from his own property, put it in park, and killed the engine. At first, the pounding rain and lightning flashing across the sky irritated him. He'd much prefer a calm and dry evening.

But as he thought about it more, the weather was perfect for his plan.

He opened the tailgate and pulled his victim to the edge by his feet. Good thing he was fairly strong and could heave him over his shoulder. Otherwise, this might have caused a glitch in his plans.

And he hated glitches.

His heart pounding in his ears, he trudged through sloppy mud puddles to a flat meadow area. A roar of thunder greeted him as he plopped the body on the ground and went back for a shovel.

Mud was heavy when sopping wet, and he'd have to really work to complete the hole and get on his way.

A flash of light caught his attention, and he instinctively ducked as a vehicle passed on the distant road. Likely, they couldn't see him through the rain, but who wanted to take chances? His own truck was obscured, but out here in the section just beyond pines and aspens, he wasn't as concealed.

Thankfully, he'd started on this project a few days ago, and it was only a matter of shoveling out the water, firming up the hole, and plunking his former friend into it.

He prided himself on using a less messy alternative to his gun. Not that he was above using his gun, because he wasn't. As a matter of fact, that would have been quicker. But the poison worked just as well.

A half hour later, he completed the task, retreated to the shelter of his truck, and started the drive back home. He'd toss his muddy boots in some dumpster in another town along the way to the city airport. Then he'd vacuum out his truck, park it in the airport parking lot, and rest and relax on the plane until he reached his destination.

Too bad the destination wasn't somewhere like Hawaii or the Caribbean instead of some dumb training for work. But it all fit together nicely since, if anyone decided to accuse him of anything, he'd have an alibi.

Besides, no one would ever find the body in the first place. His betrayer had some issues, and some might even believe—and he'd help them with believing it even more when they came to ask if he'd seen his former friend—that the man had wandered off and left town.

He chuckled to himself. Could a plan be more perfect? Add that to the fact that the burial ground, as he called it, was owned by an old codger who refused to sell it, and no one would ever find his betrayer. No one would even realize he'd met his demise.

Yep, the plan was perfect. His betrayer only had two friends, and he'd tell the cops when they asked that his former friend had talked of heading to the city for work. That he'd mentioned often about moving and looking for a better-paying job than the employment this pathetic town had to offer.

No one would ever know the truth.

Yes, betrayal did, indeed, have consequences.

ONE

TWO YEARS LATER

There was nothing like a good run to release any lingering tension from the day's events.

Harper Amerson tugged on her sweatshirt, grabbed her gym bag, and traversed the winding halls of Lake Radford Family Fitness Center. She waved at the purple-haired teen at the front desk. "Have a great evening, Bettina."

Bettina said nothing, only rolled her eyes and tapped her black-painted fingernails on the counter.

Harper stepped out of the main door of the fitness center and followed the sidewalk to the south side, where she'd parked her SUV. When she'd arrived, there had been few parking spots due to a boys' basketball tournament. Now, with the exception of three or four cars—likely owned by employees—the parking lot was empty.

An owl hooted from its perch on a telephone pole, and in the sky, dark clouds merged over a half-moon. Harper shivered at the cold, early January weather. She startled when a car on the adjacent street backfired, sending up a plume of black smoke.

Harper adjusted her gym bag on her shoulder and quickened her pace.

At least she'd parked beneath a streetlight, even if she accumulated more than her share of steps just to reach her vehicle.

Dad would tell her to keep her wits about her, which she did. She commonly exercised after work, and with the fitness center closing at eight, was usually out the door and on her way home well before that time.

Most of the time.

Tonight, she'd had to wait for a treadmill, which allowed her to do some strength training before running. Unfortunately, that wait also meant she needed to eat a snack beforehand because of the risk of a hypoglycemic attack.

She spied her SUV in the distance, peered about in an efficient perusal of her surroundings, and carefully stepped off the curb to cross to the overflow parking area.

A truck with blaring music whizzed past, going faster than prudent in the twenty-mph speed limit zone, and she jumped back onto the curb. Her chest seized, even as her pulse pounded. One millisecond later, and he would have hit her.

Thank You, Lord.

Harper glanced at her fitness tracker watch—7:45. Fifteen minutes until the fitness center closed. Tomorrow she'd make it a point to get there earlier than six, even if it meant cutting an appointment short. Clients came first, but some liked to visit far past regular business hours.

Exhaling several deep breaths in an attempt to calm herself, Harper again stepped off the curb and cut across the overflow to her car.

The wind rustled through the trees planted along the road, and the scent of moisture floated in the air. Two steps from her SUV, she noticed something attached to the driver's side door and flapping in the breeze.

Had someone accidentally hit her car and left a note with insurance information? Harper peered to the left, to the right, and behind her. No one else was in the parking lot. Whoever had left the note was long gone.

The paper on her car door flapped again. Probably a prank or an advertisement.

She drew closer and tapped the "unlock" on her key fob, expecting the interior lights to illuminate the vehicle as the doors unlocked. But the car remained dark. She held the fob up to the dimness of the flickering streetlight. Yes, she'd been clicking the correct button. She tried again, bemoaning the fact that her fob battery was likely dead and she'd have to manually unlock the door.

It shouldn't surprise her. The fob had been inconsistent lately—sometimes working, sometimes not. Harper groaned. This morning had been hectic, but this was an excellent reminder to switch it with the new one she'd just purchased.

As she drew closer, she squinted and read the words on paper, mocking her in the shadowy night.

In black marker, the words, 'GO AWAY OR ELSE', were haphazardly written in all caps on a white sheet of typing paper.

She inhaled a sharp breath as a shudder worked its way through her. Was someone attempting to be funny? Or perhaps the author of the note had the wrong vehicle. Hers wasn't the only mid-sized red SUV in Lake Radford.

Harper scanned the words once more, then lifted her head to again survey the area, her gaze resting on the doctor's office across the street. Someone lurked near the corner in the shadows, the sparks of a cigarette flickering in the dark alcove.

Probably just someone loitering, but she wouldn't take that chance.

Harper fumbled to manually unlock the door, but instead dropped her keys. They clanged, echoing in the otherwise eerily quiet night as they hit the asphalt. She was about to stoop and retrieve the clump of keys when she heard footsteps. The person from across the street had pushed off the wall and started in her direction, efficiently gaining ground with his brisk stride.

There was no time to grab her keys. No time to unlock her car and drive away. No time to…

She willed her lead-filled feet to move and sent a prayer heavenward.

Finally, in what could only be attributed to an answer to prayer, Harper pivoted and stumbled across the parking lot and back to the fitness center.

Footfalls indicated the stranger's close proximity and prodded her forward. She missed the curb, tripped, and fell forward, her gym bag crashing to the sidewalk.

Pain in her knee twinged, and with clumsy effort, she stood and limped a few paces before again hastening her pace.

Cold engulfed her even as sweat trickled down her back.

Dare she look behind her again?

Why was the sidewalk so much longer than usual? Why was it taking her forever to reach the main entrance? Her breath came out in a foggy puff as the gym bag slapped against her right leg.

She passed by a small window to one of the fitness center offices and caught a blurred glimpse of the profile of the person chasing her. Fear's dangerous tendrils crawled up her legs and settled into her stomach. Who was he? What did he want? Why was he following her? Was he trying to scare her, or was he attempting to grab her? Had he left the note? Where was everyone? Surely, she wasn't the last to leave. Where were the employees?

The questions pummeled her in tandem with the raindrops now spitting from the sky.

Hot breath brushed her neck. He reached out, his fingers skimming her arm, and she shrugged away while simultaneously screaming and propelling herself forward.

Not much farther now...

Finally, Harper reached her destination and yanked on one of the double doors.

Locked.

She tried the other.

Where was the man from across the street? Was he still following her?

Finally, Jasper Cerutti, the night janitor and maintenance man, turned the key in the deadbolt lock and held open the door for her.

"Harper? Is everything all right?"

She brushed past him, past the entryway, and into the foyer where three other employees, including Bettina, stood gaping at her.

"Can you please lock the door, Jasper?"

Jasper nodded. After double-checking it was locked, he turned toward her. "What's wrong?"

"Someone was out there chasing me."

"Chasing you?" Concern lit his expression, and he double-checked to ensure the door was locked.

Harper's heart pounded so loudly in her ears that she could scarcely hear anything else. "I just—I just need to call 911." She fumbled her phone, causing it to crash to the white-tiled floor.

"Can we just go home?" Bettina whined.

"Patience, Watson," another worker, Enzo, a young man in his early twenties, responded.

Marilyn, a sweet grandmotherly woman who assisted at the front desk, patted Harper on the back. "That's scary. Is he still out there?"

"I'm not sure, and I dropped my keys."

"I can walk you to your car," suggested Jasper. He stared out the front door. "I've got a flashlight I can bring so we can find your keys."

The man had always been willing to help out the best he could. Probably why he received *Employee of the Year* last year.

"No, I need to call 911. For other reasons too."

Bettina rolled her eyes. "You can walk *me* out, Jasper. I'm ready to go home."

Harper's hands shook as she hit the emergency button on her cell.

"911, what is your emergency?"

"I'm at The Lake Radford Family Fitness Center, and there's a suspicious person outside who was following me—and I found a note on my car."

"Are you somewhere safe?"

"Yes, ma'am. I'm inside the building."

"Please wait there. An officer is on the way. I'll stay on the phone with you until they arrive."

Dizziness distorted her vision, and Harper gripped the counter.

Jasper strode to the entryway and pressed his face against the door. "I don't see anyone," he said.

Bettina resumed her incessant tapping on the counter. "Good. Then let's go home."

"Why are you in such a hurry?" Enzo asked.

"Would you want to stay here?"

"It's my job. I'm here until we lock up."

Bettina shook her head and muttered something under her breath in her typical passive-aggressive fashion.

"I think it's best if we just wait here until the police come," said Marilyn, the voice of reason.

Jasper jangled his ring of keys. "They should be here any minute."

Marilyn draped an arm around Harper's shoulders. "You mentioned something about a note. What kind of note?"

The words flashed in her mind again. Was it from the same person slinking in the darkness?

A police cruiser pulled up directly in front of the main entrance, and Jasper unlocked the door. Two police officers entered.

A sleety mixture splattered against the windows. Harper shivered.

"I'm Officer Baldwin, and this is Officer Uchida. A reporting party called about someone chasing them and a note?"

"That was me, yes." Harper stepped forward.

Bettina shoved off the counter. "I didn't see anything, and I would like to get home."

"Yes, ma'am, and you will soon, but first we have a few questions."

Bettina rolled her eyes.

"Can you describe to me what happened?"

"Yes, I was walking out of the center when I saw a note on my car."

"What did the note say?"

"'Go away or else'."

Marilyn gasped. Jasper's eyes widened. Bettina sighed an exaggerated breath, and Enzo furrowed his brows.

The officers took notes, and Harper relayed the information about the man following her. When it became evident that Marilyn, Enzo, Jasper, and Bettina had no knowledge of the happenings, Officer Uchida accompanied them to their respective vehicles.

"Unfortunately, due to the rain, the note is likely no longer legible. Do you know of anyone who would want to leave it on your car? Perhaps as a joke?"

"No."

"Any enemies?"

Harper inhaled a sharp breath. "There's only one person I can think of who doesn't like me, and that's a coworker."

"What is the coworker's name?"

"Clark Montayne."

"Where are you employed?"

"Lake Radford Realty and Rentals."

Officer Baldwin scribbled the words. "And Mr. Montayne works there as well?"

"Yes, sir, but I doubt he would do this."

Jasper raised a finger. "Sir?"

"Yes?"

"I'm the night janitor and evening maintenance man for the center, and I did see Mr. Montayne here tonight. He comes here most nights of the week for cardio and weights."

"All right, thank you." Officer Baldwin redirected his attention to Harper. "Now, tell me about the man who followed you."

"I first noticed him across the street, hovering near the doctor's office. I dropped my keys, which are still out there..."

"Officer Uchida, would you mind seeing if you can locate her keys?"

The other officer nodded and left the building.

"Do you have a description of the man?"

"He was smoking a cigarette, and I was only able to see a blurred image of him."

"And he followed you?"

Harper closed her eyes, attempting to recall the incident. "Yes. I was trying to manually unlock my car door. I accidentally dropped my keys and noticed he was coming toward me, so I started running back to the gym. He was pursuing me and even attempted to grab my arm before I was able to get away. I caught a blurry glimpse of him in the small office window just before the front doors."

Officer Baldwin scribbled more notes. "Anyone else outside when this happened?"

"No, sir."

Officer Baldwin directed his next question to Jasper. "Is there anyone left in the building?"

"No. I believe Harper was the last member to leave. Usually, Enzo attempts to let members know at fifteen-minute intervals so the front desk workers don't have to stay late. People were pretty good about leaving on time today."

"Are there cameras on the south side of the building facing the doctor's office?"

"No cameras are pointing in the direction of the overflow parking. The board has discussed installing some, but as of yet, has not done so."

"And what about on the side where the small window is, where she said she saw the man's reflection?"

"Yes. The front of the building is well covered." Jasper scratched his head. "It wasn't too long ago that we didn't need this type of surveillance."

"Times have been changing in Lake Radford over the past couple of years with the influx of people moving in. Ms. Amerson, have you ever had any threats made against you?"

"No."

"You mentioned you worked at the realty company. Could there be someone who might have a vendetta against you for a business reason?"

Harper ran through the clients she'd served for the past two years in her capacity as an agent. "Not that I can think of. I help people find new homes or sell the ones they've outgrown. It's a positive experience for most people."

Officer Baldwin closed his notebook. "If you think of anything else, please let us know. My hunch is that the note was either a joke—albeit in poor taste—or perhaps stuck on the wrong vehicle in error. As for the man who followed you, we will be looking into this. Mr. Cerutti, where exactly are the cameras on the building?"

Jasper explained in detail where all of the cameras were located. "I'd be happy to go over the footage with you, with permission from my boss, of course."

"Yes, thank you," said Officer Baldwin.

Officer Uchida returned with Harper's keys.

"Ms. Amerson, Officer Uchida will accompany you to your vehicle and follow you home. I have your phone number, and someone will be in touch tomorrow after we've gone over the camera footage."

"Thank you, sir."

Officer Baldwin was likely correct about the note, but who was the man who'd followed her?

TWO

By the time she reached home, it was too late to call anyone, although it would have been nice to hear Mom's or Dad's words of reassurance.

Even if they were 2,000 miles away, temporarily caring for Grandma and Grandpa after Grandpa's stroke.

Officer Uchida checked the area around Harper's house and the interior and reassured her that there was nothing amiss.

Harper tossed and turned, sleep elusive as the sleet pounded on her roof. Had she made too much of the note? And what if she was incorrect about the man? What if he was just crossing the street to get across, and wasn't truly following her? But why then did he attempt to grab her arm?

Second-guessing herself and overthinking were, unfortunately, second nature. Harper lifted her worries to the Lord, prayed for Him to bless her with a good night's sleep, then rolled over once again.

Finally, at some time mere hours before she would have to arise, she fell asleep.

Early the next day, Harper replaced her former fob with the new one she'd purchased a few weeks ago and hit the remote start button on her SUV. She'd just finished getting ready for work when she saw her neighbor, Mrs. Satterwhite, with curlers in her hair, no coat, and wearing her purple nightgown and slippers.

"Mrs. Satterwhite?"

"Oh, Harper, I'm so glad you're up and about. I've lost Coco. I took her out for a bathroom break, and she bolted down the street."

Harper wrapped an arm around the woman's thin shoulders. "Why don't you go in and call animal control, and in the meantime, I'll search for Coco."

"Oh, thank you, dear. It is a mite bit chilly out here."

"Which way did she go?"

Mrs. Satterwhite pointed to the east. "Thataway."

Harper assisted the woman back into the house, then hurried in the direction Mrs. Satterwhite indicated, her heels tapping on the sidewalk as she attempted to avoid the mud-caked areas.

"Coco!"

The chocolate poodle was known to run off, and Harper had, just last Sunday, spoken to the elders at her church about constructing a fence behind Mrs. Satterwhite's house so she would have somewhere safe to let Coco out.

Harper checked her fitness tracker—7:50. She had an 8:00 appointment with some new clients looking for a four-bedroom, two-bath. But she couldn't just leave Coco out in the cold, especially since the dog was Mrs. Satterwhite's treasured companion.

"Coco!" she called several more times. When she reached the end of the block, she scanned in both directions. No sign of the dog.

It was a toss-up which way to go next, so she chose the right. She called for the pet several more times before removing her cell phone from her coat pocket. Keeping her eyes peeled while multitasking, Harper called the administrative assistant and let her know she'd be a few minutes late.

"No worries. Your eight o'clock isn't even here yet, so you're good," said Loretta.

Animal control should be there soon, provided they weren't on another call when Mrs. Satterwhite contacted them. Harper peeked behind trash cans, flower pots, and around trees.

Finally, the curly-haired dog emerged from behind a shed, her tail wagging. Harper reached over, scooped her up, and patted her on the head. "Coco, you can't run off like that. It would devastate Mrs. Satterwhite if something happened to you."

Coco responded with a yip and several licks on Harper's hand.

Fifteen minutes later, after returning Coco, Harper climbed into her car and headed for work.

The parking lot, as usual, was full. She steered toward the dedicated section for employees at the far end. That's when she noticed an expensive black car with tinted windows straddling two spots.

Not just any expensive black car, but Clark Montayne's car. The vehicle overlapped her space, so there wasn't enough room for her to park.

Typical of Clark.

But that was not acceptable, especially today when she was already late. Harper took pride in providing excellent customer service and maintaining returning clients. That wouldn't happen if she was half an hour late.

Which she was.

Harper backed out and perused the parking lot, settling on a vacant spot intended for customers. She whipped into it, exited her SUV, and ran to the front door of the building.

"Hello, sorry I'm late."

Loretta pointed to a couple talking with Clark. "That's your 8:00," she mouthed.

Leave it to Clark to exhibit his "hospitality".

"Hello, Mr. and Mrs. McAlpin?"

A man in an expensive suit turned toward her, a woman with heavy makeup and perfectly coiffed, shoulder-length, dyed blonde hair following his lead. "Are you Harper Amerson?"

"Yes, sir. I apologize for being late. Something came up, and my neighbor needed my help." She stepped to the side. "My office is just this way."

"Thank you, Mr. and Mrs. McAlpin. If you ever need anything—anything at all, please do not hesitate to reach out." Clark shook hands with them both before the couple, somewhat reluctantly, followed Harper to her office down the hall.

She led them inside, shook their hands, and offered them the two seats in front of her desk. "Once again, I do apologize."

The couple said nothing, only exchanged glances.

"On the phone, you mentioned you were in the market for a four-bedroom, two-bath home..."

"Ms. Amerson, with all due respect, might we..." The woman pursed her red-lipstic ked lips and deferred to her husband.

"Since we already started speaking with Clark, we'd prefer to go with him." Mr. McAlpin stood and pulled out his wife's chair.

"Oh. That's fine. I'll lead you to his office."

"No need. We know where it is."

Harper watched as they left. Just as well. Some people were better suited for Clark.

She leaned back in her chair, mentally listing all that she needed to do today. Thoughts of last night re-entered her mind. Had the police found anything on the gym's cameras? Would the man attempt to follow her again? Leave another note? Were the man and the note writer one and the same?

An hour later, she was preparing a comparative market analysis when she heard an abrupt knock.

"Door is open," she said before spinning around to see Clark standing in the doorway, his arms folded across his chest.

"Hello, Clark."

"Are you really that vindictive?"

"What are you talking about?"

Clark unfolded his arms, clenched his fists by his sides, and shot a fiery gaze in her direction. "Don't pretend you don't know, Harper," he hissed between gritted teeth. He stomped in, shut the door behind him, and forcefully pushed a chair aside, cornering her behind her desk.

Harper stood, her legs attempting to buckle. While she didn't believe Clark to be dangerous—narcissistic, yes, but dangerous no—one never knew for sure. And he had always intimidated her. "What are you talking about?" she asked, her voice wavering.

He breathed heavily, the acrid stench of cigarette smoke emitting from him as he growled his words. "You told the cops I was following you last night. Do you know how embarrassing that was to have them sitting in the reception area waiting for me and having Mr. and Mrs. McAlpin see them?" His face reddened, and he reached up to loosen the collar of his expensive shirt.

Right. She had mentioned to Officer Baldwin that the only one she knew who didn't like her was her coworker, Clark Montayne.

"I apologize if it was embarrassing."

"You're not sorry. You're just trying to undermine me because I'm doing a much better job here than you are."

"That's not it at all. I had a frightening experience last night, and they asked if I knew of anyone who disliked me."

"I'm quite sure I'm not the only one who, quote, dislikes you." Clark put air quotes around the word "dislike."

A knock on the door sounded, and their boss, Paulette, entered. "Is everything all right in here?"

In the instant it took to blink, Clark's persona changed. "Good morning, Paulette. Yes, everything is just fine."

"That's good to know. I thought I heard some yelling."

Clark shrugged. "No, no yelling. Harper and I were just chatting about some things."

Paulette looked from Clark to Harper. "Harper?"

"We were having a discussion."

"All right, well, just thought I'd check. When you're finished, Clark, could you meet me in my office? It seems we received another rave review for a house you sold last month."

Clark's pseudo grin lit up his face but didn't reach his hard brown eyes. "I'll be right in."

Paulette left, and Clark propped himself against the front of her desk, a vein pulsing in his jaw. "As I told the cops, I wouldn't be following you on a cold, rainy night, and I certainly would not be leaving you notes," he sneered. "You're barely worth the time it takes to speak to you."

"Tell me how you really feel," Harper managed to squeeze past him and point at the door. "Have a nice day, Clark."

Once Clark stormed out, Harper plopped back into her chair, relieved that was over. Paulette was a good boss but totally blinded by Clark's manipulative ways.

There was some sort of one-sided, unspoken competition between Harper and Clark, although Clark had been there longer, had more clients, and sold far more houses.

And, while Harper was competitive when it came to sports, she wouldn't consider herself that way at work. She was just grateful for a job she loved, an office full of coworkers, 99% of whom she liked, and a way to help clients reach their home ownership goals.

She resumed working on the comparative marketing analysis, noting that this week would be busy, not that she was complaining. Real estate ebbed and flowed, and since she worked on commissions, Harper welcomed a full schedule.

The phone rang, and she lifted the handset, grateful for a diversion. "Harper Amerson, may I help you?"

"Hello, Harper, this is Mrs. Medill."

"Mrs. Medill, so nice to hear from you. What can I do for you?"

"We were wondering if we might have a second look at the Cox property."

"Absolutely. I have an opening in my schedule this afternoon."

There was a pause on the other end of the line before Mrs. Medill spoke again. "Oh, how I wish we could see it again this afternoon, but we're getting ready to leave town. Would next Wednesday work?"

Harper checked her schedule. "I have an opening next Wednesday at two o'clock."

"That would be lovely."

"Perfect. I'll meet you there then."

"Oh, and Harper?"

"Yes?"

"Has there been any other interest in it?"

Harper noted the desperation in Mrs. Medill's voice. Whoever was able to purchase the acreage with breathtaking views would be very fortunate. "I've only had one other party interested in it so far."

"All right, well, I won't worry about it. If it's meant to be, it will happen. I'll see you next week."

Harper jotted the note in her calendar and bid Mrs. Medill goodbye. At present, that listing was her most important because the owners would benefit greatly from the sale and be able to afford the treatment their son so desperately needed.

THREE

Detective Kade Lassiter studied the minimal footage from the recent burglary at a mom-and-pop business on Main Street. The lone camera, an older model with its outdated technology, left much to be desired. That, and it had run out of storage capacity, blipped, and showed such a meager amount of footage that it might as well not been used at all. The four figures in the video were all merged together in one big blur. Kade couldn't discern body types, ages, or much about their clothing from the available material. So far, the tips hadn't led to anyone finding those responsible for vandalism and stealing armloads of merchandise.

The worst part? They obviously knew what they were doing since they'd mostly avoided the camera, which meant they had cased the place.

"Detective?"

"Hey, Baldwin, come on in."

Officer Baldwin entered and plunked down on the lone folding chair in front of Kade's desk. "Any new information on the Dumaine case?"

"None yet. Any robbery is bad enough, but it's even worse when it happens to a business where the owners have given back so much to the community."

"I remember that place when I was a kid. Hard enough to make it these days, let alone when someone comes in and steals from you."

"Exactly. So, what can I do for you?"

Baldwin lounged in the chair as if it were a recliner. "Last night we answered a call at the Lake Radford Family Fitness Center. A woman found a note taped to her vehicle door before being pursued as she ran back to the building."

Kade's curiosity piqued. "Is she all right?"

"She is. Not sure what the note was all about or if it was even related to the man following her."

"What did the note say?"

"'Go away or else.'"

"'Go away or else'? That's a new one. Probably a prank." Although Kade had, in his tenure in law enforcement, become somewhat jaded and would consider the note as a possible threat as well.

Baldwin shrugged. "Could be."

"Did we find any footage of the man following her?"

"Not much. I interviewed the night janitor, who also doubles as the evening maintenance man. He said there are no cameras on that side facing the overflow parking area, but this morning, I did stop by and view the footage of the other areas of the building."

"And?"

"The cameras on the entrance side caught a brief glimpse of the man who may have been following her. It was starting to rain, so the image was obscured, and he disappeared out of range a few seconds later. We also removed a piece of the tape from the note on the car, but there were no prints. The paper had pretty much disintegrated."

Kade steepled his fingers. "Hopefully, it was a one-time deal."

"That's what I was thinking. Ms. Amerson was shaken up, and rightfully so."

"It was probably put on the wrong car and is some sort of prank."

"I agree. However, the guy following her was concerning."

Kade nodded. "Agreed. I wonder if he's the one who put the note on her car and if he was truly following her."

"She seemed to think so. We couldn't tell much from the one camera shot that we had."

"Ms. Amerson's name sounds familiar. Have we dealt with her before?"

Baldwin shook his head. "Amerson is a real estate agent, so that's why you might recognize her name."

"That's probably it."

"Chief has been apprised, but I'm not sure anything else will come of this. We'll dive a little deeper into attempting to find the guy, but for now, we've documented it. I told Ms. Amerson to reach out if she remembers anything else or has any other concerns."

"Thanks, Baldwin. Keep me posted."

"Will do."

Baldwin rose, and Kade returned his attention to solving the burglary. When he first moved here two years ago, Lake Radford was relatively safe, but there had been an uptick in crime in recent days.

One thing was certain. He aimed to solve the case that left the Dumaines in the tough situation of having to possibly close their store.

The following evening, Harper and her best friend, Kennedy Olohan, meandered down the halls of the Lake Radford Family Fitness Center. She'd clued her best friend in on the events of the previous night when they'd first arrived. Now, an hour and a half later, they'd finished their workouts.

Kennedy bopped her playfully on the arm. "I still can't believe you didn't call me right away and tell me what happened."

"I'm sorry. It was so late, and I'm just hoping it was a one-time deal. Or maybe they got the wrong person, and the note was meant for someone else. Although I can't imagine anyone would appreciate that type of note."

"Me either. 'Go away or else'? Who leaves that kind of note on someone's car? It does sound like a threat. I mean, what does 'or else' mean? What will they do if you don't go away? And go away where?"

Leave it to Kennedy to inspect all angles of the situation. That was one of the things Harper appreciated most about her friend. "I know. It is bizarre. I could overthink it nonstop because you're right, it does sound threatening. And where does this person think I should go if I do go away?" She shook her head. "It's all so weird. I was praying last night that it would just be a case of mistaken identity. But then, I really wouldn't want anyone to feel as though they were being threatened."

"I just can't understand why someone would tell you to go away. Who would have that kind of vendetta?"

"I'm not sure. The only person I could think of was Clark, but why would he do that? He's brash, narcissistic, and irritating, but..."

They passed Jasper and exchanged greetings before passing the racquetball courts. Enzo waved and smiled, and Bettina at the front desk sat in a chair, her palm resting on her cheek as she overly dramatized her boredom. Harper doubted she'd ever heard the young woman bid anyone a good evening when they left—or when they arrived.

"Who was the man across the street who followed you?"

"Not sure about that either. It wasn't anyone I had ever seen before. Of course, his face was obscured by a hood, so I couldn't tell what he looked like." Had she mistakenly thought the man was following her when, in reality, he was just walking in the same direction? How many times had she asked herself that?

Harper opened the door, and they entered the foyer. While they weren't parked directly in front of the entrance where the handicapped, senior parking, and moms with tots parked, both of them had secured spots just to the right and slightly around the corner, well within view of the cameras.

They walked out together, the cold air a sharp contrast to the overpowering heat inside the gym. Even though the sidewalks had been cleared, ice lingered, and Harper swerved around a particularly dangerous patch.

"Any news on job prospects?"

Kennedy had just recently moved back to Lake Radford and was temporarily working part-time in retail until she found a full-time permanent position.

"No, nothing yet."

They approached their vehicles, and for a brief moment, Harper's heart lurched as she recalled the note. But today, no white piece of paper flapped in the wind. She gave her friend a quick hug, clicked the fob, which turned on the lights in her

SUV, and checked the backseat. She then climbed inside and headed home.

Ten minutes later, she pulled into the driveway of her 1940s powder-blue bungalow. The craftsman-style house with its white shutters had come on the market shortly after she'd secured her job at the real estate office. She'd been fortunate to find not only a perfect-sized home with its two bedrooms and two baths, but also one that required little fixup and was in a charming older residential area.

Harper steered her SUV under the carport, locked her vehicle, and took one more scan around the neighborhood. Nothing was amiss, just the usual quiet and peaceful surroundings that drew her to move to the area. There really was no need to worry, was there? Just a fluke circumstance that would likely never happen again.

Right?

Lake Radford was a safe town for the most part, and she'd lived here all of her life. But that didn't mean there wasn't riffraff and crimes committed. All she needed to do was take a look at the crime section in the newspaper to realize one had to be aware of their surroundings, even in a town with just over 20,000 people.

Harper reheated some leftover soup from her earlier dinner. That was the thing about hypoglycemia—she practically had to graze all day, especially after working out. She covered the soup mug and set it in the microwave when her cell rang.

Mom's picture came up on the screen. "Hi, Mom."

"Harper, hello. How are you?"

She and Mom had always been close, attended church together each Sunday, and normally went to lunch once a week. But with Mom and Dad caretaking for Grandma and Grandpa in recent weeks, Harper had missed that. "I'm fine. How are you?"

"Grandpa is doing so much better, which is a huge praise. We're fortunate your dad has been able to handle some things for the business remotely because I'm not sure how long we'll be here. Grandma was walking out to get the mail yesterday and sprained her ankle as she was going down the porch stairs."

Poor Grandma. As if seeing the love of her life suffer a stroke wasn't enough. "Oh, no! Is she all right?"

"She will be, yes. She has to take it easy for a few days and stay off it. Of course, asking her to rest is a challenge." Mom laughed. "You know how she is with the various clubs she's a member of."

Harper knew that all too well. That was one of the reasons it was an undertaking to convince her and Grandpa to move back to Lake Radford after ten years in sunny Florida.

"Please keep praying they'll be agreeable to moving back to Lake Radford. While they're still able to be independent, it would be much better to have them close by. Of course, it's ultimately their decision, but I think Grandma may be edging closer to the prospect of moving back. Any news on a possible house?"

"Actually, yes. There is an opening at The Cottages." The Cottages were a cluster of little one-bedroom one-bath homes in a safe residential environment for those sixty-five and older. A nurse was on duty 24 hours a day. Each elderly resident or couple in the senior community lived in their own home and had full independence to come and go as they pleased, but with the benefit of medical care and transportation within close reach. It was difficult to secure one of the homes because they were in high demand, especially with the growing retired population in Lake Radford, but thankfully, Harper knew the manager.

"That would be perfect!"

Mom and Dad originally offered to add on to their own home and move Grandma and Grandpa into their own space, but neither grandparent had been amenable to such a plan. Likely because they were accustomed to their own place, especially Grandma's flower garden. At The Cottages, she'd be able to be a part of the community garden, perhaps even the president of it, which would be a selling point.

"I will talk to the manager. If Grandma and Grandpa agree to move here, I can put a deposit on it to hold it while Grandpa continues to heal and they both can travel." Thankfully, it had been a minor stroke, and her grandfather had been in relatively good health before that happened.

"That would be fantastic. How are things going for you?"

Harper debated whether or not to tell Mom about the incident. Her mother had a lot on her plate with Grandma and Grandpa and worrying about Dad's accounting business in Lake Radford.

"Harper, are you there?"

"I'm here. I'm just trying to decide…"

"Is it work? Has that disagreeable fellow—let's see, what's his name?"

Only Mom, at what she termed the "tender age of fifty-five," would use the vernacular *disagreeable fellow*. Harper laughed. "His name is Clark, and he's his usual self. By the way, I secured the contract to sell the Cox property."

Way to go, Harper. Divert the conversation.

"The Cox property? I had no idea that was on the market."

"It is. Shortly after Jeff and Vanna Cox inherited it, they moved to a different state for work with the plan to someday return to Lake Radford, but now need the funds from the sale to pay for their son's cancer treatment."

"Oh, dear. I hate to hear that that's the reason why they have to sell it. I'll be praying for their little boy. Awful to be going through that at any age, let alone at six."

"It's a sad situation all the way around, but I'm thankful they do have some extended family and are members of a supportive church."

"That's a lovely property. I remember your dad and me driving out that way not too long ago. It's beautiful with the view, the forested area, and the small lake."

"Probably one of the prettiest in the county. I'm interested to see who purchases it, although I honestly haven't had that many calls to show it. Just two so far." Not that it was too concerning. January was typically one of the slower real estate months.

"Glad to hear everything is going well."

"Actually, Mom, there is something that I have been debating whether or not to tell you because I don't want to burden you anymore with what's going on with Grandma and Grandpa." Would Mom think she or Dad would need to rush home if she told them?

"What is it, dear?"

She took a deep breath. Mentioning the note, but not the creepy man following her, would be sufficient. She didn't want to worry her mother, and honestly, there was nothing her parents could do 2,000 miles away. "When I walked out of the fitness center the other night, someone had taped some weird note to my car."

"A weird note? What did it say?"

"Just gibberish. I think they got the wrong car. I've turned it into the police, and they're keeping an eye on the potential situation, but I don't think anything will come of it. The police arrived, but the note was destroyed by the rain. I sensed that they weren't overly concerned."

"Well, that's good to hear the police weren't worried. Sometimes people do goofy things, and hopefully this is just one of those times. Although I'm not sure what is with people these days."

That was one of Mom's favorite statements, and truly, the world was different from the way it had been just in the past ten years.

The microwave dinged, and Harper removed her soup. "I think it was meant for someone else."

But the man who'd followed her...

They discussed several other topics before disconnecting.

Just chatting with Mom had greatly alleviated her concerns about not only her family, but also the episode at the fitness center. What she had shared of it, anyhow.

———

Kade opened *The Lake Radford Daily*. The guys at the department teased him that he was an old soul, still preferring to read the paper version of the newspaper rather than online.

He took the ribbing well, especially since no one would consider thirty-two an "old soul". He found out a lot about people through the paper, and any time that curiosity could assist with solving a crime, the entire community was better for it.

He scanned the front page.

Lake Radford Police
Investigate Burglary

Last Tuesday evening, Dumaine's Clothing, Goodies, and More was burglarized and vandalized in a brazen attempt to destroy the business that has been a mainstay in Lake Radford for over 25 years. Thieves forced their way into the closed business and stole numerous items, including nearly all of the signature Dumaine's sweatshirts and t-shirts, shoes, socks, necklaces, baseball card collectibles, and gift items. The store was ransacked, and profanity was sprayed on the walls. One window was broken, and the display case housing the baseball cards was completely destroyed. Water was poured on the cash register, and the faucet in the bathroom was left on with the sink plugged, causing significant water damage.

Police currently have no suspects. If you have any details that may help in solving this case, please contact the Lake Radford Police Department at 555-5439.

Kade exhaled a deep breath. He hated having cases left unsolved, and the longer it took him to find those responsible, the more anxiety the town felt, and rightfully so.

Would those responsible for vandalizing Dumaine's continue their crime spree? Or was it a one-time event?

Experience told him this wouldn't be the last place they chose to terrorize.

Kade flipped through the next few pages, noting nothing of interest until he came to the fourth page.

Lake Radford Realty and
Rentals Agent Spotlight

Real Estate agent Harper Amerson is in the spotlight this month. A native of Lake Radford, Amerson has been an agent with the realty office for the past two years. She matches buyers with their dream homes and assists others with selling their current homes as they move forward in the next stage of home ownership. In her spare time, she enjoys volunteering at her church, running, reading, doing crossword puzzles, and gardening. Harper is currently accepting new clients and looks forward to serving the people of Lake Radford with all of their real estate needs.

A photo of Harper Amerson graced the page. The attractive woman, a year or two younger than Kade, smiled from the advertisement. Blue eyes, long brown hair, and wearing a stylish burgundy-colored blouse, she looked every bit the part of a professional.

He stared at the picture a few minutes longer, attempting to figure out why someone would want to leave a note on her car and follow her.

Several cases demanded his attention, and Kade again looked at the scant footage of the Dumaine case before examining evidence for a rather peculiar case that had happened at one of the local big box stores.

For the second time in as many weeks, a motorized scooter had been taken from the property and dumped in a vacant weeded area in the northern corner near the interstate. Whoever the culprits were knew enough about where the outdoor cameras were located to avoid them.

Until this time. The store had installed several more, apparently unbeknownst to the thief or thieves. Was it just kids looking to cause mischief? There had been an uptick in those types of cases as of late. Or was it an adult being destructive?

Kade slowed the video footage. It caught the back of a heavyset man in a black-and-gray coat and hat, zipping out of the store, veering around cars, and heading to the weed-infested area. In the basket of the scooter were several items. Kade paused the feed.

He'd half expected to see some of the most stolen food items in the basket, namely, packaged meat or a gallon of milk. Or some of the other highly desirable items thieves stole, including alcohol, jewelry, or clothing items. However, none of these were in the basket.

However, a zoom in on the basket indicated there *were* several video games, two packs of cigarettes, a cell phone, batteries, and a pair of boots. And...Kade slowed the video, did a second, more thorough zoom on the basket, and paused it.

Was that a prescription drug envelope? The paper with the name was facing the other direction, but it was something. Whoever was stealing the scooters, or maybe even just this scooter, had picked up a prescription. Shouldn't be too hard to narrow down those who picked up their medications yesterday.

And if there was one thing Kade always endeavored to do, it was to efficiently solve and combat crime in the town he now called home.

FOUR

Harper loved her job. Helping people find new homes and start a fresh chapter in their lives gave her purpose.

She greeted the middle-aged Medills at the edge of the Cox property for the second time at two o'clock the following Wednesday. If she sold this one, it would be a huge feather in her cap, as the saying went. This was the first time the five-acre parcel in one of the prettiest areas just outside of town had been put on the market. An expensive property, which ruled out many possible buyers, but was worth it for whoever was able to snag it.

She tugged her navy coat tighter against her, attempting to keep out the chilly January air.

Mrs. Medill gasped. "I'd forgotten in just this past week how lovely it is."

"The view of the mountains is fantastic," her husband agreed.

Harper turned and scanned the entire area. To the south, mountains rose into snow-capped peaks. To the west, a forested area, thick with aspens, poplars, and pines, and to the east, a magnificent view of the town below.

Mr. Medill, a balding man in his early sixties, reached for his wife's hand. "We've always wanted to build a house."

"Oh, yes. We've lived in several throughout the years, but we've never built our own."

"I know you are having a tough time deciding between this one and the Tippens property," said Harper.

Mr. Medill nodded. "We like that the other acreage is closer to town. At our age..."

His wife playfully jabbed him in the arm. "At our age? We're just starting our sixties. It's not like we're in our nineties."

He laughed, and the two of them walked with Harper past the flat building area and into the grove of trees.

Even in the cold of winter with no foliage, the acreage was stunning. Harper could imagine the Medills walking their dog through the area on a sunny day. "We didn't walk back here last time since it was snowing, but we can walk the length of it if you'd like. Just watch for the mud." She pointed out other aspects of the acreage before adding, "Perhaps one of the best amenities is that there are no nearby neighbors. It has a country feel, despite being in the city limits."

"Oh, yes, we like how private it is, and we would like to see the entire property," said Mrs. Medill. "Seems it didn't get as much moisture here as it did at our rental."

Harper recalled the sleet last week as she'd hovered in the fitness center answering the police officer's questions, and shuddered. Hopefully, nothing more would come of that incident. So far, there had been no more notes on her car and no more sightings of the man who'd opted to chase her. She returned her attention to the Medills. "There's a small creek at the edge of the property and a natural pond as well."

"Wouldn't the grandkids love the creek?" Mrs. Medill clutched her husband's arm as they traversed through the damp weeds.

"And the pond as well. Do you know if there's fish in it?"

"Back in the day, Mr. Cox stocked it."

The Medills conversed between themselves, discussing all the plans they'd have for taking the grandchildren fishing and then sitting beneath the stars for s'mores. "Almost like camping," added Mrs. Medill.

A branch snapped, and Harper startled.

"Probably just a critter," said Mr. Medill. "Harper did say the wildlife was abundant."

The clouds drifted across the sun, causing a gloomy ambiance in contrast with the former mostly sunny conditions.

A gunshot crackled through the air.

Harper dropped to the ground, pulling the Medills down with her. The hairs on the back of her neck stood on end as her heart pounded in her chest. It sounded so close.

"Is someone hunting this time of year?" Mr. Medill asked.

"I'm not sure. This land butts up to county land on the far boundary, but this is still in the city, so no hunting allowed." She cautiously stood and perused the area before another shot sounded, and she dropped to her knees again.

A forceful gust of wind howled through the trees, the arctic cold lapping against Harper's exposed cheeks and hands.

Mrs. Medill's face blanched. "I think we should probably go."

From her crouched position, Harper scrutinized the area again, attempting to discern where the shot came from. Could be anything. Could be someone on the neighboring county land shooting a pheasant. She saw nothing, until...

A flash of someone running between the trees caught her attention. Branches crackled, footsteps pounded. She squinted, losing track of whoever it was after mere seconds. The breath-pinching fear sucked the air from her lungs.

Could it be the same man from last week at the fitness center?

She needed to call 911.

But her phone was in her SUV.

Harper and Mr. Medill assisted a panicked Mrs. Medill to their car. They drove away, leaving Harper fumbling with her fob. She slid inside her vehicle, locked the doors, and snatched her purse from beneath the seat. With trembling hands, she withdrew her cell phone.

Glancing about her, she started the SUV. The cold from the vents, along with the high adrenaline from the situation, chilled her face. Snow began to fall. Wind rocked her vehicle.

She pressed in the password for her phone.

Entered a wrong digit.

Tried again.

Then a third time.

The message on the screen above where she entered her password bluntly reminded her that she had two more tries before being locked out of her phone.

Finally, her screen saver, along with all of her app options, filled the screen.

Her hand trembled as she hit the green "phone" button.

Then something hit her SUV, hard enough to make a plinking noise.

A rock, perhaps?

Harper pivoted to see the man in a hoodie approaching her. He shot another shot into the air as he bolted in her direction.

She shifted the SUV into reverse, the tires spinning in the mud. Fumbling for the windshield wipers, she simultaneously put the car in drive while turning on the rear wipers.

The man continued toward her.

Her heartbeat sounded in her ears, and beads of sweat formed on her forehead, despite the cold.

Harper sped from the lot and onto the main road. She took a brief glance into the rearview mirror. The man had disappeared.

Would he follow her in his own vehicle?

But she'd seen no other car on the Cox property besides hers and the Medills's.

Who *was* he?

Staring ahead, but not really seeing, she nearly drove off the road and into the borrow pit before correcting herself and causing the SUV to jerk.

Harper flipped on her turn signal and barely stopped at the intersection before heading west into town and to the police station.

Should she instead pull over in a nice neighborhood? Call 911 from there?

A tan car pulled in behind her on Alberta Avenue and rode her bumper.

Harper strained to see the driver through the fogged-up back window and the continual snow. She pressed the defroster button.

Finally, heat escaped the vents.

Still, she shivered. Where were the Medills? They'd left before she had, so the man couldn't be following them.

"Lord, I don't know what is going on, but please don't let that man be following me. Please keep me safe." Her breathless plea was interrupted when she noticed the tan car had not relented in its overzealous tailgating. She pressed on the gas slightly, cautious of obeying the speed limit in the oncoming residential neighborhood.

The snow grew thicker, and she slid on the slushy street.

Houses lined either side of the working-class neighborhood with older, ranch-style homes.

The car remained on her bumper.

Harper tugged on her seatbelt to ensure it was secure.

Lord, please keep me safe.

A minivan pulled out from a side street directly in front of her. She slammed on the brakes to avoid hitting it, her SUV fishtailing as she did so.

Her pursuer nudged her bumper, and she jolted forward.

Without taking her eyes from the road, she felt for the defroster button and increased the airflow. A blast of air hit the windshield, helping to remove the condensation on the fogged-up window. She kept her attention focused on the road ahead and in the rearview mirror.

The tan car veered beside her on the left-hand side in the no-passing zone. She overcorrected and nearly hit a parked vehicle before righting her SUV.

The vehicle zipped past her and nearly hit an oncoming truck before careening into the proper lane ahead of Harper. She squinted, attempting to see if it had a license plate. Hard to tell with the snow, but she could see that it was a local plate and the first three numbers were four, nine, and three.

She slowed as the car disappeared from her sight. Turning on her blinker, she safely pulled to the side in front of a red-brick house. Her heart hammered loudly in her ears. Would the vehicle be back?

After offering a prayer of gratitude, Harper gradually inched back onto Alberta Avenue. Turning onto Main, she proceeded several blocks before sliding into the Lake Radford Police Department parking lot.

Kade entered the interview room. Harper Amerson sat at the table with the cup of coffee Officer Baldwin had brought. Her face was ashen, and her brown hair in disarray. She tugged her navy coat tightly around her. He pivoted and clicked the button on the thermostat on the wall to add a few degrees.

Standing in front of the table, he extended a hand. "Ms. Amerson, I'm Detective Kade Lassiter, and I will be assisting on this case." Her hand was cold in his, but her handshake firm. "I do want to inform you that I will be recording this interview."

Her gaze focused on the high-definition camera mounted on the wall. She then nodded mutely and stared at the folder on the table.

From his experience, the sight of a camera and a folder was often intimidating as it revealed that the situation was serious. Especially nerve-racking when the person you interviewed was the innocent party.

Her gaze remained fixed on the folder, which so far only contained a few sheets of paper. He hoped to solve the issue of who was harassing Ms. Amerson before it grew to the typical one-inch-or-more thickness. "Whenever we have a situation such as this, we open up a case," he said, hoping to alleviate some of her anxiety. "Hence the folder. But really, it also helps me keep all of the facts about a case straight." He offered a smile, and her lips slightly curved upward. "Officer Baldwin mentioned he took your statement regarding what happened at the Cox property."

Ms. Amerson blinked rapidly and gave a slight tip of her head. "If it was just what happened at the fitness center, I would think maybe it was some random thing, but now with the Cox property…" her voice trailed.

"I understand." To avoid adding to her distress, he wouldn't go so far as to say he thought someone might be targeting her. "I assure you that we *will* get to the bottom of this matter." He meant it, and he hoped his voice sounded reassuring. "I read through Officer Baldwin's notes from both today and the incident at the fitness center. Is there anyone you can think of who may be behind this?"

"No, and I don't consider myself as having any enemies. My coworker, Clark Montayne, doesn't like me, but I can't imagine he would go to these lengths to scare me." Something indiscernible flashed across her face. Was there more to the coworker story than she let on?

Montayne's name had been brought up before during Baldwin's interview the night of the fitness center incident. Although Baldwin had already spoken with him, it might be worth Kade asking Montayne a few questions as well.

"Do you think Mr. Montayne might have been the one at the property today?"

Ms. Amerson shook her head. "No, it wasn't him. This man was thinner and, I'm confident, the same one from the fitness center. Although I couldn't see any facial features because he was wearing a full-face mask." With a shaky hand, she lifted the disposable cup full of coffee to her lips. She returned it to the table, the remaining liquid sloshing to one side. "Besides, he is out of town at a seminar with several other coworkers today."

That ruled out Montayne, at least for this incident.

"While I was attempting to drive away from the property, the man threw something—maybe a rock?— at my car."

"Officer Baldwin did find a dent in your passenger side door that would be consistent with a rock being thrown at it."

"I'm just thankful it wasn't at my window and that when the tan car nudged my bumper, it didn't do any damage."

"Yes. I agree." What had been the motive behind the rock? To intimidate Ms. Amerson into staying? Or to scare her into leaving? "We will be gathering evidence, including checking for any spent shell casings, since you mentioned he did fire some rounds. Unfortunately, we probably won't be able to get much by way of footprints because we have received enough snow to cover the ground since the incident happened." Kade jotted a few notes on one of the sheets of paper. "Can you think of anyone who might not want you to sell the Cox property?"

"No. It's a beautiful piece of land, and while there are no restrictive covenants, I imagine whoever purchases it will want to build an aesthetically pleasing home there. If the owners weren't desperate, I doubt they'd even part with it since it's been in the family for nearly a century."

Kade held up a leaflet with pictures of the Cox property. Breathtaking mountains rose behind a thickly forested area, their tips alternating between snow and a bluish-green tint indicating plentiful timber. The forested area edged against the entrance to the property. At this time of year, the branches of the leafless trees spread their arms, inviting the visitor to investigate the canopied area toward what the brochure mentioned was a small pond. "Can you tell me a bit about the property and the current owners?"

Ms. Amerson seemed to relax a bit, and she folded her hands into her lap. "It's now owned by Jeff and Vanna Cox. Jeff is the grandson of the former owner, who inherited it from his father. Originally, it was used to run cattle on, and given the pond and creek, provided water for the animals.

Nearly a hundred years ago, it was purchased as a two-hundred-acre piece of land that was subsequently divided into several five-and-ten-acre parcels. Most have been developed over the years and annexed into the existing city limits. There aren't any close neighbors, which is part of its charm, and this is the first time this parcel has been listed for sale."

"Any idea why the owner decided to sell it after all this time? I would assume since it's been in the family for so long, there is some sort of sentimental value, not to mention it would be an excellent place to build a home."

"Yes, there is sentimental value attached to it for certain, but Jeff and Vanna are desperate since their son is battling leukemia and they need the funds to pay for his medical treatment. The community has come alongside them in their time of need, as have many in the city where they are staying for their son's treatments. Still, the Coxes lost their medical insurance when Jeff lost his job three months before their son's diagnosis. Were it not for the dire need for funds, I think it would have stayed in the family perpetually, although from what they've mentioned in the past, the Coxes are not interested in building on the property."

"Do you have the Coxes' phone number?"

"I do." She scrolled through her phone and rattled off the number.

Kade wrote himself a note to call Jeff and Vanna Cox and personally speak to any neighbors. "Have they ever seemed to want to change their minds after putting it on the market?"

"No, they've actually dropped the price twice now in an effort to get it sold. Our real estate office is sponsoring the upcoming 5K Valentine's Day run at Lake Radford Park as the fundraiser on the Saturday before Valentine's Day, in an effort to raise additional funds for them and for another individual in need."

Kade had heard about the fundraiser, especially since some of the funds would be helping his best friend, Trace. He and several of his fellow officers planned to participate, although it had been a while since he'd done any sort of intentional running.

Ms. Amerson's eyebrows furrowed. "Did Mr. and Mrs. Medill by any chance stop by?"

"Yes. Mrs. Medill was understandably shaken up after the incident. Officer Baldwin took their statement as well, although they had no idea who might have fired the shots or who was trespassing on the property today."

Ms. Amerson took another sip of her coffee, but from the way she wrinkled her nose, it had already cooled.

"Can I get you more coffee?" he asked.

"I'm fine, thank you."

Kade tapped his pen on the table. "In Officer Baldwin's report, he mentioned a tan car tailgating you and then erratically passing you in a no-passing zone. Can you tell me a little bit more about that?"

"I didn't recognize the vehicle, and I didn't get a good look at the driver, but I think there may have been more than one person inside. I first noticed them when I pulled onto Alberta Avenue. Initially, I thought it might be my imagination, but then I realized they were tailgating me."

"Do you think it was the man with the gun?"

"No, I don't think so. I didn't see that car at the property, and I would have noticed that. If he had climbed into a tan car after the fact—maybe someone came and picked him up or something—that could have happened. But honestly, I was in such a hurry to get out of there." She shuddered. "I suppose it's entirely possible that he had someone drive him, or maybe someone brought the car, and he drove it..." She rolled her shoulders. "I honestly wouldn't have thought anything of it until it was right on my bumper."

"Did you notice anything else about the tan car?"

"Just that it was an older model, two-door sedan." She tilted her head and peered at the ceiling, then returned her attention to him. "It was a local plate, and I did notice the first three numbers were four, nine, and three. I also noticed that it only had two doors."

Ms. Amerson's recollection of the first three numbers was impressive. The two-door mention definitely helped, as only some years had that type of distinction. It shouldn't be too difficult to locate the vehicle, given its make, model, and the partial, unless they'd used a stolen plate. Was the owner the one from the property who'd fired the shots? Maybe the same one who'd chased her and left the note? Was someone truly harassing Ms. Amerson, or were these happenings all a string of unrelated coincidences?

Not that Kade believed in coincidences. "Do you happen to have any family in town?"

"My parents normally live here, but they are currently in Florida caring for my grandparents. My grandfather recently had a stroke." Her eyes glistened with unshed tears. "We nearly lost him."

Kade knew what it was like for a family member to have health issues. "I'm sorry to hear that."

"Thank you. It's been an ordeal, and I wish I could have gone with them. But they will be staying there for at least another month. They are hoping to maybe move my grandparents back to Lake Radford after Grandpa is fit enough to travel." She inhaled a deep breath, then released it slowly and paused as if pondering her next words. "Were you able to figure out who left the note on my car and followed me outside the fitness center?"

"Not yet. Unfortunately, the available camera footage was smudged due to the weather. And the man, for the most part, stayed outside the line of sight." Which made the case all the more interesting because whoever it was likely knew the location of the cameras.

Ms. Amerson's face fell, and he wished he had better news to share. Regrettably, these things took time. That and add it to his pile of recent cases, and the likelihood of it being solved immediately grew dimmer, much to his regret.

"So, nothing at all on that? I know the paper from my car door was saturated, so they couldn't examine it closely, but anything?"

Desperation sounded in her voice. Most didn't realize all that went into solving any type of incident, mainly because they hadn't been a victim before. That was a good thing—Kade wished there were fewer victims, but his sense of justice and the desire to follow in the footsteps of his dad and grandpa made him more than tenacious in wanting to solve any type of crime that came his way.

"Unfortunately, there are no windows on the south end of the building that faces the overflow parking lot because that's where the gyms are, so we didn't have any witnesses to either someone putting the note on your car or the man hiding by the doctor's office before following you. The blurred image from the front of the building wasn't much help. From my understanding, the fitness center board is considering putting cameras on the south side but has yet to do so. Neither the doctor's office nor the adjacent empty office building had cameras. I would highly recommend you avoid parking in the overflow parking when you visit the gym, at least until we find out who is behind this."

"Yes." She ducked her chin in agreement.

"We will have an officer do several drive-throughs in your neighborhood tonight and in the coming days." Kade handed her one of his cards. "Please contact me if you think of anything else, if you see the man again, or have any other concerns."

Her wary glance told him she wished he could offer more.

"We will get to the bottom of this, Ms. Amerson, and I am sorry you're going through this. I've been here in Lake Radford for two years so far, and it's a relatively safe place compared to other towns the same size."

"I do appreciate all your help." She pushed the chair back and stood.

"I'll see you out."

Kade accompanied her down the main hall and through the door to the reception area. He watched as she left the building and climbed into her SUV.

If he had anything to say about it, whoever it was harassing Ms. Amerson would soon be apprehended.

FIVE

The kid had better text.

He'd waited nearly an hour now to hear how it had gone. He checked his phone one more time just in case a text came through, and he didn't realize it. He rarely worried about anything, but he did have second thoughts about the three teens. Especially the one. Flighty as all get out. But that kid had been the first to open his hand for the money.

Dumb kids. Anything for fifty bucks.

Fifty bucks each.

This investment was costing him more than he'd like.

The one he'd worried about was the only one who'd had reservations and the only one who likely took his threat seriously—the threat to hurt his family if the teen ratted him out.

He chuckled to himself. That kid's expression—horror-stricken was a good word for it—with his face all ashen and his words shaky. *"Please don't hurt my mom."*

"Yeah. Okay." He'd laughed inside but said nothing. Only offered his sternest glower. The other two had some lame excuses.

"My parents aren't even in the country right now."

And the other one with his nonchalant attitude. *"Doubt my parents would even care what I'm doing anyway. My mom and stepdad are too concerned with my half-brothers and sisters. They wouldn't know if you even did go after them.*" The teen started chuckling.

The latter kid sounded like *he* didn't even care about his mom, stepdad, and half-siblings. What a sicko to not even care about your family.

He shrugged. The teens wouldn't be able to identify him if they chose to be stupid and talk to the cops. Not with his disguise. And not with a meeting in the usual place where he hired the people necessary to do his bidding.

He laughed to himself. The numerous lost and founds in town were useful and became his regular shopping mall when it came to camouflaging his identity. Who would think to snatch things from the boxes of dirty, worn, and forgotten clothes at the grocery stores, a few churches, and the fitness center?

The cowboy hat was a bonus.

Too bad he'd actually liked it. He would have kept it instead of throwing it out with the rest of the garbage into the commercial dumpster.

The black trench coat? That really wasn't his style, but with the hat and mask, had done the trick.

Nope. There was absolutely no way anyone could identify him.

The ticking of the clock reminded him he'd have to leave in half an hour. Those teens should have done what was asked of them by now. How had Harper Amerson taken it? Would she finally give up on selling the Cox property, or would he have to take additional steps? It would be to her detriment if the woman didn't relent.

He unwrapped the frozen dinner meal, followed the instructions he knew by heart, and popped it into the microwave. He stood in front of it, impatiently watching as the numbers counted down. It dinged, and he waited for the calorie-laden food to cool before eating.

Finally, twenty minutes later, the text notification from the flighty teen chimed. The words peered up at him from the screen.

Finished.

Did all go well?

Yeah.

No spectators?

Nope.

He wanted to know the details, but also knew he'd better keep the conversation short. By having it be as innocuous as it was, no one would know who or what he was talking about or be able to prove anything. Not that they could anyway. Especially not with the burner phone.

He'd have to toss it and get another one soon.

He scowled. The sooner Harper gave up, the better, as this was costing him far more than he'd like.

SIX

Today was gearing up to be a busy day.

Just the kind Kade lived for.

He poured a bowl of cereal, topped it with a sliced banana and milk, then added a side of toast with peanut butter, and included his usual first cup of coffee. Should carry him over until lunch, which, if his day proved to be as hectic as he figured it would be, a dash through Olsen's drive-thru for a burger was on the menu, no pun intended.

The Amerson and Dumaine cases filled his thoughts. And whenever he thought about the Amerson case, another *failed* case entered his thoughts as well. With effort, he shoved it aside, prayed over his meal, ate, then glanced at the clock.

A quick call to Mom and Dad was in order to see how Dad's appointment yesterday went.

"Hello?"

"Hey, Mom."

"Kade! So nice to hear from you."

"You too. How are things going? How was Dad's appointment?"

"The doctor said your dad hadn't declined any further. He was also able to extend his physical therapy appointments."

"That's good to hear."

"A definite praise, for sure. Your sister got the job she applied for and starts next Monday. Let's just say she's ecstatic."

His sister was tenacious, and her getting the job didn't surprise Kade. "I'll have to call and congratulate her."

"I guess twelve other nurses were applying for the same position."

"If anyone could land that job at the hospital, it would be Kalinda."

Mom laughed. "Very true. Your dad and I raised very ambitious children. By the way, your dad is here if you'd like to chat with him before he heads to his monthly elder board breakfast."

"I'd like that. Thanks, Mom. Love you."

"Love you, too, honey. Be careful, and we'll talk again soon."

Mom, perhaps more than most, knew the danger involved with being in law enforcement, having been married to a cop for so many years.

"Hey, son, how goes it?"

"Hey, Dad. Mom said your appointment went well?"

"It did, although I don't think my neurologist knew what a stubborn old coot I am when he first diagnosed me."

Kade laughed. "You're far from being an old coot, but as for stubborn…"

This time, Dad chuckled. "The good news is that I may be stubborn, but I wanted to be sure and share that trait with my favorite son."

"That may or may not be true."

They shared another round of laughter before Kade continued. "I'm just glad you had a good checkup and that your physical therapy was continued."

"Yeah, always have to dot all the *i*'s and cross all the *t*'s when it comes to insurance stuff."

"And the elder position is going well?"

"It is. I've, of course, had to step back due to my health, but I'm hanging in there. They can't get rid of me that easily."

Dad had served on the elder board on and off over the years for as long as Kade could remember. He had a heart for the congregants and the gift of shepherding.

"How's work going?"

Kade propped his feet up on the chair beside him, but kept an eye on the clock on the microwave. "Going well. It's been busier than usual, especially for winter."

"I know how that goes. Just wait until summer, right?"

"Exactly. I do like it here. Lake Radford is a cozy little town with plenty of amenities."

"Well, if you ever tire of law enforcement, you could snag a job in tourism."

Kade chuckled. "No, thanks. However, there have been a lot of new people moving in. At some point, I hope to find a house to buy instead of continuing to rent, but so far there hasn't been anything that really captures my interest."

"In due time. I know you can't talk to me specifically about cases, but any interesting ones?"

If Dad could have, he would have continued in law enforcement for the rest of his life. Kade knew the importance of vaguely sharing about cases as that kept his dad feeling as though he was "in the loop" but not giving away any private information. "Two cases in particular right now, a burglary with a side of vandalism and a potential stalking case."

"You okay with the latter?"

No, not really. "Yes, I just want to stay on top of it so that…"

"I know I sound like a broken record, as the saying goes, but, son, that wasn't your fault."

"I appreciate that, Dad, but you know how it is."

"I do, and if you need to talk about it some more, I'm here."

Kade had discussed it with Dad ad nauseam, but it might be helpful to, at some point, hash over it again, especially if that's what the Amerson case evolved into. "Thanks. I appreciate that."

"It's not easy being in law enforcement, and if I haven't told you before, your mom and I are proud of you, not only for carrying on the family legacy, but for being so dedicated and good at what you do."

"Thanks, Dad." His parents had told him a dozen times, but Kade never tired of hearing it. "Well, I'd better go. I'll be hitting the ground running today." He bid Dad goodbye, grabbed his notebook, stuffed it into his pocket, and drained the remnants of his cold coffee. He gathered his coat and keys, then headed to the big box pharmacy.

The subpoena had already been served, so talking with the employees should be no big deal. At this particular pharmacy, there were two pharmacists and four techs on duty when he strode inside just as the drugstore opened for the day.

He introduced himself, mentioned the subpoena, then started with the two pharmacists, who, unfortunately, weren't much help. The cameras, which normally were fully functioning, hadn't been working that morning, but had been fixed by the afternoon. One of the techs called in sick the day of the heist. One tech said he was managing inventory, so he hadn't dealt with many customers that day, and another said he was unloading shipments in the back at the time in question. That left one more tech, a motherly woman in her early fifties with a vivacious personality.

"Yes, I remember that individual," she said after Kade referenced that the individual in question was a heavyset man in a black-and-gray coat and hat, potentially riding a motorized scooter.

"What can you tell me about him?"

The woman beamed. "I just have to tell you that this is so exciting. I watch those mysteries on TV all the time and never imagined I would be a part of solving one." She squealed before regaining her professionalism. "Well, for one, he was extremely crabby. He was riding a scooter but was able to stand while I tallied his total."

"Did you see his face?"

"Yes. He was probably in his thirties."

Kade hadn't figured him to be that young.

The tech tapped her chin. "If I could just remember his name and his prescription, I could probably find him in the computer and give you more details."

"That would be extremely helpful."

"He had a black mustache and beard, thick, wire-rimmed glasses, and a round face with dark eyes. And I don't mean the color. He was a large fellow, and I don't mean muscular." She paused and closed her eyes for a second. "If I remember correctly, he had two prescriptions, one for a digestive issue and one for a mood issue. Hold on a second."

The tech typed in some information into her computer. "We prescribed five digestive prescriptions on the day in question. Let's see...no, wouldn't be him, wouldn't be her, wouldn't be...aha. Yes, I think this is the name of the man you are looking for. Give me a second to verify." Her fingers flew across the keys. "Yes, he also had an additional prescription that day." She gave Kade the man's name and address from the computer.

And five minutes later, Kade was that much closer to solving the case.

The best part of being a real estate agent? Matching up those looking for a house with their dream home. On one of three separate showings today, Harper met the family of four to show them a bilevel with a fully finished basement. The beige, brown-trimmed home, built in 1985, boasted four bedrooms, two baths, a two-car garage, and ample space for children to play, with its nearly half-acre yard.

Harper instinctively perused her surroundings. Would whoever had been at the Cox property show up here as well? Did she need to be concerned each time she showed a listing? Never before the recent events had she had to worry about doing her job. But now, a tingle of anxiety wrestled through her.

She met the next family at the residence at three o'clock and proceeded to show them the interior, which had been freshly painted. But while the home was well-maintained and boasted no problems, Harper figured it was the yard that cinched the deal for the young family.

"We'll be in touch with an offer," the husband said.

If only she could match all potential buyers who came to see her with the perfect home, lot, or land. And if only she didn't have to worry about whoever it was who seemed to be stalking her.

SEVEN

The druggie was really getting on his nerves. Hopefully Harper hadn't caught a good glimpse of him as the druggie—Motta—stumbled through the woods after shooting rounds into the air. The guy couldn't run to save his life.

And he wanted to hire Motta for another "job"?

He shook his head. If he wasn't desperate and if the druggie didn't work for such meager pay, then he'd find someone else.

He rolled down the window, threw out his cigarette butt, and drove across town to the vacant building across from the Shabby Motel.

It was shabby, all right.

The two-story rust-colored motel boasted cranberry-colored doors and two junked vehicles parked off the side. He'd been inside once—shower curtains hung on the windows, mold lurked in the crevices, and there was green shag carpet throughout. The smell of cat urine and sewer was enough to turn most people away. That or the bed bugs.

He was surprised the place hadn't been condemned. Especially since Lake Radford was basically a clean town.

Well, except for the north end.

Snow flitted through the sky, illuminated by the one lone streetlight. He left the vehicle running while he waited for Motta, but made sure to lock the doors.

No telling what kind of creeps were out at this time of night, even with a winter weather advisory in effect.

The clock on his dashboard read 9:29. Motta should arrive any minute.

A gust of wind blew, swirling the snow and pelting the windshield. For once, the weather forecast proved correct. Perfect for his plan.

Also perfect for the plan was the fact that he owned two vehicles. Helped that he made decent money. Although his car was by far his preferred mode of travel, with its leather seats and expensive radio.

Motta pounded on the passenger side window, and he unlocked the door. Motta leaped inside, slammed the door, and huddled in front of the heater.

He promptly turned off the car.

"Hey, man. Turn that back on. It's cold."

"Yeah, well, I don't need to waste gas, and besides, the less attention I draw to us, the better." He resisted the urge to retch at Motta's stench of a combination of body odor, urine, pot, and some obscure foulness that smelled like rotten fruit.

Motta threaded a shaky hand through his long, brown, greasy hair. "What you got for me?"

At least whenever he needed the druggie's help, he could just text him. That worked well. Although a homeless guy, Motta owned a brand-new, expensive cell phone—go figure. A phone that he made Motta delete all messages from every time they met.

Just to cause Motta a little more angst, he stared straight ahead, waiting before he shared his plan. The vacant building boasted a new clump of graffiti. Foul language was spray-painted in red, along with a gang symbol. Never had there been gangs in Lake Radford until recently.

Cops needed to get with it and do something to thwart it. Crime had no place in his hometown. Not to mention it brought down property values.

"So, what you need, man?"

"I need you to pay a visit to a house."

"Yeah, okay."

Motta jittered about, causing the entire car to shake. The guy couldn't sit still to save his life.

"Tomorrow, after there's plenty of snow on the ground, I need you to go to 127 E. Washington Avenue."

"What? Never heard of it. Is that on the north end?"

Far from the north end. But then, Harper Amerson wouldn't live on the north end. "Nope."

Motta tapped it into his phone. "That's not even close by."

"You have legs. You can walk."

The druggie jiggled his knee and stroked his wiry brown tuft of a goatee. "It's cold outside in case you haven't noticed."

He tossed him a side glance. The guy needed to buy a new coat. One warmer for the Lake Radford winters. Didn't he realize he was in the Rocky Mountain West, not in some beach town? "You'll go to the house, walk around the perimeter, up to the front door, and check the handle. Then mosey around back and try the back door. Try a window or two."

"What?" Motta's dark eyes bulged from his pimple-covered face.

"Just to each door and a couple of windows, then you're finished. The weather forecast is calling for four inches. Make sure there are at least two before you go there, and be sure it's in the dark."

"What about cameras?"

"No cameras." He'd checked.

Motta flung himself against the seat and reached for his vape pen.

What was it with some people's unhealthy choices? "None of that in my vehicle."

The druggie snarled and shook his head before returning the vape pen to his pocket. "What about my footprints, huh? The cops could trace me through that. What then?"

"Yeah, they could, and we need your tracks to be seen."

Harper would freak out if she knew someone was tramping around her yard and trying to get in. The thought brought him immense satisfaction.

Served her right.

"You want me to get caught?"

No, because then I'd have to find someone else to do my dirty work. "You won't get caught. You'll toss your shoes afterward in a black garbage bag. No one would have any reason to suspect you."

"Do I look like I have extra pairs of shoes? This is my only pair."

Motta's worn boots with a rip in the side had seen better days.

Not his problem.

"I can't get caught. I'm on probation. If I break it, I go to prison. Like that." Motta snapped his fingers.

"Don't worry. I have an idea."

That settled the druggie for a minute. He reached into the backseat and, with his gloves on, lifted a grocery sack with a pair of boots in it. "Use these when you go."

Motta cringed. "Whose are those? I don't know if I like the idea of wearing someone else's shoes."

He shrugged. "Found them in the lost and found at the grocery store over on Sixth. Choose if you'd rather keep the shoes you have on or these shoes, and wear the others for the job."

Motta removed one shoe from the bag and inspected it. He sniffed the inside, then checked the tread.

Whoever lost these shoes would miss them.

"These are name brand."

"Yep."

"Okay, but what if I try the door handle and the door's unlocked?"

"Don't go in."

"That makes no sense. I could steal something while I'm there."

He shook his head. Motta was such an opportunist. "You're not there to steal. Just do what I ask if you want the job."

Motta replaced the shoes in the sack. "Kinda risky since someone could see me."

Tension infused his jaw and facial muscles. Time to bring out the important stuff. He reached into his pocket and retrieved the baggie with two thirty-milligram oxycodone tablets. "Guess you won't be needing these, then."

The druggie reached for the bag, and he jerked it away. "These are for you *if* you do the job right."

"I'll do it right. I need those. I've already used the other ones you gave me."

He lacked an endless supply, but at least the doctor *had* renewed his prescription twice after his surgery last year. He hadn't needed them. Hadn't wanted them. Not when the over-the-counter stuff worked. "*If* you do the job right and don't get caught, these are yours. Then and only then."

"All right."

He reiterated the plan one more time, then nearly shoved Motta out of the vehicle. "Text me when you complete the job."

"Yeah, okay, man. Sure. But you promised those pills."

He didn't answer, only started up the car and drove away, leaving Motta in the fumes. He immediately hit the button to roll down the window. With any luck, the druggie's stench would be gone before he reached home.

EIGHT

Kade took a break from the Dumaine case and did some investigating on the tan car with the partial plate that Harper Amerson had identified as the one trying to drive her off the road.

After a bit of computer sleuthing, he found the vehicle registered to an April Malles, who resided at Shuford Trailer Park, #33. He grabbed his coat, and he and Detective Gossett headed to the trailer park on the north end. It wouldn't surprise Kade if the car truly was at that location. It was typical for someone to be arrested in the area at least a couple of times a month. The state criminal investigations had an eye on one of the trailers as a potential drug house.

The snow eased when he reached the entrance to Shuford Trailer Park. This past November, he and the men in his men's Bible study at church delivered Thanksgiving food baskets to several of the residents here. Some of the people had merely fallen on hard times, and it was always rewarding to be able to help those who were otherwise unable to have a Thanksgiving meal.

The first trailer on the left was the manager's trailer. The shabby and faded maize-colored trailer with rust trim and a white door was probably the best-kept one in the entire park.

His GPS told him they were nearly to their destination. He took a right, edged around a curve, then a left, and parked in front of a beige-colored trailer with turquoise trim. Someone had attempted to put shutters on the front windows. Two faded wood flower pots stood on either side of a rickety staircase leading to a small porch. An inch of snow filled the top of the whiskey barrel flower pots, and the green dented trash can had blown over. To the side was parked a tan older model sedan with the local license number four, nine, three, seven, two. Just as he'd figured when he'd punched in the information earlier.

Maybe this case would be an easy solve.

Gossett unclipped her seatbelt. "Well, let's see if the residents know anything about harassing Ms. Amerson."

Kade appreciated teaming up with Gossett. Her valuable communication skills and her attention to detail made her an effective detective, one of three on the force. An added bonus? If they had to interview a woman, Gossett excelled at putting a fellow female at ease, hence making the suspect more willing to cooperate.

Kade and Gossett emerged from the service vehicle and walked up the wobbly stairs. A painted "welcome" sign greeted them. It was as if someone had tried to make the place look the best it could despite the dismal circumstances.

Gossett rapped on the door, and a woman peeked through the faded curtain before cautiously unlocking and opening the door.

Kade and Gossett both flashed their badges, "April Malles?" Gossett asked.

She hesitated. "Yes?"

"Hello, ma'am. I'm Detective Gossett, and this is Detective Lassiter from the LRPD. Could we ask you a few questions?"

The woman wore a Sheila's Restaurant uniform—a white shirt and black skirt with a magnetic nametag featuring her name. Had she just returned home from her shift?

"Is there something wrong?"

"We just have a few questions. May we come in?"

Ms. Malles stepped aside and ushered them into the 12'x46' mobile home. The house screamed of the 1970s with its avocado-green-and-white linoleum, golden-yellow fridge and matching stove, and dark wood cabinets in the kitchen. The open floor plan boasted flattened dingy brown carpet in the adjoining living room. Paneling and wallpaper with enormous yellow flowers in the kitchen completed the style. It reminded him of his uncle's old house, which they'd visited years ago when Kade was a kid. Except for a stack of papers and odds and ends on the catch-all orange counter, the mobile home was otherwise tidy. Something boiling on the stove caused Kade's stomach to rumble, and he remembered he hadn't eaten since breakfast due to the hectic day.

"Please, have a seat." Ms. Malles waved a shaky hand to the faded navy couch.

She took a seat in the adjacent green recliner and rubbed her hands on the front of her skirt. "How can I help you?" Dark circles beneath her eyes and wisps of blonde hair, graying at the temples, fell over her thin face.

"Thank you for taking the time to speak with us," said Gossett. "Is that your tan car in front of the house?

"Yes, it is.

"Were you by any chance driving on Alberta Avenue a few days ago at about four?"

"No, I was at work, but..." her face paled. "Can you give me a moment?"

Kade nodded, and Ms. Malles stood and pivoted down the hall. He heard a knock on a door, followed by a, "Yeah, Mom?"

"Zephyr, I need you to come out here for a second."

"Is it time to eat?"

"Just come out here, please."

The door creaked open, and a few seconds later, a lanky teenage boy followed Ms. Malles into the living room.

"Take a seat," she directed, pointing to one of the two chairs at a splintered dining room table.

The boy did as she requested. "What's going on? Why are these guys here?"

"Detectives, this is my son, Zephyr."

Kade repeated the introductions. "Zephyr with the same last name as your mother?"

"Yes."

"And your age?" asked Gossett.

"Just turned eighteen last month."

"Can we refer to you as Zephyr, or do you prefer Mr. Malles?"

"Zephyr is fine." The teen shifted his feet from side to side, and his gaze darted from Kade to Gossett, and back to Kade.

Ms. Malles didn't return to her seat but instead planted her hands on her hips. "They need to know if we were driving the car on Alberta Avenue a few days ago. Since I was at work, it wasn't me, but were you driving in that area?"

The teen blanched. "Y-yeah, we were driving around in that area. So what?"

"Zephyr, so help me..."

"Mom..." But his rapid blinking told Kade all he needed to know. The young man knew something.

Kade lowered his voice and spoke calmly. "We just need to ask you a few questions."

Zephyr bounced his knee, causing the entire table to wobble. "Yeah, okay."

"Is the car in front of the house yours?"

"No, it's my mom's."

"Were you by chance driving on Alberta Avenue a few days ago?"

"Yeah, a couple friends and I…"

"Please tell me you were not driving around with Orion and Talon."

Zephyr cleared his throat.

"Do not tell me you were driving around with Orion and Talon," Ms. Malles repeated.

"Mom, it was just for a little while after school."

Ms. Malles plopped down on the couch as if defeated. "I thought you weren't going to hang around with them anymore."

"They *are* my friends."

"And bad influences. How do you ever plan to rise above this," she gestured around the room with her hands, "if you make the bad choice to hang around those two?" Ms. Malles closed her eyes for a brief moment. "Those two boys have been in trouble with the law. Why Zephyr thinks he needs to hang around them is beyond me."

"It's not like there's anyone else to hang around. I don't exactly fit in with the athletes, the brains, or the cool kids. I'm not an arts guy or a goth. And I'll never be popular. As a matter of fact, most kids consider me trailer park trash. That leaves me the option of being a stoner or hanging around with Orion and Talon." He cocked his head to one side. "Which would you prefer?"

"Don't you dare get disrespectful with me. I'm not going to deal with your sarcasm right now."

Zephyr lowered his voice and had the decency to apologize. "Sorry. Look. We were just hanging out for a little while, nothing major." He shrugged. "We drove through and got some burgers."

"Being a teen these days isn't easy," said Gossett. "It's hard to find what friend group you belong to."

"Yeah, it is." Zephyr stared down at his lap and avoided eye contact.

Frown lines creased over Ms. Malles's mouth, and she swiped at her cheek. She focused her attention on Kade and Gossett. "It's just us."

Kade knew that meant there was no father in the home, which he already knew from looking into the family situation before he and Gossett arrived. "I understand, ma'am, and that's hard."

"Yes, it is, and it doesn't help when your son thinks hanging around the wrong crowd will get him out of this situation. I have loftier plans for him than him becoming a criminal."

"I'm not a criminal, Mom," scowled Zephyr.

Gossett leaned back on the couch. "Zephyr, did you and your friends drive down Alberta Avenue after grabbing some burgers?"

"Yeah."

"Did you happen to see a red mid-sized SUV traveling down the road?"

Zephyr scraped a hand over his shaggy blond hair. "Look, we were only trying to scare her. It wasn't a big deal."

Kade scribbled the information on his notepad. "Zephyr, we'll need you to come down to the station to answer a few questions."

"Is he being arrested?"

"No, ma'am, but we do need to conduct a formal interview." Gossett prefaced her words with a kind smile meant to ease some of the apprehension Ms. Malles surely felt.

Water splashed over the side of the pot on the stove, and Ms. Malles bolted from the couch to turn off the heat and remove it from the burner. "I'm coming with you, Zephyr."

"You don't have to, Mom."

But his words belied his expression, and the way Zephyr peered up at his mother with wide eyes told of his fear and apprehension.

"We haven't eaten yet. Could you give me a minute to put this in the fridge?"

Kade and Gossett nodded simultaneously as Ms. Malles strained the water from the noodles in the pan, poured them into a bowl, covered it, and stuck it into the fridge. Then she and Zephyr followed Kade and Gossett back to the station.

"Just a hunch, but I don't think he's the one who chased Ms. Amerson or left her the note," Kade mused as he pulled out of the trailer park.

"No, but it will be interesting to find out why he and his friends thought it was a good idea to follow Ms. Amerson and nudge her bumper."

"And it will be good to find out if Zephyr can give us any clues as to who might be responsible for the gunshots being fired."

They rode the rest of the way in silence, Kade deep in thought. When he'd first become a detective in Fairmont, his first assignment was a stalking case. A case that hadn't ended well, with an innocent victim dying at the hands of a crazed maniac.

If it were up to him, Kade would never allow that to happen again. He'd err on the side of caution. And if the man really *wasn't* chasing Ms. Amerson, and the note *wasn't* meant for her, but was a case of mistaken identity, if the gunshots fired were merely some hunter disobeying hunting laws on private property, and if the ones following her were just a bunch of problematic teens that didn't mean any harm, then Kade would happily close the case and go on his way.

But if someone was stalking or harassing Ms. Amerson, or anyone in Lake Radford for that matter, Kade would do all he could to make sure the outcome didn't resemble that of his first case.

He pulled into the station parking lot, and within minutes, Zephyr Malles was in the interview room. He Mirandized Zephyr, reminded him that they would be recording his statement, and then Kade and Gossett tag-teamed with their questions while Ms. Malles sat beside her son across the table.

Kade then reiterated what they'd spoken of at the Malles residence before adding, "Why don't you start at the beginning and tell us what happened?"

Zephyr chewed on his thumbnail. "So, we were just driving along Alberta Avenue and saw this red SUV and thought it would be fun to maybe scare her a little bit."

"Zephyr!"

"Mom, it wasn't really any big deal. It was just a joke."

"Not a big deal? It's not a big deal to scare someone? Would you like that done to you? Would you like someone to do that to me?"

"No, I wouldn't, and if anyone did it to you—" Zephyr squared his shoulders.

The boy might be rebelling, but he loved his mother, that much was clear.

Gossett asked the next question. "What happened next, Zephyr?"

"So, yeah, we were just driving along and maybe riding her bumper for a bit. The roads were a little slick, and we may have nudged her bumper, not meaning to, but she stopped really fast." The boy stumbled on his words.

"You nudged her bumper?" Ms. Malles's mouth twisted. "Why would you think that is okay, and why would you blame it on the icy roads? If you were following that closely, it was entirely your fault."

Zephyr's voice wavered. "Mom. I don't need a lecture right now, okay?"

Ms. Malles looked from Kade to Gossett with a pleading look. Kade's heart went out to her. It couldn't be easy raising a boy on her own.

Gossett, in the usual serene tone she likely used with her own kids, added, "Zephyr, your mom is just concerned."

The boy lifted his head slightly and peered at his mom. "Yeah, I know. Sorry."

"Did you try to pass her in a residential area?" Gossett asked.

"The chick was going way too slow. It would have been next year before we reached the intersection."

"You do realize that is a no-passing zone?"

"Yeah, we realized that when a truck almost hit us head-on."

"Zephyr!"

The boy started on his other thumbnail. "We got back over on the correct side of the road. It's all good."

Ms. Malles narrowed her eyes. "It is *not* all good. You could have been killed. The people in the truck could have been killed. Not to mention the woman you were harassing. I knew these boys were bad influences. Why would you think this was a good idea?"

"Like I said, it was all in fun, not a big deal. We're sorry, okay?" Zephyr folded his arms across his chest.

Kade maintained his focus on Zephyr. "Do you happen to know anything about the acreage known as the Cox property?"

"Cox property? No, never heard of it, why?"

"The Cox property runs along Cox Road, which intersects with Alberta Avenue. It's a plot of land for sale. Were you and your friends there before being on Alberta Avenue or before getting burgers?"

"No, we weren't at a property. We skipped..." He again avoided eye contact.

"You skipped school, too?"

Zephyr ignored the question, unfolded his arms, refolded them, then continued. "After we left school, we were grabbing some burgers, then we came off of Main and waited alongside the road at the very edge of Alberta Avenue where it intersects with Martin Street."

"Do you mean to tell me you are waiting for this woman? Stalking her?" Ms. Malles's voice rose several octaves. "I have clearly not raised you right."

Zephyr peered down at his hands before intertwining them so forcefully that his knuckles turned white. When he didn't answer his mom's question, she asked another one. "Not stalking, Mom," he mumbled.

"Do you even know who this person is?"

"The chick?"

Mrs. Malles crossed her arms. "Yes, the 'chick.'"

"No, we were just told..."

Kade jotted down more notes. "You were just told?"

"Yeah, Orion, Talon, and I were just told."

Kade would get to that line of questioning next. "Can you tell me their last names?"

"Look, I don't want to rat them out."

He wouldn't tell the boy it would take him less than five minutes to determine the last names. "Do you realize withholding information is illegal?"

"Fine. Orion Levendoski and Talon Roberts."

"And you go to school with them?"

"Yes."

"Seniors?"

"Yep. Gonna graduate. Well, hope to."

Ms. Malles arched an eyebrow.

"I *am* gonna graduate, Mom."

Kade continued his line of questioning. "You were driving along Martin Street, pulled over onto Alberta Avenue, and were waiting for the woman in the red SUV?"

"Yes."

"But you don't know her?"

"No, none of us know her."

"And you want to just play a trick on her?"

"Yeah. It was just a quick way to make a few bucks. Mom, you said you were having a hard time paying the electric bill this month, so I found a way to help us out a bit."

Ms. Malles shook her head. "Committing crimes for money is not what I meant when I said we were short on funds for the electric bill. Besides, you have a job at Sheila's washing dishes."

"That doesn't make much, especially since I can only work there a couple of days after school and on Saturdays. I thought you'd be happy for the extra money."

"Happy if you had earned it *legally.*"

Zephyr opened his palms and splayed his hands toward the ceiling.

His mom continued. "I will not have you doing illegal things. You need to graduate unless you want to spend your life in jail, which is where I think Orion and Talon are going to end up."

"They've already been in—"

"Yes, I know they've been in the juvenile justice system before they turned eighteen. I am *well* aware."

"It was just a one-time deal, Mom. Nothing to get upset over." But even as Zephyr attempted to act cocky about the whole ordeal, Kade knew better. The kid was stumbling all over himself, his voice shook, and his restlessness indicated guilt. "You mentioned that someone asked you to do this. Can you elaborate?"

Something indistinguishable flashed in Zephyr's eyes. He answered a little too quickly. "Just some guy."

"Could you tell us more about him?"

Zephyr's narrow shoulders went rigid. "Like I said, just some guy."

Interesting how the teen was protecting whoever put him up to this.

There were other ways to prod, and that was Gossett's strength. "Zephyr, I know this is an uncomfortable situation. You and your friends likely hadn't anticipated getting caught when you decided to have a little fun."

"N-n-no, we didn't. Plan to get caught, that is."

"Right. I'm guessing, because you had your mom's car, you were nominated to be the driver."

"Yep. Orion and Talon have cars, but we chose my mom's."

Ms. Malles's eyebrows rose into her forehead. "Whose idea was it to have some fun at the woman's expense? Yours? Orion's? Talon's?"

"None of ours. It was the guy. I don't know much about him."

Kade leaned forward and rested his chin on his hands, hoping to come across as casual, rather than authoritative. "Tell us what you know."

The teen's face flushed. His words first came out as a rapid jumble. "Yeah, so there was this guy. He met us here on the north end by that vacant building across from that dive of a motel and asked us if we would be willing to do something for some cash."

"Again, I do *not* want you doing illegal things just to get money."

Zephyr ignored his mom and proceeded. "The guy just asked if we would scare this chick. Not anything major, just freak her out. He said maybe we could tailgate her, follow her, try to pass her—that sort of thing. Not hurt her. Just frighten her. Which we thought didn't sound too bad for fifty bucks apiece."

Ms. Malles rubbed her temples.

"Do you remember what this guy looked like?" Kade asked.

"It was dark, and I don't remember a whole lot, just that he was probably a little taller than me, was wearing a brown cowboy hat, and some sort of trench coat."

"Did you see his face?"

"No, not really. He had on one of those ski masks, which I didn't really think anything about because it was cold that night."

Ms. Malles lifted her head. "This was at night? What time of night?"

"It was last week. You were working the late shift at Sheila's, and I was riding around with Talon and Orion in Talon's car."

"Do you remember who it was who told you about this job?" Gossett asked.

"Talon was the one who heard about it, and he told us."

Kade scribbled down more notes. "Did you happen to see the man's vehicle?"

Zephyr glanced up at the ceiling, his breathing erratic before stalling into slow, deep breaths. He moistened his lips. "No, I didn't see his vehicle, and I did see his eyes, but it was dark, so I couldn't tell you what color they were."

"How old did he sound?"

"He sounded older, but I don't know how old. Older than me."

"Back to the vehicle. Truck? Car? Van? Bus?"

"Didn't see it."

"Anything you can tell us will help," offered Gossett. "Even if you don't know the make or model, just whether it was a car or truck."

Sweat dampened Zephyr's armpits, causing a wet circle to grow on his t-shirt. "Don't know what he was driving. When we saw him, he was on foot."

"Is there anything else you can tell us that might be helpful?"

"I sent him a text telling him we did what he asked."

"Do you still have it?"

Zephyr shook his head. "No, I deleted it, but he asked if there were any spectators."

"And you said..."

"No."

"I'm going to need to check out your phone. I can get a warrant or—"

Zephyr removed his phone from his pocket and handed it to Kade. "You can look at it if you want."

"Thanks. I'll get this back to you as soon as possible. I'll also need the phone numbers of your friends who were with you that day."

Zephyr provided them, and Kade took notes. "Did the three of you discuss this matter via texts?"

"No, we just talked about it at school."

The teen was ultimately cited for reckless driving and would have to appear before a judge. But there was something about Zephyr that gave Kade hope. He'd add the teen to his prayer list. A niggling in his gut told him there was still time to turn this kid around.

NINE

Thankfully, there had been no issues in the past several days. Detective Lassiter called and informed Harper that he'd found the young men responsible for following her on Alberta Avenue, but hadn't yet any luck with the identity of the man firing his gun on the Cox property, and no further information about the man at the fitness center. As the days passed, Harper was more and more convinced that the note was nothing more than a case of mistaken identity and meant for someone else. And that the man who'd followed her wasn't *actually* following her, but instead was just walking behind her.

Or at least that's what she would attempt to convince her at-times "overthinking" mind to accept.

She still hadn't wanted to return to the Cox property. Detective Lassiter had collected some spent shells and had interviewed the neighbors. No one had seen anything, which hadn't surprised Harper, given the distance between the houses. One neighbor had heard the shots but just assumed it was someone on the adjacent county land target practicing or hunting grouse.

Life returned to normal. Today had been productive. Harper had, with Grandma's go-ahead, put a down payment on a house in The Cottages for her grandparents, had closed two real estate deals, and had secured a contract to sell a duplex near the park. An efficient, later-than-usual workout yielded her a step closer to being ready for the upcoming Valentine's Day 5K. Running had always brought out her somewhat competitive nature. Competitive even more so with herself than with other runners. She hoped to beat her previous time from last year's event and support a good cause while doing so.

Harper peered outside. Miniature swirls of snow fell from the sky and landed peacefully on the already several inches of snow on the ground. If the temps eased up a bit and climbed out of the negatives, she could foresee snowshoeing with Kennedy. It had been a few years since they'd participated in one of their favorite pastimes.

She flipped the switch on the electric fireplace in her living room. The fireplace roared to life, complete with the imitation orange flames and faux logs, and she held her hands in front of the vents. Harper closed her eyes briefly before reopening them, her gaze settling on the frames lining the mantle. One of her, Mom, and Dad; one of her and her grandparents; one when she won a medal in a 5K two years ago; and finally, a wood-framed photo of her and her two best friends from high school. Harper picked up the frame. It seemed so long ago now—more than eleven years since they roamed the halls of Lake Radford High. It was good to have Kennedy back in town again.

They'd each gone different directions since that time. Harper remained in Lake Radford, Kennedy left the state and had only recently returned, and Laurel still resided out of state. They'd all stayed in touch relatively well via social media, phone calls, and texts, and Harper was thrilled when Kennedy returned to Lake Radford. Perhaps someday, Laurel would come back as well.

In the photo, they linked arms, their smiles bright.

She replaced the frame just as the old family heirloom clock Grandma had given her chimed, indicating the late hour.

Harper climbed into bed, reached for her Bible, and flipped to First John. As always, she allowed the words to seep into her soul before reading the commentary at the bottom of the page. She set it on her bedside and lifted her prayers of gratitude and concern to the Lord. Her eyelids grew heavy, and she fell asleep within minutes, the promise of a new day on her mind.

Sometime later, crunching snow sounded just beyond the wall in her room.

At first, she thought it was just a figment of her imagination or a dream. She rolled over, tugged the covers to her chin, and attempted to fall back asleep.

The crunching continued, seemingly just on the other side of the wall, followed by the sound of the train somewhere in the distance. Harper checked the time. Three a.m.

No one would be walking around in the snow at this hour.

Probably a dog. She strained her ear for any barking.

None.

Silence now, but for an occasional car in the distance.

She rested her head back on her pillow. Hadn't she just earlier been reminiscing about snowshoeing? About her and Kennedy traipsing through the nearby park, burning some serious calories before stopping at Sheila's for a cup of hot chocolate?

Yes. That was it. She was probably even dreaming about that and imagining the sound.

Harper reached up, fluffed her pillow, and attempted to fall back asleep. A backyard fence was on her list of wants once she had some extra money. Could be that a dog was wandering around the area.

She grimaced. Hopefully, it would find its way home soon. The frigid temps were no place for furry pets.

Her breathing evened, and relaxation consumed her. That delightful time just before a deep sleep, as her mind settled and her heart rate decreased.

Until...

Was that someone walking around on the deck just off the dining room?

A thumping noise, almost like boots.

Another dream?

Harper regretted being a light sleeper. The stomping continued. Why would someone be plodding around on her deck?

She needed to settle this once and for all, or her mind would never allow her to return to sleep.

Harper swung her legs over the side of the bed, slipped her feet into her fuzzy slippers, and moseyed from her bedroom into the hallway, taking a left turn into the dining room.

The commotion on the deck ceased, and the ticking of the clock and an owl somewhere outside were the only sounds she heard.

Good.

But she'd double-check just to make sure.

Harper reached over and was about to push the curtain on the glass door aside when she heard the sliding glass door screen screech.

She froze.

Through the curtains, she could see the outline of somebody on the deck.

Someone familiar.

Familiar because he looked similar to the one who'd followed her at the fitness center.

Her feet remained planted in place. Breath caught in her throat as her heart pounded in her ears.

Lord, please keep me safe.

The scrape of the screen door sounded as whoever it was tugged it along, combating the snow in the door's track.

The masked lurker peered at her through the curtain. His eye caught hers.

She gasped and released her hold on the edge of the curtain.

There was likely no way for him to get inside without picking the lock or breaking the glass, but hadn't she heard somewhere that if one was determined enough, one could break into any home? Locked door or not?

Harper willed her frozen legs to move. Finally, receiving the message her brain sent to her feet, she stumbled before racing back into her room. She shut and locked the door and reached for her cell phone.

"911, what is your emergency?"

"Someone is trying to get into my house!"

"What is your location?"

Her voice trembled in her own ears. Was the man still on the deck? Was he devising a way to get in? "I'm at 127 E. Washington Avenue."

"An officer is on the way. Please stay on the line."

Whoever it was on the deck tried the door handle and knocked on the window. Another chill ran up Harper's spine. Would he get in before the police arrived? Who was he? *Why* was he doing this?

She did as she was told but tapped "speaker" on the phone and tossed it on the bed. She'd need to find something with which to defend herself if the intruder got in before the police arrived.

Rummaging beneath her bed, she located the document-sized safe she kept for important items. Someone clocked on the head as she swung it would have—at the very least—a headache. It would distract him long enough for her to escape.

Lord, please keep me safe.

The flyer about the women's shooting event on her nightstand caught her attention. The event was held twice a year, and she *really* needed to make the time to attend and learn how to properly shoot a gun. It had just never been a priority before now.

She was strong. Kept herself in tip-top shape. Ran, used the elliptical, strength trained, and could bend into a pretzel from her days in gymnastics as a kid. But she was no match for a man bent on hurting her.

Not that she wouldn't fight to the death.

Harper cautiously slid to the side, twirled the wand affixed to the blinds on the window slightly, and peered outside into the darkness.

Nothing.

She closed the blinds and huddled beside her bed, the safe in her grasp.

An eternity passed. Was whoever had been on her deck still there?

She jumped at the loud knock on the door.

"The officer has arrived," the 911 operator told her.

"Thank you," she breathed.

Relief flooded her, and Harper unlocked her bedroom door and bolted to the living room. She peeked through the peephole. Sure enough, an officer stood on her porch. One she didn't recognize, but an officer all the same.

Her hands shook as she flipped the lock and opened the door.

He introduced himself, and she told him what had happened, described the potential intruder, and informed him that she believed it to be the same man who'd followed her at the fitness center last week.

"I'm going to check the perimeter and your house. Please stay inside and lock the door behind me."

She did as she was told and anxiously awaited his return. Would he find whoever it was?

The officer returned about fifteen minutes later. He came in, and she shut the door behind him.

"Did you see anyone?"

"No. Whoever it was is long gone. I did, however, take some photographs of the footprints. While it's still snowing and some of that snow has already filled in the prints, it could be helpful as far as helping us estimate a few things about this person, things like estimating height and weight, which will be helpful in addition to your description of him."

He took her statement before agreeing to conduct another perimeter check after he'd finished his initial investigation.

Harper crawled back into bed and shivered beneath her blankets. Fear surged through her. Was the man lurking around her house tonight and attempting to get in the same one who'd chased her outside the fitness center and fired the shots at the Cox property? Who was he, and why was he harassing her?

She rolled over to one side and stared at the illuminated clock on the wall. There would be no sleeping tonight.

TEN

True to his word, Griff McKown met Harper at her house at 10:00 a.m. on Saturday. He pulled to the curb in a white Chevy truck with the words *All Things Safety and Security Company* emblazoned on the side. They attended school together, with Griff being two years ahead of her. Despite living in a smaller town, she hadn't seen him in at least a year. He looked much the same as she remembered, with his short blond haircut, square jaw, and hazel eyes.

Had it really been all these years since high school? Since her friend, Laurel, crushed on the star football player?

"Harper! How have you been?"

"Good. And you?"

"Doing well. The business has really taken off. In a way, kind of sad, I guess, that someone could make a living installing security systems and teaching self-defense."

She wouldn't have thought one would be able to make a living in that profession until recently. Harper chewed on her bottom lip. "Did Detective Lassiter give you any details about why I needed you to install cameras and a security system?"

She wouldn't even think about how much the cost would set her back.

All because someone decided it was appropriate to stalk her for whatever reason.

"He couldn't say much due to your case being an active investigation. When he told me your name, I told him I knew you."

"I've had some problems with someone harassing me."

"I'm sorry to hear that." His brow furrowed. "I don't know what it is about Lake Radford, but it seems like there are a lot more crimes lately. Did you hear about Dumaine's getting robbed not too long ago?"

She'd read about it online and felt sorry for the kindly couple who owned it. "I remember going there as a teenager all the time. I can't believe someone would break in and rob and vandalize it."

"You and me both. Last week, I installed cameras and a security system to replace the paltry one-camera, outdated system they had. I hope the PD discovers who did this soon. That's the second business in a week that I've done installs for."

"I hope so, too. It's always been that the north end was sketchy, even when we were kids, but now we have to worry about the downtown area?" Harper shuddered. "And my little neighborhood." *And walking out of the fitness center and showing properties.* She glanced from one end of the street to the other.

Was her stalker watching her even now? Would he return?

Harper was grateful that the police department offered to do patrols of her formerly safe neighborhood. But was it enough?

Griff stroked his clean-shaven chin. "Do you remember that time we decided to live on the edge and cruise around on the wild side on the north end after one of the football games?"

"I remember that. We were all crammed into your mom's minivan."

"That thing was sure smooth, and it could fit eight passengers, so it worked well for us. Of course, how we fit all of us in there is still beyond me."

"It helped that we weren't all wearing seatbelts, not that I would admit that to just anyone."

Griff chuckled. "Yeah, we're much older and wiser now and have seen the statistics. But back in those days, we were invincible."

Harper and her friends had always been on the straight and narrow and didn't engage in drinking, smoking, and partying, as some in their high school had, but they had pulled a few harmless stunts in their day. "If I remember correctly, we got lost that night."

"Why were we driving around over by the tracks? The north end was bad enough, but why did we drive all the way over there?"

"I think it was you who said we wanted to live on the wild side?"

"Yeah, true. The van died, and we weren't able to get it started again. We guys were doing our best to try to figure out what was wrong with it—tinkering around with the engine in the dark near the tracks. No wonder I decided to go into security." Griff laughed. "It wasn't out of gas, but we figured out it was a dead battery. And then we were all trying to figure out who we'd call—whose parents would be the best about calmly coming and getting us even though we had all broken curfew by that point."

"I think we ended up calling my dad in the end."

"He was pretty cool about it as I recall, but we all ended up grounded."

Harper recalled the evening clearly. She, Kennedy, Laurel, and two other friends were hanging around the senior football players after the homecoming dance.

Dad's lecture.

Mom's lecture.

Followed by her parents telling her she'd done the right thing about calling them in her predicament, which shortened the grounding period. But…the lying about being at Kennedy's and spending the night, and instead driving around on the north end…

"I haven't seen you around much. You must be super busy."

Griff nodded. "I have been busy. With the installations and then teaching self-defense, I get a lot of groups from here and other places wanting to take classes."

"Do you still go to Lake Radford Community Church?"

She hadn't seen him there in forever, but the church had gone to two services, so he might attend second service.

A flash of sorrow crossed Griff's face. "I don't even remember the last time I went to church. I think it was shortly before Dad passed last year."

"I'm so sorry to hear about your dad. I remember his funeral."

"Yeah, I don't think Mom was ever the same after losing him so suddenly."

While she and Griff hadn't been close, Harper regretted that she hadn't stayed in better touch with him after the loss of his dad. "How is your mom doing now?"

"She's doing all right. She's thrown herself into her job and babysitting my sister's kids when she's not working."

"I will remember to pray for her. When you see her next, would you please tell her I said hi?"

"I will tell her that. Thanks. I'm going to walk around and see where the best place is to install the cameras. I'll be back in a few minutes and provide you with the details of my plan of action."

Harper watched him as he rounded the corner to the west side of the house. While it wouldn't be foolproof, it would be beneficial since she'd read a while ago that cameras did deter some wannabe criminals.

She loaded the dishwasher, folded the clothes from the dryer, and started paying some bills at the desk just to the side of the living room when a knock at the door indicated Griff was back. Harper welcomed him in, and he gave details on how much it would cost, where he planned to place the cameras, and how long it would take. She figured Griff was giving her the friend discount, which she appreciated, since it cost less than she'd anticipated.

Griff drained his mug of hot chocolate before launching into another topic, one that Harper was surprised he hadn't broached sooner. "Have you heard from Laurel lately?"

Back in the day, Laurel and Griff briefly dated before Laurel broke it off. Did Griff harbor any resentment? "We text each other regularly."

"That's good. How is she doing?"

"She's doing well, but I wish she'd move back here."

"Probably not with all the memories."

Griff was right. Lake Radford held so many memories that Laurel would rather forget. But what Laurel didn't realize was that not everyone held what her dad had done against her.

"Well, tell her I said hi if you talk to her again." A mesh of worry and confusion etched Griff's expression. He, just like Harper and Kennedy, likely wondered why Laurel broke up with him. He cleared his throat. "I'll be back Monday to install the cameras. If you ever need some self-defense tips, let me know. I'll be offering a refresher course in the summer."

"I will." The thought had occurred to her more than once that she needed to refresh her memory on some of those tactics. While such knowledge was always a beneficial thing to have in one's arsenal, she never imagined it would be something that she should.

Not until the recent events.

Harper waved as Griff pulled out of the parking spot in front of her house. She'd spent an ample amount of time praying for Laurel that God would heal the pain she carried with her and that Laurel would turn back to her Savior.

She'd pray the same for Griff.

ELEVEN

Some people were such idiots. They just didn't get the hint.

He paced the area of his living room. Harper would have to somehow learn that the Cox property needed to remain in the hands of the current owners.

But nothing had worked so far. Not the note on her car, not hiring the druggie and paying him pills to chase her, leave a note on her car, fire gunshots on the property, and lurk around her house. Not paying some dumb kids looking to make an extra buck to follow her and freak her out.

The listing had not been removed, and the land was still on the market.

The last thing he needed was someone buying it and finding things they shouldn't.

That wouldn't do. He'd worked far too hard for what he had to lose it all just because someone signed a real estate contract. Not that the new owner would start building until they secured all the permits, and he knew the city was notoriously slow when handing out those permits. And it would likely be thirty days until the property closed from the day the paperwork was signed.

But still...

He tugged on a pair of gloves, opened the newspaper, and flipped through it, resisting the urge to yawn in boredom. Nothing ever happened in this town. Until recently, he'd rarely purchased *The Lake Radford Daily,* but as he'd thumbed through the last several issues, he had to admit he really did enjoy keeping up with the police reports—that and he needed it for his next plan.

Nothing much about the first incident other than "suspicious person on 422 Fifth Avenue," where the fitness center was located. Good. They could just keep it at that. Made it easier for him.

"Prowler" was what they'd called Motta when a report on Washington Avenue was made, and "shots fired" on Cox Road. The designation of "careless driving" was given to the teens who'd followed Harper and nudged her bumper.

Didn't sound like the cops had a clue about what was going on. They couldn't even solve the Dumaine case, which he personally had no stake in, but thought it interesting that someone would target the worthless mom-and-pop store.

Unless the druggie talked. In that case, action would necessitate said druggie spending more than a few minutes on the Cox property.

More like an eternity. Underground.

But Motta would be in good company.

The best part of this whole plan? That no one would ever suspect someone like him. Upstanding, professional, and skilled. Oh, sure, the cops thought they knew, but he'd never share the truth.

Ever.

He tossed the paper aside and picked up the issue he'd purchased earlier from the dispenser outside the post office. He'd saved it just for a special occasion such as this.

Harper Amerson stared up at him from her picture in the paper on page four. How she ever got to be a real estate agent was beyond him. She couldn't even accurately describe someone chasing her. Or someone standing on her deck.

If she had, Alan Motta, the elusive druggie, would have been apprehended.

Oh, well. Not like he figured anyone would believe Motta's incoherent gibberish if he did try to pin anything on someone other than himself. Someone like him. No, the cops would take one look at the criminal who'd been in jail, and now on probation, more times than he could count, and discount anything Motta said.

He chuckled to himself. Likely, when and if they *did* catch Motta, the guy would be so doped up he'd be useless. Helped that his last payment was a mixture of the painkillers he loved, along with some meth to give him that rush of euphoria. The combination would probably kill Motta at some point, but who would really care about some scumbag lowlife no longer existing?

He certainly didn't. As a matter of fact, he'd be doing the world a favor by ridding it of one less vermin who roamed the streets abusing drugs and committing crimes.

Lake Radford would be better off without the likes of Motta.

Except that he needed the druggie for a little bit longer. Then, like just about everyone else in his life, Motta would become dispensable. Unnecessary. Nonessential.

With a pair of scissors, he cut out her photo and the information about how she wanted to help aid people looking to buy or sell homes. Selling didn't matter, but the buying part did—if it meant the Cox property where the body was.

He studied her photo. Saw her nearly every day, walking around like she was better than everyone else.

"Harper, Harper, Harper," he sneered. "It's time to warn you again."

He opened the new pack of typing paper he'd purchased during his trip to the big box store yesterday. He cut out the letters from the newspaper and worked at pasting them onto the sheet of paper. He released a stream of his favorite curse words when the letters kept sticking to his latex gloves. It took him twice as long as it should have.

He let the letter dry before fitting it into an envelope.

How to write the address so it wouldn't be in his handwriting?

He tapped his foot on the floor and thought about it for a minute. Ah, yes. That would work well.

With his left hand, he formed the letters and words and affixed a stamp. Tomorrow, he'd mail it in that mailbox in the residential area on Second Avenue.

A residential area that had none of those annoying porch cameras. He knew because he'd looked.

And those cops who were always looking for stuff to do in this uneventful town? They'd not find one of his fingerprints on the letter or the envelope.

TWELVE

Harper met the Geller family at the Lake Radford Title Company. Their profound excitement at closing the deal on their new home brightened her day. They signed papers from buyer to seller, then Harper joined them in the foyer and congratulated them once again.

An idea occurred to her...perhaps gifting new homeowners with a basket of goodies, including a gift card or two from local merchants, would be a welcoming touch. She'd be sure to mention it at the next staff meeting.

Sarah, a woman she'd attended high school with and who had worked at the title company since she interned there during her senior year, closed and locked the door behind them. "Have a great evening."

Harper and the Gellers returned the farewell greetings before she and the family went their separate ways. She climbed into her SUV and watched as Mrs. Geller strapped their little one into his car seat in their older model minivan. Another happy ending for a family who'd been looking for the perfect starter home for the past year and a half. They didn't have much money, and Harper, with the permission of her boss, reduced her commission fees.

It was worth it to see the joy on their faces.

Harper checked the clock on her dashboard. Just enough time to grab a quick bite to eat and then head to the fitness center with Kennedy.

As she drove down Washington Avenue, she passed an officer on patrol. She was grateful that there were eyes on her street periodically throughout the day, especially given that the police department was shorthanded.

Harper parked her SUV in the carport, then traipsed through the wet grass to her mailbox. Thankfully, the snow had once again melted. That's how it was this time of year in Lake Radford—snow, then that snow would melt, then it would rain, then more snow, which would again melt.

She scrutinized the area, noting the cameras Griff had installed—one on her porch and one on the front of the house. He'd also mounted one on each side of the house and one in the back, noting that there were now no vulnerable spots in her yard.

That gave her relief. At least if the lurker returned, whoever it was would be caught on video.

Harper peered both ways down Washington Avenue before waving at Mrs. Satterwhite, who stood with Coco in her arms at her expansive front living room window. Harper smiled at the cheerfully decorated mailbox on which multiple daisies had been hand-painted by the former owner. She opened the latch and retrieved a hefty stack of envelopes, including a magazine and a 9"x12" manila envelope.

While it was tempting to verify that the manila envelope was indeed from Mom, Harper kept her wits about her, scanned the area once more, and made her way up the stairs and to her front door. Once inside, she immediately locked it.

She detested having to be this paranoid.

Never again would she take calmness, serenity, and safety for granted.

Harper strode to the counter while simultaneously thumbing through the abundant stack of mail. A water bill, an electricity bill, a credit card bill, and several pieces of junk mail. She tossed them on the counter before opening the manila envelope, which was indeed from Mom, who loved to send fun little gifties in the mail.

She retrieved her envelope opener from her desk and slid open the seal. Inside, Mom had stuffed a note and a box of Harper's favorite candy hearts. Harper didn't have many sugary weaknesses, but this was one of them. She did enjoy candy hearts, especially around Valentine's Day.

She unfolded the note with Mom's loopy handwriting:

Thought you might enjoy this fun little treat. Grandma's ankle is healing, and Grandpa is doing better every day. Dad and I love and miss you.
Mom

Harper lifted the tab on the box of miniature candy hearts, popped one into her mouth, and savored the sugary taste.

Might as well sort the mail since she had a few minutes before meeting Kennedy at the fitness center. She slit open the bills, took a peek at the balances, then stacked them in the black wire tray to be paid in the next day or so. She grabbed the junk mail and thumbed through it one more time before setting it on her portable shredder just to be sure she hadn't missed anything. A white business-sized envelope with squiggly handwriting and no return address caught her eye. Was this just another ploy attempting to sell her something? Perhaps one of those pieces of mail with the marketing goal of making the recipient believe it was a personal letter rather than a company attempting to sell her a better deal on high-speed internet or invite her to a used car sales event?

She glided the envelope opener along the top edge, expecting something else to set on the shredder when she pulled out a white piece of paper. Harper unfolded it and skimmed the words, her heart rate ticking up several notches as she did so.

Someone had pasted individual capitalized alphabet letters of typed print on the paper spelling the words, 'THE SPOT-LIGHT IS A DANGEROUS PLACE TO BE'.

She released the piece of copy paper as though a hot potato, and it fluttered to the floor. The words mocked her, and she read them again from her standing position. Why would the spotlight be a dangerous place, and what did it mean?

What spotlight?

Had she received this and only this, she might have dismissed it. But in conjunction with everything else, it was obvious someone was sending her a threatening message.

Harper regretted having touched it, mixing her fingerprints with those of the sender.

Shaking, she withdrew her cell phone from her purse and punched in Detective Lassiter's number.

"Lassiter."

"Hello, Detective?"

"Ms. Amerson? Is everything all right?"

"I received a strange letter in the mail, and I believe it's related to the other happenings in my case."

THIRTEEN

Kade was not impressed with Clark Montayne.

He hadn't been the one to interview Montayne that first time at the realty office, but now, since the case was officially Kade's, he had the pleasure—or displeasure—of interviewing the arrogant real estate agent.

Montayne agreed to stop by the PD during his lunch hour. Kade met him in the lobby and led him to the interview room. Montayne strutted his way through the hall before settling into the chair, and Kade closed the door. "Will this take long?"

It wasn't so much the first words out of Montayne's mouth, but the tone in which he said them.

"That depends on you." Kade took a seat across from him, a brand-new file folder in front of him. "Just so you know, it's standard procedure to record every interview."

"Whatever." Montayne sprawled out in the chair, taking up the space of two men despite his slim stature.

Kade maintained eye contact for a moment before Montayne looked away.

For a man who supposedly hoped to present himself as a professional businessman, Montayne was sorely lacking in his body language. Yet his clothing presented a wealthy up-and-coming executive with his button-up, classic-designed pale green shirt, tan slacks, and expensive black pointy-toed loafers. When he sat, he crossed one leg over the other at the ankle, exposing black socks that matched his shoes, and wore one of the pricier fitness trackers on his wrist. His fingernails were clean and trimmed, and his short-permed hair combed. He boasted a five o'clock shadow of a beard and perfectly straight, chemically brightened teeth.

"Tell me how well you know Harper Amerson."

"You people have already interviewed me once. Remember that? You came to my place of employment," sneered Montayne.

"Sometimes we do follow-ups." If Montayne was looking for an apology, it wasn't happening.

"It's like you're harassing me. I had nothing to do with any of her issues."

Kade ignored his statement. Whether Montayne had anything to do with harassing Harper remained to be seen. "Tell me how well you know Harper Amerson," he repeated.

"We're coworkers."

The words uttered through pursed lips told Kade all he needed to know about Montayne's opinion of Ms. Amerson. "How long have you worked together?"

"I don't know. Couple of years?" Montayne crossed his arms. "Why the interrogation?"

"Would you consider Ms. Amerson to be a friend?"

"No. Just coworkers. We have a job to do, and we do it."

Kade scribbled his thoughts on a piece of paper. Sure, he was recording, but the notes added an extra layer he might need later. "Do you and Ms. Amerson interact much during your workday?"

"Our offices are at opposite ends of the building."

Not *quite* the answer Kade sought.

Montayne leaned forward, and Kade caught a whiff of cigarette smoke. He jotted that down.

"Mr. Montayne, have you ever sent Ms. Amerson a letter?"

"A letter? Who sends letters?" Montayne tapped on the table and released an exaggerated sigh.

"Do you ever send her texts?"

"Texts?"

"Yes, with your phone?"

Montayne leaned his head back and rolled his eyes. "I know what texts are. I just want to know why you're asking me if I'd send her letters or texts."

"Answering the questions would be appreciated." Kade had underestimated a stalker once before, and an innocent life had been the cost. Every angle had to be pursued, even if that meant dealing with the obnoxious and mannerless Clark Montayne.

"I could get a lawyer."

"That is your right."

Montayne appeared to consider his options before finally speaking. "No. I don't think I've ever sent her a text, and I for sure wouldn't send her a letter. I don't even like her."

Bingo. "Mind if I ask why not?"

Montayne checked his watch. "With all due respect, I do have a showing in a half hour."

"Does this look familiar?" Kade removed the plastic evidence bag with the note and envelope Ms. Amerson had received in the mail.

Montayne cocked his head. "What is that?"

"Feel free to inspect it, just don't remove it from the bag."

The man did as he suggested and lifted the bag from the table and turned it over. "'The spotlight is a dangerous place to be'?" What appeared to be genuine confusion flashed across his face.

"Ms. Amerson received this in the mail yesterday. Do you know anything about it?"

Montayne set the bag on the desk and flicked it away. "No idea at all."

"Would you say there is any competition between you and Ms. Amerson?"

"Maybe from her point of view. In my mind, she's nowhere as proficient as I am."

"At the realty office, is it important to secure sales?"

"What do you think?"

The disrespect was irritating, but not surprising. "I would imagine there is a competition among real estate agents. Didn't you get Agent of the Year last year?"

"And the year before, yes."

"Do you know anything about the Cox property?"

"Sure. Everyone knows about the Cox property. First time it's been on the market. Nice setting for a home, forested, view of the mountains, still in city limits. What's there not to like?"

"Sounds like the perfect place to live."

Montayne shrugged.

Kade continued with his questioning. "I would imagine it's listed at a hefty price."

"Not sure. It's not my property."

But the lack of eye contact told Kade differently. Montayne knew exactly how much the property was listed for.

Montayne's lips drew back into a sarcastic smile. "Anyone in the office can show it. The Cox property is a multiple listing, so even agents outside of the office could do so as well."

"So, maybe selling for a hundred thousand?"

"Higher."

Kade keyed the property into his cell phone. "Says here it's listed for $495,000 for the five acres."

"Sounds about right."

"That acreage would garner a healthy commission, am I right? Let's see, close to $30,000 on the asking price if my math is..."

"Why are you asking me this?"

Kade ignored the interruption. "If my math is correct, that's a sizable commission."

"Yeah, so? I've had better commissions than that."

"I can't imagine that's the norm. Lake Radford's real estate prices have increased in the past few years, but there are still plenty of affordable options for those looking to buy. Am I correct?"

Montayne scratched at one of his generous black eyebrows. "There are a lot of affordable options here, but there are also a lot of pricier ones as well, especially in the Oxbow area. And because you're so curious about the real estate market, the only places not selling well are those on the north end."

More than he needed to know, but it could be helpful. "Have you been to the Cox property in the past week?"

"No."

"No showings there?"

"Not my listing."

"You mentioned that, but also that any agent can show it because it's nonexclusive."

"Yes."

This was getting nowhere. "Have you *ever* shown the Cox property?"

Montayne threaded a hand through his hair. "I may have shown it once. It's Harper's listing, and I have plenty of my own."

"As pricey as that one?"

"Pricier. Besides, not everyone wants to build. Some would rather have a house already built."

Montayne had a point. "So, you haven't been there in the last week?"

"Again, no."

"And this letter doesn't look familiar to you?"

"Nope." Montayne again checked his watch. Or maybe he was checking his heart rate, which seemed to have escalated due to his jittery movements.

"How do you feel about Ms. Amerson being in the spotlight in the paper?"

"The realty company does that all the time. Shows the public who the agents are. I couldn't care less if it was her turn to be in the..." he air-quoted, "spotlight." Montayne released an exaggerated breath. "Are we finished yet?"

"Just one more question." Kade had saved the best for last. "Do you know the man in this photo?"

Montayne glanced down at the blurred image of the man outside the fitness center the night he'd chased Ms. Amerson. "Never seen him before in my life."

"All right. How about this one?" Kade pushed the paper toward him with the image of a thin guy in a knit cap, one of whom surveillance of Montayne showed him speaking to the other day outside the real estate office.

Montayne's eyes narrowed into slits. Could be he was hiring someone to harass Ms. Amerson. He could well afford it. "He was probably asking for money."

"And did you give him some?"

Montayne shrugged. "Who knows? Probably not. I try not to give away my hard-earned cash to some sleazeball leech."

"What's the man's name?"

"How should I know? If he was asking me for money, I wasn't going to stand there and chat with him."

"It looks like you're handing him something."

Montayne lifted the photo and perused it closely. "Yeah, okay, I remember this guy. He was asking for money, and I handed him a couple of ones and a cigarette."

"Not your usual M.O., though, is it?"

"No."

"So you weren't paying him for maybe a job he did for you? Maybe shoveling snow or something?"

"I don't need to hire homeless bums to shovel snow. I live in a neighborhood with an HOA. I pay $100 a month to have those services provided."

"Just handing a guy a couple of ones and a cigarette, even though you're not known for making donations."

"Yep."

"Ever seen the guy any other time?"

"Nope."

"Do you think you'll give him some money another time if he needs it?"

Montayne pierced Kade with a hard glare. "Nope."

The other footage Kade examined had showed Montayne and the unknown man going their separate ways, the unknown man lighting the cigarette and disappearing into the night.

Kade nodded. "All right. Well, that should be all for now."

Montayne stood up so fast that the chair fell backward. "Good. I need to get to my meeting."

Kade extended a hand, which Montayne reluctantly shook. For someone who rated himself as a strong and fit athlete in his bio on the real estate website, the man had a weak and clammy handshake. "We'll be in touch. I'll show you out."

Montayne had the audacity to hand Kade a card. "In case you're ever in the market for a new house."

FOURTEEN

The time on the dashboard revealed it was ten to eight. Harper zipped up her puffer coat and stepped from her SUV, planning to arrive early to tend to a few matters before the monthly staff meeting. A gust of wind whipped against her face, threatening to tug loose the bun she'd fashioned her long hair into before leaving the house. She hoped the weather would improve by the time the Valentine's Day 5K rolled around. Out of all the years she'd participated, only twice had the weather been too frigid and nasty to enjoy the fundraiser.

She opened the door to the office, the wind catching it and whipping it against the wall. With effort, she heaved it shut and stood just inside the door, shaking off the chill. She kept her coat zipped for the time being until the warmth of the business seeped through her. Finally, she edged her way inside and paused at Loretta's desk.

Loretta, still in her coat, conversed with someone on the phone—likely a customer from the way her normally bubbly vernacular switched to an all-business tone. While she waited, Harper perused the multitude of knickknacks and pictures crowding her friend's desk. Not that the items weren't all organized, because they were. As a matter of fact, Loretta liked to refer to it as organized chaos. Numerous photos of her grandchildren, plastic and glass figurines, two painted rocks, an abundance of sticky notes, and a mug with coffee drew Harper's attention. A former food can that one of her granddaughters had decorated with silk flowers, buttons, wallpaper, and foam shapes doubled as a pencil holder, but was overcrowded with too many pens and pencils.

She was about to forego chatting with Loretta when the woman bid the person on the phone goodbye, jotted something down on an already-filled purple sticky note, and took a sip of her coffee.

"Good morning, Harper."

"Good morning. Busy day already?"

"I barely got in the door, and the phone was already ringing." Loretta rolled her eyes.

"Any interesting news while I was away?

Loretta laughed. "You were just here yesterday, but nothing too interesting. I made a new pot of coffee for the staff meeting, and Zelda's delivered some fresh donuts for the staff meeting."

Their boss, Paulette, always went all out when she ordered doughnuts from the bakery. Most of the time, Harper could resist the delectable maple bars that brought her back to her elementary school days when she and Mom would stop by after school and grab one for the two of them to share. But today, Harper would have a challenging time foregoing the tasty treat and might just relent, much to the disturbance of her healthy habit mantra.

She leaned on the gray cubicle wall that surrounded Loretta's desk. Knowing the administrative assistant's penchant for whimsical decorative items, she'd likely love to hear Harper's idea. "The other day during a closing, I had this great idea. What if we presented a welcoming basket to new homeowners at the time of closing? Wouldn't that be awesome?"

"Oh!" Loretta's eyes enlarged beneath the reading glasses perched on the bridge of her nose. "What a great idea! I would love to help with that."

Just as Harper figured. Loretta did an exceptional job greeting customers, transferring phone calls, and handling any miscellaneous overflow the agents asked of her. But Harper knew, both from working with Loretta for the past two years and from teaching Vacation Bible School with her three summers in a row, that the sweet woman in her early sixties thrived on anything crafty and imaginative.

"If Paulette agrees to it, I think it'd be something to add to your work duties."

Loretta laughed and removed her coat, slipping it onto her rolling chair. "Normally, I would say I have enough on my plate, but I'd never turn down something creative like that. What are you thinking of having us put in it? I learned how to do origami at a class at the senior center last month for the craft club. I'm also quite proficient in constructing little tissue paper roses."

"The flowers would be a nice touch. I was also thinking about maybe some gift cards from local businesses, and if it were summer, maybe a few seeds for the homeowners to plant in their new yards. Perhaps maybe a candle or a plant or even one of those directories the Chamber of Commerce publishes with a listing of all of the local restaurants and things to do in Lake Radford."

Loretta clasped her hands together. "It's fabulous! I think you should bring it up in the meeting today."

"I think I will. Perhaps the other agents have some suggestions for things to add to the baskets."

"Speaking of which, the meeting starts in just a few minutes. I guess I'd better go in there and make sure everything is all set." Loretta flipped the phone switch for calls to go directly to voicemail, took another sip of coffee, all in a matter of seconds, and started toward the conference room. Harper turned around to see Clark standing close by, leaning against the wall outside his office. He glowered at her, his mouth pinched.

"Good morning," she said, doing her best to be cordial.

But instead of a greeting, he spoke terse words between gritted teeth. "Quit telling the cops lies about me or I'm going to have you sued for slander and harassment."

Dread gnawed at her insides. The last thing she needed was a frivolous lawsuit from Clark Montayne. "I have no idea what you're talking about."

He leaned closer, his face inches from hers, and his eyes darkened. The stench of cigarette smoke, along with fear, choked her. "They questioned me again about some dumb letter you got in the mail. I didn't send it, and I didn't have anything to do with whatever it is you are accusing me of. Got it?"

"I never said you did. You are the only enemy I have, so logically they are going to question you." She wished her voice sounded more confident.

"I'm not your *only* enemy, and if I was going to do something to you, it wouldn't be sending you some dumb letter with words cut out of the newspaper. This is your last warning before I go to my attorney."

She said nothing, but attempted to rein in the pounding of her heart. Clark took a step back, pivoted, and, keeping his eyes on her, methodically walked in the direction of his office.

Harper rushed to her own office to deposit her coat and purse before meeting in the conference room. Paulette was a great boss, but she didn't appreciate lateness, especially to the monthly meetings.

But before she switched gears, she needed to calm herself. While she never truly imagined Clark to be physically dangerous, something in his sinister glare and harsh words had rattled her. Detective Lassiter must think he was somehow involved to interview him.

Harper perched in her chair and folded her hands. *Lord, please calm me. Settle my racing heart. Please keep me safe and let them find out who is harassing me. Be my refuge and uphold me with Your righteous right hand.*

It was the same prayer she'd prayed numerous times in light of recent happenings.

Less than five minutes later, she entered the small conference room with eight padded chairs around a white table and slid in between Loretta and Angie, the rental property manager. The aroma of donuts filled the air, and someone propped open the donut box to reveal the tasty selection of maple bars, glazed donuts, and jelly rolls.

The other employees staggered in, including Paulette, the owner and broker, who took her place at the head of the table, and the other agents, Jamila, Ean, and Enrique. Clark entered last and took the remaining seat directly across from her.

Clark visited with Enrique, and they laughed about something. Paulette tapped on the table with her pen, a sign that the meeting was about to begin. "Good morning, everyone." Her cotton-blonde hair, as usual, was coifed into the perfect bob, and Paulette looked every bit the part of a successful businesswoman. A nasty divorce nearly caused her to lose the business she had worked so hard for, and Harper greatly respected the woman who not only was a fair employer but also actually cared about her staff.

"First off, please do help yourself to a doughnut or two." She flashed one of her dazzling smiles. "Loretta also made us a fresh pot of coffee..."

To which Ean offered a slight groan. "Not so sure I'd like to drink it if Loretta made it." He scrunched up his bulbous nose.

Loretta playfully swatted his arm.

The forty-something man's eyes twinkled beneath stylish glasses. His thick British accent added to his charm, and few found it difficult to dislike the personable fellow with the excellent sense of humor.

"If you absolutely can't bear the taste, Ean," teased Jamila, her ebony face glowing, "there is bottled water over on the corner desk over there."

Ean chuckled. "You're always the helpful sort. And, truthfully, it's always good to know there's a choice of beverage."

Harper watched the interaction between her coworkers. Were it not for Clark, the place would be as near perfect as a workplace could be.

Everyone grabbed a doughnut, with Enrique, a jolly Hispanic man who rarely turned down food of any kind, plucking two from the box. "Does anyone want either of these before I eat them?"

Everyone shook their heads in response.

"Thank you all for coming today," said Paulette. "This will be a shorter meeting, but we do have a couple of items to discuss. First off, I know it's a little bit slower right now, but I have every confidence it will pick up in March. We do have quite a few listings, and we closed on a few houses already this year, so that's good news. We do have a shortage of acreages, and it's been a struggle to sell anything on the north end, but other than that, we are selling properties, so I want to encourage you all to keep up the good work."

Paulette discussed several other matters before she opened the meeting to her employees for anything they wished to discuss. Harper was about to suggest the baskets when Clark set his donut on his napkin and slightly raised his hand. Before Paulette could acknowledge, he started speaking. "I have a suggestion."

"Yes. What is it, Clark?"

Because Paulette rarely saw anything but the good in others, she had yet to realize Clark painted an excellent façade and was not the man some people—she—thought he was.

"I was thinking…" his attention veered briefly to Harper, and something cold flashed in his dark-brown eyes before he continued. "When people buy a new home, it's an exciting experience. It doesn't matter if it's upgrading, downsizing, first-time homebuyers, someone new to the town, or someone who's lived here for decades. I was thinking it might be good PR to have housewarming baskets. I've seen these before at other real estate agencies and was surprised when I started working here that we didn't have them to offer to our clients."

Harper's jaw went slack before a surge of anger burned within her. She felt Loretta nudge her arm gently. As if he wasn't annoying enough, now Clark was attempting to undercut her and steal her idea? Should she say something to Paulette? After all that had been *her* idea.

Paulette offered a broad smile. "I really like that idea, Clark. I am surprised, just as you are, that we haven't thought of it before. It would be a nice gesture and an excellent marketing tool, too. You know I am all for effective marketing."

Clark puffed out his chest and weaved his fingers through his black hair. "Great! Perhaps we could even include a few gift cards from local merchants and that business directory from the Chamber of Commerce."

"Keep talking. I like what I'm hearing," said Paulette.

A bitter taste filled Harper's mouth. It was one thing to bring up an idea, but to claim it as your own when it was clearly someone else's—someone who had just been talking about it less than fifteen minutes ago—was another thing altogether.

Loretta tipped her head in a slight nod toward Paulette as if encouraging Harper to tell their boss where the idea originated. But it was likely Harper wouldn't be able to get a word in edgewise because Paulette and Clark were discussing the finite details of the housewarming baskets, and Ean had chimed in to say it would be an excellent addition to add some tea bags.

Perhaps later she would have the opportunity to speak with Paulette. The woman was—as so many were—enamored by Clark's façade.

Or maybe it didn't really matter as long as the clients received the baskets and Loretta was the one who got to make them.

Whatever the case, Harper did not need to deal with a vengeful Clark Montayne on top of everything else.

FIFTEEN

Harper entered the Lake Radford Family Fitness Center. Some stress relief was in order. She shuddered at the recollection of the man on the Cox property and the letter she'd received.

The whys and how-comes infiltrated her mind. The only person she could think of who might be out for some type of revenge was Clark, but he hadn't been the one in the woods.

However, Clark had been extremely offended that he'd been interviewed by the police.

How many times had she thanked the Lord that she and the Medills were safe that day at the Cox property? That the man hadn't come *toward* them with the gun?

How often had she thanked the Lord that whoever it was on her deck that night hadn't actually gotten inside her house? That the group of teens, one of whom would have his court date soon, hadn't run her completely off the road or caused an accident?

God was faithful and had kept her safe thus far. She breathed a prayer of gratitude. Things had again been quiet since she'd received the letter. Perhaps whoever it was would now leave her alone.

A notification sounded, and she glanced at the text from Kennedy.

Sorry, I can't make it tonight. I got stuck late at work.

No worries. I don't plan to stay long.

Be safe.

I will. Chat with you soon.

She'd be here just long enough to get a good run in and then leave early.

Harper swiped her membership card, said hello to Bettina—who didn't return her greeting—and hurried back through the hallways to the main cardio area. At least she was here earlier today. It was six when she pulled out of the real estate parking lot. A necessary and quick bite to eat, and she was on her way to the gym.

The place was hopping, but fortunately, she'd found a space to park beneath a streetlight.

She looked up to see Clark brush past her. Too bad most people in Lake Radford preferred this gym over the other two options.

She increased her pace and rounded the corner by the racquetball courts and dashed through the weight room. Three treadmills remained, including her favorite one—the older model on the far end with the smoothest running surface.

Harper switched her bag to her other shoulder, grabbed a few hand wipes, and was about to reach "her" treadmill when Clark hopped up on it. He turned, glowered at her, and hit the "quick start" button.

The man was a challenge, and Harper did her best to remember to pray for him. And for herself in how she dealt with him.

She found an available treadmill second to the end on the far right-hand side. Ten minutes later, she was past the warm-up stage and well into her run. Several patrons left, but a quick perusal told her Clark remained.

A forty-something man beside her slowed his pace and swiped at the sweat on his brow. He teetered slightly to one side, reduced his speed, and then gripped the side handles. "Are you all right?" she mouthed.

Instead of answering, the man slowed his pace even more before hitting the "emergency stop" button. He wavered before collapsing on his treadmill.

Harper stopped her own machine and rushed to the man's side. "You—call 911!" she shouted to a nearby woman. When the woman instead just stood there, swaying with eyes bulging, Harper directed her order to another. She then kneeled beside the man. Thankfully, he was still conscious.

Lord, please help me know what to do!

"Sir, can you hear me?"

He nodded, and she assisted him into a more comfortable position. "The ambulance is on its way."

Sweat dampened his forehead, arms, and chest. Normal since he'd been running, and the fitness center wasn't known for always keeping the gym as cool as it should be.

Jasper hurried toward them, the first aid kit and AED in his hands. "The ambulance is on its way. Is he all right?"

A sigh of relief escaped her lips. "I think so. He's still conscious."

"It's my blood sugar," said the man. He rubbed his head. "I got dizzy and lightheaded."

"Are you hypoglycemic?"

"Yes."

Lord, please let the ambulance arrive soon.

She knew exactly how he felt. "Is there a glucose pill in the first aid kit?"

Jasper rummaged through the plastic bin. "Someone forgot to replace them."

"No worries. I have some in my bag." With a sense of urgency, she hoisted her gym bag onto her treadmill and foraged through the front zippered part. She removed the slim bottle of glucose pills and popped the lid.

Together, she and Jasper propped the man into a sitting position. "I'm hypoglycemic as well. Here's a glucose pill."

He opened a shaky hand, and she deposited the orange-flavored tablet into his palm. "I should have these in my bag," he muttered, popping it into his mouth and carefully chewing it.

"Someone is going to be in trouble for not replacing them in the first aid kit," muttered Jasper.

A small crowd had gathered, including Enzo, one of the other gym employees. He motioned for everyone to take a step back so the paramedics could get through. Clark ignored him and stood right behind Harper. "You shouldn't give him that. You could be sued."

She turned to look into his cold eyes. His black hair matted to his forehead from exercise, and his hairy and thin muscular legs boasted a scar on his knee, probably from some type of surgery. His apathy irritated her, although it wasn't unexpected. Harper bit back a retort and instead focused on the man. "How about another one?"

He nodded.

EMTs arrived seconds later, and Enzo again directed traffic.

A tall paramedic in his twenties squatted beside the man and began his observation. "Sir, can you tell me your symptoms?"

"Yes, I was running, and I started to feel dizzy, started shaking, was lightheaded, and experienced double vision."

The other EMT, an older woman, peered up at Harper. "You were here when this happened?"

"Yes. I gave him two glucose pills. He mentioned he was hypoglycemic."

Less than five minutes later, the man agreed to a trip to the ER. The crowd disbursed, except Jasper, Enzo, Clark, and two other people.

"Glad you were here. Quick thinking on the glucose pills," said Jasper. "And thank you, Enzo, for your help."

"I'm just thankful it wasn't a heart attack. I've had CPR and first aid training, but have hoped never to use it." Harper glanced at her fitness tracker. Her heart rate was still elevated from the eventful evening.

Clark wiped his face with a towel. "Don't be surprised if you get sued."

He was relentless. But Harper was just grateful it hadn't been worse.

Enzo shook his head. "She won't get sued. Haven't you ever heard of the Good Samaritan Law?"

Clark snorted. "Better to leave people as they are than to get involved."

"Maybe for you." The words left her mouth without a second thought, and elicited a reddened face and curled lip from her coworker. He turned on his heel and stomped away.

"Thank you, Jasper and Enzo, for being here. The gym is lucky to have you both." Harper's voice shook as she said the words. The episode with the man hit a little too close to home, reminding her of the few times she'd lost consciousness from her own hypoglycemia.

Enzo smiled, and Jasper shrugged. "It's our job," he said.

Harper cleaned her machine, stretched, and left the fitness center, her heart still racing in her chest. It could have been so much worse for the man. He could have hit his head when he fell, or worse. *Thank You, Lord, for watching over him.*

The following day after work, she headed into the parking lot and started the trek to her SUV. Clark had taken her spot again, and she'd had to park farther away than usual. In this case, behind the neighboring store.

She'd gotten caught talking with an investor who was interested in a triplex on Fourteenth Street and hadn't been able to leave as soon as she'd like. At least it was staying light later, and the sunset was now edging toward 5:30.

Still, as she walked out, the gloomy and cloudy ambience gave her pause. There was a camera behind the realty office, but camera or not, if someone planned something nefarious, that surveillance wouldn't protect her.

A horn beeped from Main Street in front of the realty office, but in the back, all was quiet. She hastened her pace, weaving in and out of the remaining vehicles, and made her way between a jacked-up truck and an older model, pointy-nosed van. Not much farther now. Just a few steps to the adjoining parking lot, and her SUV was just beyond that.

She scanned her surroundings and gripped her purse against her body. In her right hand, she carried her keys, the SUV key prominent in case she needed to use it to protect herself.

Use it to protect herself? Who was she kidding? She needed to update her self-defense skills and sign up with Griff for a refresher course. And she needed to take the women's shooting course next time it was offered.

Her purse brushed softly against the jacked-up truck, and she was about to emerge from between the vehicles when a man jumped in front of her.

Harper screamed.

She backed up, preparing to exit through the other end, but the man rushed toward her. "Go away!" But her voice did nothing to deter him. Harper stumbled over a crack in the asphalt and nearly fell backward. She grabbed the van's mirror to right herself. She teetered, and the man grasped her arm. Harper kicked him as hard as she could in the shin.

He muttered an oath and doubled over, but didn't release her. Instead, the thin man in the threadbare winter coat and knit cap pulled a knife and held it to her chest.

The bolt of panic hit her so forcefully, she wasn't sure how she'd maintain her balance. Her first thought was prayer. *Lord, please help me!* Her second thought was emerging victoriously from the situation. The knife was close. So close to her skin.

Was anyone else around? Would anyone hear her? But what was she thinking? If she screamed, he'd likely plunge the knife into her. Her heart pounded in her ears as the nausea roiled in her stomach.

Had she seen this man before? He looked vaguely familiar.

Yes, that's who it was. Detective Lassiter had stopped by last night and had asked her if this man could potentially be the one who'd been lurking around her house. The camera had captured a picture of him behind the realty office, talking with Montayne.

Was he the one? She'd told the detective she couldn't be sure. Same slim build, same shabby clothing, although not the same coat. And this time, the man didn't wear a face mask. Anxiety eclipsed her thoughts. The longer she stood here with this crazed lunatic, the more at risk she was. Her gaze darted to the knife, then to his face.

She would memorize his appearance so she could accurately describe him.

If she survived.

Lord, please help me!

The stench of an unwashed body, intermingled with a rotten food smell, filled her nostrils. *Please, Lord, let the owner of the truck or the van return to their vehicle.*

"What do you want?" she asked, wishing her voice didn't tremble with raw panic as she muttered the words.

"You better quit."

"Wh-what?"

"You better quit." His mouth hung open, revealing black chewing tobacco bordering his two front teeth. Was he awaiting her confirmation?

"Yes, I will quit," she said, desperate to get him to leave.

"You promise?"

"I promise."

"Now give me some money."

"Some...money?"

The man kept the knife on her with one hand, then held out his other hand as if waiting for her to extract cash from her wallet. With shaking hands, she unbuttoned her purse, unzipped her wallet, and extricated the only cash she had—a five and four ones.

Her assailant wadded up the money and shoved it into his coat pocket. Then, backing away from her slowly while keeping the knife aimed at her, he exited the area between the two vehicles and disappeared into the shadows.

Harper's legs shook, and for the next several seconds, her leaden feet planted her solidly in place. Then, a bolt of adrenaline pumped through her, forcing her to launch forward, running the remaining way to her vehicle.

Her hands trembled as she hit the fob, opened the door, climbed inside, and clicked the lock button. She sat, shaken and rattled, gripping the steering wheel.

Thank You, Jesus, thank You, Jesus. She fought the rising panic and dialed 911.

SIXTEEN

Kade met his informant to discuss the man Montayne had spoken to that night and had supposedly given a few ones and a cigarette to. Something told Kade that wasn't the only thing Montayne had told the man.

The informant, a scruffy man in his thirties named Padgett, whom Kade pretty much sat on the fence about when it came to whether or not he was truly informational, seemed to ponder Kade's inquiry. "I might know who you're talking about."

"Might or do?" Unfortunately, with Padgett, you had to be blunt.

"Any way we can shorten my probation?"

"Not for me to decide."

Padgett scrubbed his filthy beard with his hand. "But you'll put in a good word for me, right? Tell the judge I'm always one to help out the cops when they need me?"

"Depends on whether or not the details you give are helpful."

Padgett blew out a deep breath that overrode the smell of coffee in the shop and reeked of menthol vape. "All right, yeah, I know who he is. Name is Fontenot. He's a homeless guy here in town. Surprised you haven't heard of him."

Kade hadn't, but that didn't mean anything. He was still getting to know the townspeople. "Where can I find him?"

Padgett gave an exaggerated shrug. "He's homeless, so how should I know?" But the way Padgett blinked ninety miles an hour and drummed his fingers on his stained jeans, Kade figured he wasn't being truthful.

"Are you protecting him?"

"Why would I protect him?"

Typical Padgett, answering a question with a question. "Where can I find him?"

"Look, man, you didn't hear this from me, but I heard he was couch surfing and was staying at Nunez's place."

"Kirtis Nunez?"

"The one and only, or at least we hope he's the only one." Padgett uttered a nervous and annoying laugh.

"Is Nunez still living in the Shuford Trailer Park?"

"Last I heard. But look, man, you can't say I told you."

"Are you being straight with me?"

"You bet I am." Padgett thumbed a finger toward the door. "You done with me? Because I need to go."

Kade nodded, and Padgett scurried out the door, coffee and donut in hand.

If Fontenot was the one who'd been stalking Ms. Amerson, then all Kade had to do was find out who put him up to it. Odds were it could be Montayne.

Kade returned to the office, did a mountain of paperwork that he'd been putting off, and three hours later was ready to leave for the day at a decent hour when Baldwin stuck his head in the door. "Ms. Amerson just called dispatch about being threatened and robbed in the realty office parking lot. She's at home now."

"Let's go." Kade simultaneously grabbed his keys and coat and hurriedly followed Baldwin. Had Ms. Amerson been injured? Was it the same person who'd been stalking her? Did they have any footage of the crime?

Ten minutes later, Kade and Baldwin sat in Ms. Amerson's living room as she detailed what had happened when she'd left work.

"Can you give us a description?"

"Yes. Thin, disheveled, brown eyes. One eye was slightly bigger than the other. Dark brown facial hair. He was wearing a knit cap. Maybe 5'8" or so."

Kade brought up the photo of Fontenot on his phone. "Is this him?"

"Yes, that's him!"

Baldwin took Ms. Amerson's statement, and Kade told her he'd be paying a visit to the man. He also promised that a patrol would be making more frequent drive-bys.

As Kade bid Ms. Amerson good night, he thought about the cases still yet to be solved. So much for thinking that events in the Amerson case had slowed. Ms. Amerson's rose to the top position, followed by the Dumaine case.

Could be an easy solve if things went the way he hoped they would after he spoke to Fontenot.

The man wasn't anywhere to be found that evening when he stopped by the Shuford Trailer Park and surveilled trailer #18. People came and went, but no sign of Fontenot. Kade wouldn't play his hand just yet. Knocking on the door and asking Nunez or one of the other felons who typically resided there would only encourage them to warn Fontenot.

And if this man was the one who'd caused Ms. Amerson all this trouble, Kade wanted to have all his *i*'s dotted and *t*'s crossed.

He left after a two-hour stakeout. It was time to call Montayne in again and put the pressure on about his *real* conversation with Fontenot.

Early the next morning, he headed back to the Shuford Trailer Park, this time with Gossett. If Fontenot had come in sometime during the night, chances were the man was still there. Patrol officers hung back at the entrance sign for backup. Kade planned to arrest Fontenot, and if there was any trouble with Nunez and his classy group of friends, assistance wasn't far away.

Nunez's trailer was among the worst in the park. A yellow 1950s single-wide with two doors on the front, a weathered roof, and a boarded-up window made it stand out. A makeshift shed, built but never finished, stood at the far end of the lengthy home. Perhaps once upon a time, someone thought to make a clever add-on, but they hadn't finished the job. Garbage littered the yard, and a rusted vehicle with three wheels was parked beneath a rotted tree.

"Nice place," commented Gossett.

"Thinking of moving?"

Gossett laughed. "Sure. My husband would love this place. There's even a car in the yard for him to tinker with."

Kade parked his service vehicle, and he and Gossett monitored their surroundings before emerging from the car and walking up the two rotted steps to the front door. Kade knocked.

Kurtis Nunez opened the door, his gray hair sticking up at odd ends. "Whaddaya want?"

"We're looking for a man by the name of Fontenot."

"Ain't seen him."

"Come on, Nunez. We know he's couch surfing here."

Nunez's mouth twitched, but his stare remained steadfast. If Kade could list one person he wished were behind bars, it would be Nunez. A felon whose rap sheet included possession with intent to distribute, grand theft, assault, and burglary should be locked away. But somehow, someway, he was still a free man.

"He ain't here." Nunez began to shut the door when Kade stuck his foot in it to keep it from closing.

"If you're harboring a criminal, things won't go well for you."

Nunez snickered. His coarse gray beard swayed when he did so. A beard that sported some type of leftover food in it. He sobered just as quickly. "Do you think that scares me?"

"It should."

"I can count on one hand the years I've spent in the slammer. Go away, cop. Fontenot ain't here."

Kade removed his foot, and Nunez slammed the trailer door. As if on cue, the door at the other end of the trailer opened, and a man leaped out of the house and started running.

It would have been nice to be able to warm up before running after Fontenot, but at least after two cups of coffee, Kade had an excess of energy. He chased him down the main road, behind a garbage can and over a fence, before he tackled Fontenot to the ground, handcuffed him, and he and Gossett took him to the station.

A half hour later, Fontenot admitted to attempted assault and robbery, but vehemently denied any role in the other incidents regarding Ms. Amerson. He also denied that Clark Montayne had anything to do with his choice to commit the crime against Ms. Amerson.

Harper had tossed and turned that night, grateful that Kennedy had offered to come over and sleep in the spare room. Not that her best friend would be much protection if the man who'd pulled the knife on her returned, but just having someone else in the house did help.

They stayed up until eleven o'clock watching a chick flick and eating popcorn. All was quiet, and the police car she'd seen at least four times through the window lent some reassurance that the man wouldn't be prowling around tonight.

"Do you think it's the same man?" Kennedy asked as they cleaned up the kitchen after the movie.

"I think it could be. I didn't get a good look that night at the fitness center, and both times, he was wearing a mask. Interestingly, Detective Lassiter mentioned that the man who was in my yard left a size twelve print in the snow, so it's someone with larger feet."

Kennedy had the grace to change the subject to Laurel and how they hadn't heard from her this week, which launched into a topic regarding the good old days when the three of them did everything together. They chatted about a variety of things until Kennedy brought up a completely unexpected topic out of the blue.

Leave it to her best friend to broach a subject that may or may not have been on Harper's mind.

"So, what do you think of Detective Lassiter?"

"He seems thorough and like he really cares about the town and its residents."

"And…"

"And what?"

"He is kind of cute." Kennedy jabbed Harper in the arm with her elbow. "I know you've noticed."

Harper shrugged. Yes, she *had* noticed his appearance. Rugged. Muscular. Short, dark brown hair, amazing eyes. "All right, maybe. There aren't a whole lot of good-looking guys in Lake Radford, so I guess he does stand out."

"Is he married?"

"How should I know? He's attempting to keep me from being stalked and harassed. I haven't asked if he has a wife."

Kennedy laughed. "He's not."

"Then why ask? And how do you know?"

"I asked someone who knows someone who knows someone else, anonymously, of course, and no, he's not married. Or even seeing someone. How's that for good investigative skills?"

"I might be impressed, but honestly, Kennedy, that hasn't even been on my radar."

"Uh-huh, and I'm working my dream job."

"A part-time job in retail is your dream job? Who knew?"

They shared a few more laughs before Kennedy sobered. "Have you told your parents about all that's going on?"

"Only the note that I received at the fitness center. They have their hands full with caring for Grandma and Grandpa, and I can't just lay this on them."

"You're kidding, right? Your parents would want to know."

"Have you met my mom? I love her to pieces, but she is such a worrywart. I can't do that to her, especially not right now. Did I tell you that Grandma sprained her ankle?"

"You did, and now you are changing the subject. You really should tell your parents, and you really should entertain the idea of maybe considering Detective Lassiter once all this is over."

"I'll pray about both suggestions."

"And speaking of praying, I happen to have it on good authority that the handsome detective attends second service."

"Oh, really. Now, who told you that?"

Kennedy pretended to zip her lips. "I'll never tell."

"Why don't you consider him?"

"No thanks. Totally not my type."

After checking the door twice, Harper told Kennedy good night, then headed to her room. Her best friend had been a great diversion from nearly being stabbed tonight, but even so, sleep would be hard to come by.

Harper prayed for God's peace, opened her Bible, and read through the Psalms about how David had been pursued by his enemies and how God had kept him safe. Then she'd thought about the timetable regarding all that happened.

Harper had never been threatened. Never had to worry about being a victim of a crime. She loved her town. Loved her job. Loved the people in the town where she'd been born and raised.

Why then? Why now?

Nothing had happened until she'd listed the Cox property. She didn't believe in coincidences, but it did strike her as odd. She'd need to tell Detective Lassiter about her suspicions.

Detective Lassiter. All right, so she did think he was cute, and she did appreciate that he did go to second service. Hopefully, that meant he had a relationship with Jesus.

Clark Montayne denied having anything to do with Fontenot's attempted assault and mugging of Ms. Amerson. Kade wasn't fully convinced. Montayne had lawyered up, Fontenot was in jail, and now, hopefully, things would settle down a bit.

But the niggling in Kade's gut told him there was more to the story. He laced up his running shoes and started down the quiet neighborhood he called home. If he was going to successfully run in the upcoming 5K, he needed to practice more than just apprehending slow-moving criminals like he had when he'd chased Fontenot.

God had provided a cool but clear February day, and it wouldn't be long before jogging would be an every-night occurrence. Well, every night that he was home at a decent hour, which wasn't always. His hours as a detective were insane sometimes, but he wouldn't trade the job for anything.

He zipped around the first part of the cul-de-sac, then down a connecting street before returning home, stretching his calves and quads, and microwaving a plate of leftovers.

A thought popped into his mind. He'd be seeing Harper Amerson at the 5K in a few days. Perhaps when all of this crazy stalking stuff was over, he could connect with her on a more personal basis.

SEVENTEEN

Harper finished eating breakfast, pinned her bib onto the front of her long-sleeved pink, sweat-wicking athletic shirt, and tucked her phone, lip balm, granola bar, and glucose pills into the pink-and-white striped running belt. After she parked her SUV, she'd insert her car keys into the belt as well. A few sips of water, and she was ready for the event she anticipated each year.

It would be refreshing to focus on something other than the happenings of the past few weeks. Detective Lassiter mentioned that the creepy man who'd pulled a knife on her and robbed her in the realty office parking lot was in jail. The relief had melted off her shoulders at the news. No more notes, no more letters, no more prowling around her house, and no more being stalked. She'd thanked the Lord profusely for His protection and the good news that she'd not have to worry about her life being in danger, at least not while Mr. Fontenot was in jail.

But she still wasn't one hundred percent sure it was the same man. Harper shoved the thought aside. The day was too full of excitement and promise to ruin it with a passing thought that maybe her eyesight had deceived her.

Harper arrived at the 5K location, eager to not only participate but especially to help raise funds for a worthwhile cause.

Thankfully, the weather was a warm 45 degrees, sunny, and with no breeze. The snow from last week had already melted, and the pathway was clear. The pleasant day hinted at spring, but while the weather may not dip below zero, spring would not arrive in Lake Radford for at least three or four more months. Snow had arrived as late as the first week of June, although that wasn't typical. Still, February and March saw plentiful opportunities for abundant snowstorms.

An entrance with pink and red balloons taped to it arched over the starting line, with a replica of it at the finish line. She saw several people she knew, including her neighbor, Mrs. Satterwhite, who had brought Coco to the pet-friendly event.

"Well, hello, dear." Mrs. Satterwhite snuggled a pink-sweatered Coco, who, for the moment, appeared calm and content resting against her owner.

"I'm so glad you were able to come."

The elderly woman's lips curved into a smile. "I've never been what you would call an athlete. As a matter of fact, I was the girl with her nose in a book during my school years. But I love the thought of being able to walk the loop for a good cause and, of course, Coco didn't argue when I suggested it." As if Coco understood exactly what her owner was saying, she bobbed her head and offered a doggy kiss to Mrs. Satterwhite's wrinkled cheek.

Harper scanned the area. How many years had she attended the event? The fundraiser had assisted everyone from those struggling with cancer and other medical issues to those recovering from car accidents, residents who had fallen on hard times, and more. This year, the event would help two separate people in need, including the sweet little Cox boy who suffered from leukemia, and medical bills for a member of local law enforcement, and was sponsored by the realty office. She wouldn't have missed it for anything...

Except this year, before Mr. Fontenot's arrest, she'd had a slight reservation about attending due to the man who'd decided it was a good idea to stalk her. Detective Lassiter reassured her that the place would be crawling with law enforcement and that he would offer protection as well.

That cinched the deal.

Harper's attention focused on Detective Lassiter across the parking lot. He looked up just as their gazes connected. He smiled, and something fluttered in her stomach. She waved and returned his smile. Today, he wore a blue shirt that highlighted his athletic upper body and the firm sculpt of his muscles. The guy was definitely in shape.

"Hello, Harper," Jasper's voice interrupted her thoughts about the detective.

She reluctantly tore her gaze from Detective Lassiter, who was making his way toward her. "Hi, Jasper. Perfect day for a 5K."

Jasper reached up and stroked his gray-tinged beard. "I won't be running," he said with a chuckle. "I plan to walk the one mile."

Clark Montayne and a group of his friends stood near the water station. When he saw Harper, he lasered her with a scowl and assumed a defensive stance.

The only thing she could figure out about his obvious animosity toward her was her declining his offer for a date soon after she'd started at the real estate office. But that had been nearly two years ago. Obviously, he still held a grudge. Sure, he might see her as competition now, but he'd made it clear she was his enemy not long after they'd met. Detective Lassiter mentioned he'd secured a lawyer. Could he really be guilty of some of the tactics used on Harper as of late?

Harper stared for a moment. He definitely wasn't the man in the hoodie, and doubtful he'd fired the shots at the property, although Mr. Fontenot denied chasing her at the fitness center and being at the Cox property. For one thing, Clark was much more muscled and broader-shouldered than the skinny man who made it his mission to harass her. Mr. Fontenot and the man in the hoodie—who were now suspected to be one and the same—were likely about 5'8" tall and 125 pounds based on Harper's description. Clark was about 6' and probably twenty-five pounds heavier.

No. It wasn't him, but was he, as Detective Lassiter had mentioned, behind the harassment? And while Clark *wasn't* the one who'd followed her at the fitness center, tried to break into her house, or who'd been at the Cox property that day, that didn't mean he hadn't left the note on her car or sent the second one.

He was at the top of her suspect list for that, and she'd indicated as much to the detective.

Speaking of which...

Detective Lassiter walked toward her. He greeted Jasper and Mrs. Satterwhite before his attention focused on her.

"Ready for the big race?"

"I am. I've always looked forward to this. Such a great way to raise money for those in need."

The detective perused the area, and Harper followed his gaze. Nothing seemed amiss.

The recreation manager, who was announcing the race, mentioned there were ten minutes before the start of the race, and Harper launched into some dynamic stretches—lateral leg swings, high knees, and some ankle mobility heel-toe rocks. The detective joined her in stretching.

"I've never really been a runner," he admitted a few minutes later.

He could have fooled her. "Really?"

"Yeah, played football and some basketball in school, but nowadays I like to spend my time on the racquetball court."

The announcer's voice came over the loudspeaker again. "Thank you for coming to this year's Lake Radford Parks and Recreation 26th annual Valentine's Day Competition. Will you look at this crowd?"

The participants clapped, and Harper's gaze roved over the immense number of people of all ages, from seniors to kids; from students on the track team to moms and dads with strollers, and many with leashed dogs.

The announcer continued. "This is a walk-run event where you can choose to do either of those things on the 5K or the one-mile route. This year, the proceeds for our event will go to two separate recipients. First, the son of Jeff and Vanna Cox, who is undergoing treatment for leukemia. As many of you know, they didn't have insurance, and the medical bills have been mounting. Several of you have already donated and have been a part of other fundraisers. The other recipient is one of our local law enforcement detectives, Trace Tucker. Trace also volunteers for the Lake Radford Search and Rescue and was in a snowmobile accident recently while attempting to locate a lost hunter in the Radford Mountains.

"Before we begin, I just want to mention a couple of things. First, please note that our 5K runners will make their way up to the starting line. Behind them are 5K walkers, followed by our one-mile runners, and finally, our one-mile walking participants, as well as those with strollers and dogs. Please remember to keep your dogs on a leash for the entire race, as well as afterward. There will be medals awarded for first place in each age category for both the 5K and one-mile for male and female winners in each division. Please stick around and join us for the free barbecue after the races conclude." He then listed off the sponsors, which included Lake Radford Realty and Rentals, among others.

Harper and the detective edged their way through multiple people to get to the front with the other runners. "I'm going to do my best to keep up with you," he said with a smile. Her stomach flip-flopped, and she accidentally punched into her fitness tracker that she was doing tennis rather than running. She hurriedly started over and hit the proper exercise icon, her finger prepped to hit the start button when the air horn sounded.

She looked over and noticed he was setting his fitness tracker as well.

"I love these things," she said. "It's probably one of my favorite possessions."

"Yeah, I just got this new one and am still setting up the app on my phone."

She nodded, noting he had a similar tracker. "I found that it's so much easier to connect it to my laptop rather than my phone."

"Oh, really?" He didn't look convinced.

Harper laughed. "Yes. I guess you could call me an old soul in that way. I don't mind some of the other apps on my phone, but this one just seems easier on my laptop."

"That's all right. My coworkers rib me about being an old soul when it comes to preferring the print newspaper over the e-version."

He held her gaze a moment longer before the announcer's voice filled the air again. "Please remember we have aid stations along the way, and there will be a barbecue and music beneath the big white tent after the race."

She adjusted her earbuds, tapped on her playlist, prayed that everyone would emerge injury-free, and prepared to start.

"Take your marks, get set..." The airhorn sounded, and Harper launched into a run, pacing herself as several other runners passed her. There was time before she needed to quicken her pace. Grateful that today she could just run with no worries at all, even on the off chance that Mr. Fontenot hadn't acted alone, no one would dare try anything with all of these people around, especially all of the law enforcement officers here in support of one of their own. For the next several minutes, she wouldn't allow herself to worry about the recent frightening events.

Harper listened as the first song, one by her favorite Christian recording artist, sounded in her ears. She inhaled the scent of fresh air. The entire course for the race was the pathway surrounding the actual Lake Radford for which the town had been named at its founding. She glimpsed the lake with its intermittent frozen patches of ice contrasting with the areas of cold, shimmering water where the ice had either cracked or had fully melted. Within a few months, ducks, geese, herons, and cranes would be joined by turtles basking in the warm sun.

She nudged her dark sunglasses that had fallen slightly down her nose and pumped her arms as she passed by the first aid station. So far, the detective was matching her step by step. A thought slipped into her mind. Wouldn't it be nice if he were matching her pace because he wanted to run with her rather than feeling like he had to protect her? If it were the former, she could certainly get accustomed to it. From her side-eye, she glimpsed a peek at him. He wore his baseball cap backward and black rimmed sunglasses. A day's growth of facial hair peppered his chin, and he had his own earbuds. He grinned at her, and she nearly lost her footing.

What was wrong with her? He likely only saw her as someone to assist. It didn't help that Kennedy had made it a point to mention him and suggest Harper was interested in him. Which, yeah, she was.

Harper returned her focus to the course. In another five minutes or so, she would need to shove the sleeves of her shirt up to her elbows to accommodate for the warmth from running and from the sun beating down on her.

Several minutes later, Detective Lassiter had taken a place behind her, and she continued on as she passed several other runners. It didn't really matter so much if she won, but she did want to beat her time from last year. Her feet thumped in perfect rhythm on the cement pathway. She passed one of two water stations and, without stopping, took the cup from the helpful volunteer and hastily swigged it down before depositing the cup in the nearby trash can. All without losing any time.

Numerous songs on her playlist later, she passed through an area with a canopy of bare branches overhead, crossed the bridge over the river that connected to the lake, and turned the corner to the last leg of the race.

The finish line was in sight, and she increased her speed, hoping to finish strong. She stepped over the line at just over twenty-three minutes. Several runners who'd finished before her gave her a high-five, and she continued walking as her heart rate returned to a normal rhythm. She breathed in the aroma of barbecued hamburgers and hot dogs.

Mrs. Satterwhite rounded the corner of the one-mile, Coco walking her rather than the other way around. Harper waved before settling into a conversation with several friends, many of whom she'd known since high school.

Clark stepped over the finish line, and a sense of pride filled her that she'd bested him and scored a better time. He might sell more houses, but she could run faster.

<hr>

Kade beat the guy next to him by about two seconds as he raced to the finish line. Not a bad time, considering running really wasn't his thing.

Several coworkers who had beaten his time patted him on the back and congratulated him, some even teasing him about how proud they were that he finished the race. He didn't mention that some of them had only done the one mile with their wives and kids. His stomach growled, and he fixated on the white tent canopy where smoke billowed into the air from the grills just beyond. The police chief was flipping burgers, and his wife was bustling around setting out plates of cookies. The mayor tended to the hot dogs, and a few members of the city council assisted with other miscellaneous duties.

While he'd only lived in Lake Radford for two years, he enjoyed the small-town atmosphere. Much smaller than his hometown of Fairmont, which boasted a population of upwards of 60,000.

His attention gravitated to a group of people where a bright pink shirt caught his eye. Not that there wasn't a plethora of pink-and-red-clad participants in celebration of the upcoming Valentine's Day holiday, but she stood out with her long, flowing brown hair pulled into a loose ponytail and the pink tennis shoes that matched her shirt.

Unfortunate that he hadn't met Harper Amerson somewhere other than the police station. She drew him to her, and not just her pretty face and slim athletic figure. Most importantly, the fact that he'd heard through the grapevine from a reputable source that she was a Christian. Her back was to him, but as he approached, he heard her vivacious laugh at what someone in her circle had said. He wiped his brow on the sleeve of his shirt and hoped he'd applied enough deodorant. The circle disbursed, and he nearly ran into her when she took a step backward.

"Oops! Excuse me."

"Ms. Amerson, hi again."

"Oh, hello, Detective." Her brow crinkled. "I'm fine if you call me Harper."

"Harper it is." He extended his hand. "Kade."

After all, they were at a community function. Formalities could fall to the wayside, right?

And maybe when he closed her case, he could ask Harper out.

He shrugged to himself. Would she accept? Kade mentally ticked off the things they had in common. Their faith, love for the outdoors and sports, and the fact that they both lived in Lake Radford.

All right. That last point was grasping a bit.

"Going to stay for the barbecue?" he asked.

She nodded. "Yes. I wouldn't miss it. The mayor's wife bakes the most delicious cookies. I've always been surprised she didn't open her own bakery."

He pointed to one of the few tables not yet taken. "Want to snag a seat over at that picnic table?" Or maybe she'd rather sit with her friends. Kade mentally kicked himself for being so presumptuous. "I mean, that way I can keep a closer watch in case there's more than one guy who's been harassing you." He had ulterior motives, besides just wanting to protect her, but that was the most important. Spending time with her took second place, even though he looked forward to that too.

"Sure."

He gestured for her to go first and followed her to a picnic table where people had already perched as they waited for the chief and the mayor to announce that the hamburgers and hot dogs were ready.

Harper took a seat across from him. "Is this your first time running the race?"

"Was it that obvious?"

"Oh, no, that's not what I meant."

A pretty blush covered her face, and he laughed. "I'm just giving you a hard time. Yes, this is my first time here, although not my first time running a 5K." Kade paused. "It is my first time running a Valentine's 5K, but I couldn't exactly miss it when a portion of the proceeds is going to my best friend and the other portion goes to help a little boy struggling with cancer."

"I guess that would make sense that you and Detective Tucker would be friends."

"Yeah, we go way back."

"I was really sorry to hear about the detective's accident."

"Thanks. It was a fluke for sure. He's been with search and rescue for years and has ridden snowmobiles even longer than that."

"You mentioned you two go way back. But you didn't grow up here." It was more of a statement than a question.

"No, we both grew up in Fairmont. A job opened here and I..." he thought of the stalking case that plagued him, sometimes even via nightmares, despite constant prayer and speaking with the department psychologist. The entire situation had drawn Kade closer to the Lord, and he had become dependent on Him for peace and for help with the residual guilty feelings. "I landed the job first, and when they were looking to add a detective to the force after one of the seasoned detectives retired, I suggested Trace. He was already contemplating a detective post, but there weren't any open positions in Fairmont. His cousin moved here a few years ago after marrying a Lake Radford native, so it all worked out."

The chief bellowed that the hamburgers were ready, and a line formed that wound around the tent canopy. Harper chatted with a few other people and introduced him. He grabbed two plates from the stack on a makeshift table that housed cups, plates, utensils, and condiments, and handed one to her.

They both wandered over to a picnic table that housed potato salad, chips, carrots, celery, and some out-of-season, lackluster pieces of watermelon, along with pop, bottled water, and miniature milk cartons awaiting participants. Plastic utensils and paper napkins covered the remaining space on the table.

When they returned to their seats, Chief spoke again through the megaphone and offered to lead the prayer before the meal. That's one of the things Kade really liked about his boss—that he was a fellow Christian and not only talked about his faith, but lived it as well.

Kade placed a paper napkin in his lap. "Glad the weather held."

Nothing like talking about the weather. Perhaps he could find a way to be a little more interesting.

"It's perfect weather. I wasn't so sure how it would be when I first checked the forecast."

"Have you always lived in Lake Radford?

She scooped a bite of potato salad. "Yes, I was born and raised here."

"And through all those years, no reason for anybody to be causing you problems?

She arched her eyebrows, and only after looking at her expression did he realize he lapsed into work mode. "Sorry about that. Sometimes I can't seem to leave work at work."

Harper smiled, and her entire face lit. "That's all right. I appreciate that you're dedicated to your job."

Almost too dedicated sometimes. He thought of the long hours he spent on cases, especially the Dumaine burglary. But it wasn't like he had a wife and kids to go home to each night. It was working, attending church functions, working out, or volunteering as a mentor for at-risk boys. Those were the things that filled his hours.

"Did you always want to go into real estate?"

"No, believe it or not, I at one time wanted to be a nurse. But I quickly realized that the sight of blood and I don't really get along. And what about you? Did you always want to work in law enforcement?"

"Actually, yes. Both my grandpa and my dad were law enforcement. Unfortunately, Dad had to cut his career short because he was diagnosed with MS several years ago."

"I'm so sorry to hear that."

"Thank you. It's been rough on him and on my mom. But he handles it well. He's strong in his faith and has a good outlook, but there are days when he really struggles." Were it not for the fact that Fairmont was only two hours away and he could return home as often as his schedule allowed, Kade might have never considered moving.

"I can understand that. My grandpa recently had a stroke, and he hasn't appreciated not being able to do the things he once could. My grandma may have even taken it harder than he has. She hasn't liked having to see him struggle with doing the things he used to do. It's amazing how we take things like that for granted."

"I agree. Good health is precious." Kade took a bite of his hamburger. He could probably live on hamburgers, although with this one, he could barely taste the beef with all the condiments and lettuce, tomato, and sliced cheese he'd layered on it.

"Do you have any siblings?"

"A younger sister. You?"

Harper shook her head. "Nope. I'm an only child."

They continued in pleasant conversation until the mayor announced the winners in each division, including Harper taking home the medal for her twenty-three-minute, nineteen-second time in the women's age 25-35 category.

"Good job, Harper." She accepted his fist bump when she returned with her medal.

Her face glowed. "I'm so excited about this. I wanted to beat my time from last year."

"And did you?"

"By a couple of seconds."

Kade peered over his shoulder and noticed Clark Montayne scowling at Harper, reminding Kade that he was still very much a person of interest in Harper's case.

EIGHTEEN

Kade texted Trace that he would be stopping by with some burgers from Olsen's in fifteen minutes. Trace responded in less than five seconds.

I'll be here.

Kade chuckled. Poor guy hadn't been out of the house since he returned home from the hospital. Trace was likely going stir-crazy, and Kade could relate. He'd be climbing the walls if he had to sit in one place for too long.

He paid for the meal at the drive-up at Olsen's and proceeded down Eighth to the row of gray two-story condos. A few minutes later, he was unlocking the door and stepping inside Trace's bachelor pad.

"I'm up here," yelled Trace. Kade shut the door, locked it behind him, removed his shoes, and bounded up the stairs.

"Oh, man, how did you know I was craving one of Olsen's bacon burgers?"

Kade passed the kitchen area with its obnoxious turquoise walls that the former occupant had painted and found his best friend lounging on a brown recliner. Kade set the bags of food on the rustic log coffee table and moseyed to the corner where an out-of-place orange, yellow, and brown flowered vintage TV tray leaned against the wall. The thing was hideous and clashed with the masculine furnishings of the living room.

"You really need to get some new décor. Not sure about this granny look."

"Very funny. It's one thing in a sea of many possessions. Besides, Adriana found that at the thrift store, and it's actually kind of growing on me."

"Yeah, I'll bet because flowers have always been your thing."

Trace chuckled, then clutched his bandaged ribs. "Don't make me laugh. Besides, it goes well with the whitetail deer mounts."

Kade veered his attention to the taxidermy collection on the east wall in the living room, some of which had also been left by the previous resident. Thankfully, Trace owned the condo. "Maybe the turquoise walls can be revamped next."

"I'll be tackling that eyesore tomorrow after lifting some weights and going for a run."

Kade laughed. At least Trace was keeping his sense of humor. He removed the burgers from the bag and set Trace's on the flowered TV tray along with a box of onion rings and a medium pop. He assisted his friend into a more comfortable position on the recliner and prayed over their meal before taking his own seat on the cloth couch across from Trace.

"I have something to ask you," said Trace.

"Go for it."

Trace shook his head. "We'll wait until after we've eaten."

Kade's curiosity bested him. "I can wait."

"Yeah…no. I'm starving to death. Just remind me to ask you." Trace waited until he was halfway finished with his bacon burger before uttering his next words. "This is delicious."

It was clear to Kade that his friend couldn't down his favorite meal fast enough. "Haven't eaten in days?"

"Yeah, something like that. This sitting around makes a guy hungry *and* hangry."

"I'll bet. Any visitors today?

"Pastor stopped by for a little bit after the physical therapist this morning. Mom and Dad were here this past weekend, and Adriana and her husband will be here tomorrow. Speaking of my cousin..."

"Yes?"

"The doctor is going to be inducing her on Wednesday."

Kade didn't know much, if anything, about pregnancies and births, but he knew Adriana had already endured a difficult pregnancy. "I'll be praying it all goes well."

"Thank you. She'll appreciate that." He cleared his throat. "About that...I have a favor to ask you."

Kade downed another onion ring and drank some more pop. "Sounds serious."

"It is."

The suspicious glint in Trace's eyes concerned Kade. He and Trace had been best friends since second grade. More like brothers, and whenever Trace got that expression, it usually meant one thing... that he was up to something.

"What is it?"

Trace smirked. "Patience, my friend."

"The suspense is killing me."

"I'm sure." Trace shifted and groaned, no doubt from the pain. "Adriana has to be induced, so she'll need some additional help at her store."

"Won't her employees be there?"

"They will, but as you know, Valentine's Day is one of her busiest times."

That didn't surprise Kade, seeing as how Adriana owned a florist and gift shop.

Trace took another drink of his pop. "It pains me to have to ask you this, but know that it's for a good cause."

"You're avoiding the topic. Do I need to launch into an interrogation?"

Trace wadded up the paper from his bacon burger and tossed it onto the coffee table. "As you know, Adriana has added a few items to her florist menu."

"Florist menu?"

"Besides the usual flowers, candies, and balloons."

"All right…"

"Things like singing telegrams for special occasions."

"Singing telegrams?" Kade did not like where this was going. Years of training pointed to this particular perp—Trace Tucker in this case—about to share something dubious. "Out with it, Trace."

"Man, you're impatient. Adriana's singing telegrams have been hugely popular, and you know that she and James are saving up for a down payment on a house."

"Yes." He gestured for Trace to continue.

"The singing telegrams have been so popular that she has too many orders for her two other employees to handle on Wednesday, on top of delivering all of Valentine's Day bouquets and balloons."

"And that affects me how?" Did Kade even want to know?

"She called me and asked if you might be willing to help her out on Wednesday since you're off that day."

"Sure, I'll deliver some bouquets and balloons."

Trace cocked his head to one side. "That's not exactly what she had in mind."

The hairs on the back of Kade's neck stood on end, just like they did when he was about to encounter a criminal. Something didn't bode well about this entire conversation.

"What exactly does she have in mind, then? Or do I even want to hear the answer?"

Trace chuckled again, this time wincing. "She was hoping you might be able to help her out with the singing gorilla telegram."

"What? What's a singing gorilla telegram?"

"It's where a customer has placed an order for a singing telegram—in this case, someone dressed as a gorilla does the singing, along with the balloon or flower delivery."

If Trace thought Kade would be the singing gorilla, he had another thing coming. "I'm sure her employees will do a great job, although I can't say I'd want to be on the receiving end of that."

"Apparently, it's a popular request. And, no, her employees can't help with this. One of them is recovering from bronchitis and will just be returning to the shop on Wednesday. She'll only be arranging flowers. One will be handling all the foot traffic, and the third will be up to her eyeballs in deliveries. She was hoping you would be the gorilla."

"No and no."

"It's for a good cause, and Adriana doesn't have a ton of customers who requested the gorilla...probably just five or six."

"Five or six?" Kade narrowed his eyes at his friend.

Trace squirmed and avoided his scrutiny.

"You're a terrible liar, Trace."

"All right, she may have said she had ten orders."

"Ten?"

Trace did his best to shrug, although Kade could tell it caused him pain. "It's immensely popular, what can I say?"

"I cannot sing to save my life."

"You're not as bad as you could be. I've heard you singing a few off-key songs at church."

"Yeah, off-key being the key word, no pun intended. Besides, that's worshipping the Lord. It's different."

"Look," said Trace, "it's only for one day, and she wouldn't ask if she wasn't absolutely desperate. If it makes you feel any better, she did ask a couple of other people before you, but they are working."

"Why would she even think about asking me?"

Trace's gaze darted about the room. The guy better always stay on the right side of the law because he would give away any criminal intentions if he were on the wrong side.

"Don't you dare tell me you suggested me."

Trace rubbed the back of his neck. His lack of eye contact told Kade all he needed to know.

"You didn't…"

"She was desperate, and you are off on Wednesday, so I thought it would be a great idea. You can thank me later."

"After I die of embarrassment? Oh, I'll be thanking you."

"This from a guy who reveled in going undercover when he first moved to Lake Radford."

Kade shook his head. "That's totally different, and you know it. That was to catch some drug dealer. This is…" The thought of dressing up as a gorilla and singing caused him worse indigestion than downing two full onions. "There goes my stellar reputation."

"Can't fault a guy for dressing up like a gorilla and screeching a Valentine tune."

"Unless said guy is permanently traumatized from the ordeal."

Trace brushed aside his concern. "Nah, we'll just schedule you some time with the department psychologist."

"Funny. I already see the psychologist. I'll do this under one condition."

"And that is?"

"You let me borrow your new truck to drive around in while I'm in the monkey costume."

"What? No way. Take your own truck."

Kade shook his head. "Nope. If I do this for Adriana, I'm driving your truck. But I'll leave mine here so you have it in case you have to go somewhere."

"In case I have to go somewhere. With a broken leg, broken ribs, a concussion, and a dislocated shoulder. Sure. I'll just run some errands."

"No way will I drive my own vehicle through town in a gorilla costume with the cab full of red heart balloons."

"You've only lived here two years. No one even knows your truck yet."

Trace had a point, but Kade had his pride. He raised his eyebrows and waited for his friend's answer.

"All right. You can take my truck. The windows are tinted anyway."

"It's a deal then."

"I'll owe you one."

"Yeah, you will."

"Does this mean you'll help her out?"

He sighed. "What does it entail?

"I thought you'd never ask. You just have to go to a couple of homes or places of business. You'll be singing 'Happy Valentine's Day' to the tune of 'Happy Birthday', offer a handful of heart balloons, or in some cases a little bucket of cookies or chocolates, and then be on your way."

He wanted to say no. To make up an excuse. But the truth was, he wasn't busy on Wednesday, and he'd known Adriana for almost as many years as he'd known Trace and thought of her as a pesky little sister. He would forfeit his pride—albeit begrudgingly—and do what he could to help, even if it meant dressing up like a gorilla and singing a dopey song to people on Valentine's Day.

"So, will you do it?"

"All right. I'll do it."

Trace raised his elbow up slightly and did a fist bump in the air. "Thanks, dude. Now I don't have to ask anyone else."

"There were other people to ask?"

"Not that would be as good as you. I think you'll make a great singing gorilla telegram and just think...no one will even know it's you."

"Very funny." Kade popped another bite of onion ring into his mouth to take his mind off what he had just promised.

"How are things at work?"

"Way to change the subject."

"Hey, I wish I were there. I am going stir-crazy in here. Chief could have put me on some sort of desk detail."

"He knows you, and he knows you wouldn't be content sitting behind a desk and would want to get back out into the field."

"True. How are the cases going?"

Kade updated him on the cases he was working. "Things aren't going as quickly as I'd like on the two main ones."

"The Dumaine burglary?"

"That's one of them. I do have some plans on that one. Maybe once you're up to it, you can look through some surveillance footage for me."

Trace's tired face perked up at that suggestion. "Just tell me when."

"I'll talk to Chief and see if we can get you set up with a laptop or something here because it would help me out.

Things have been busy since the other detective has been slacking."

"Ha ha. Slacking. Yeah, that's it. Just sitting here twiddling my thumbs. So, what's the other case that's been keeping you so busy?"

"The one with Harper Amerson. The pieces just aren't fitting together."

"The real estate agent?"

"Yes."

"The woman you find attractive?"

Kade nearly choked on an onion ring. "What?"

"I know you find her attractive. When you called me after the 5K, she was all you talked about."

"She's all I talk about because she's one of my biggest cases right now."

"If you say so. Don't forget I've known you for a really long time, and I think you like Harper Amerson."

"It doesn't matter if I like her or not. Right now I'm working her case."

"But after the case is solved…"

"I think I'll bring you broccoli and sauerkraut next time I come for a visit."

But Kade knew Trace was right. He did find Harper attractive, and when this case was over, perhaps he'd consider asking her out.

NINETEEN

Harper slid into a parking spot in the customer area after a showing since Clark again decided to straddle both his and her parking spots in the employee section, this time by angling his expensive car diagonally across the lines.

She sighed. She could call the tow truck, but that would for sure cause strife she didn't need. In the broader context, Clark's decision to occupy the parking spots was not a significant issue. Especially considering she had to deal with some crazy person intent on harassing her. The thing that annoyed her most about her coworker, however, was when he thought it was funny to take her snacks from the breakroom's mini-fridge and set them on the table to spoil.

Snacks that not only needed to be refrigerated, but that she also relied on to keep her blood sugar from getting too low throughout the day. Thankfully, she had a stash of granola bars, but the apple slices, sliced strawberries, and already peeled oranges that she routinely stuck in the fridge were foods she depended on. His animosity toward her had garnered him many prayers. While his hostility was frustrating, she truly hoped he wouldn't go as far as to attempt to stop her from selling the Cox property via threats and stalking.

She reached for her purse on the passenger side, then took a quick scan of the parking lot. Never before recent events would she have thought she would need to practice extreme situational awareness in her small hometown. The thought saddened her. The sooner they caught whoever was intimidating her, the better.

A shiny, deep gray pickup truck breezed into the spot beside her with semi-tinted windows, partially rolled down. At first, she couldn't see the driver since numerous red and pink balloons filled the cab. But it was that time of year.

The customer parking lot served several different businesses; however, it wouldn't be out of the realm of possibility for someone in the realty office to be receiving a delivery. Jamila had recently become engaged. Perhaps the balloons were for her. Or they could be for a number of other employees in surrounding companies.

A twinge of longing briefly pervaded her thoughts. She wouldn't mind being thought of by a significant other on this particular holiday. Of course, while she had always imagined herself someday getting married and having children, those thoughts didn't usually invade her mind. However, today, with love in the air and red and pink balloons filling cabs, chocolate deliveries, and candlelight dinners, it was something she hoped to someday have. She inhaled a deep breath and reminded herself that there was a time for everything. And she would wait patiently until the man God had planned for her entered her life.

Why did a fleeting flash of Kade's face enter her mind?

The guy was doing his job by protecting her. He wasn't someone she'd ever entertain the thought of dating.

Right?

Not that he wasn't charming and handsome. And this past Sunday, seeing him at church across the sanctuary during first service after Kennedy mentioned he went to second service…just seeing him added to her interest in him.

Interest in him?

Lack of sleep could do bizarre things to already-exhausted minds.

Like making one think about a certain brown-haired, blue-eyed, handsome detective with a nice laugh and muscular build.

She needed to focus on getting inside and working on some new advertisements to pump up some business on her newest listings. Not sit here and daydream about an employee of the Lake Radford PD.

Not that she hadn't already entertained the thought of dating him after Kennedy's comment. If the interest was mutual.

She was about to exit her SUV when an unlikely sight unfolded beside her. Someone dressed in a black gorilla costume with a brown cowboy hat and a red open vest stepped out of the truck. Likely a man, due to the person's build—tall with broad shoulders. His handful of balloons bobbed in the wind. In his other hand, he held a bouquet of flowers and a festive pink polka dot box with a squished bow.

She'd read something about the new singing gorilla telegrams in the online version of the newspaper recently. She covered her mouth to stifle a laugh. Could this be such an occasion?

And the poor person he would be singing to…

There was only one way to find out. She closed the door, clicked the fob to lock it, and hurried after the gorilla. "Here, let me get that door for you," she said, holding open the real estate office door.

"Thank you."

His looming face with oversized nostrils, brown marbly eyes, black fake fur, and oversized teeth caused her to smile.

"Nice costume."

He yanked and tugged on the balloons, attempting to get them to bow beneath the doorframe. "Yeah, I got roped into it."

His voice sounded oddly familiar, though it was somewhat muffled and altered through the mask. Harper wanted to offer her condolences to him for having to wear the costume, but she couldn't stop laughing. Especially when one of the cellophane balloons bopped him upside the head.

She followed him through the door as he ventured to Loretta's desk.

Loretta pushed aside a bowl of wrapped chocolates. "Are those for Jamila?"

"I'm looking for someone named Loretta." The gorilla nearly dropped the box, and efficiently caught it before it tumbled to the floor.

"Loretta?" She held her hand to her heart. "That's me! I'm Loretta!"

Paulette strolled around the corner, followed by Jamila, Ean, and Enrique.

"Who are the goodies for?" Ean asked.

Loretta offered a dazzling smile. "Yours truly."

The gorilla clumsily handed her the flowers and wrapped box and unfolded his large paws from the multitude of strings tied to the balloons clutched in his hand. He took a step back, nearly colliding with Harper.

"Sorry about that, uh, ma'am."

"Excuse me." She shuffled out of the way.

Loretta beamed, her enthusiasm enhancing the multitude of wrinkles fanning her eyes and mouth. "Oh, I just can't believe he would think of me on Valentine's Day. He's such a precious sort. I think I'll keep him."

Paulette laughed. "Well, you should keep him, since you've only been married for how many years?"

Loretta tapped her chin. "Oh, about forty years today, but who's counting?"

Jamila swooned. "Today is your anniversary?"

"It is. We were married on Valentine's Day."

"You might ought to make sure that they're from your husband," suggested Enrique.

Loretta's brown eyes bulged for a second before she quickly recovered. "I guess I should, now that you mention it. Was there a card?"

The gorilla fumbled around and finally produced a small rectangular envelope from his vest pocket and handed it to her.

Loretta read the card, then held it to her chest. "He is such a dear man to have a gorilla bring me such a wonderful surprise."

Enrique lifted the box and shook it gently. "What's in here?"

"Aren't you the nosy one?" Ean shook his head. "Probably chocolates."

Enrique took a whiff of the box. "I think you're right."

Loretta took the box from him, untied the ribbon, and opened it. "You're right, Ean." She held it out for everyone to have one. Enrique plucked two, unwrapped them, and popped them into his mouth.

"Happy Valentine's Day, ma'am. I'd best be on my way." The gorilla pivoted and attempted to escape from being wedged in between the agents.

"Hey," said Ean, "aren't you the singing gorilla telegram? My wife was telling me something about that."

The gorilla hung his head. "Yes, I am."

That's who his voice resembled! Detective Lassiter.

But surely...

No, he would be at his office investigating crimes, not delivering balloons and flowers and singing tunes.

Loretta, who had been inhaling the flowers, set them down on her desk and clasped her hands together. "Ooh, you sing too? Did my dear husband pay for a special Valentine song as well?"

"Yes, he did."

At least he was an honest gorilla.

Even if he didn't act thrilled about this part of his job. The gorilla cleared his throat, and in a low, off-key voice, he began to sing:

Happy Valentine's Day to you!
Happy Valentine's Day to you!
Happy Valentine's Day, dear...

"Loretta," Paulette offered.

Happy Valentine's Day, dear Loretta,
Happy Valentine's Day to you!

The crowd cheered. Loretta clutched the gorilla's arm. "You did wonderfully, dear."

Ean leaned an elbow against the wall. "Are you taking any more orders?"

"You'd have to call the florist shop, but I don't think so." The gorilla spun slowly around and eyed the door. "Well, I have seven more of these to do, so I'll be going now."

Loretta folded her hands in a prayer position and begged. "Could you sing the song one more time?"

"No, ma'am, I cannot. It was a one-time deal."

Loretta pooched out her lower lip. "All right, but I'm going to keep you in mind for birthdays."

Beneath his hairy façade, did the gorilla cringe?

Ean punched in the numbers on his cell phone. "Yes, I'd like to order a singing gorilla telegram today for my wife."

***

Kade thought that he might either die of humiliation or sweat to death, or both. He bolted out of the real estate office, thankful that Harper hadn't recognized him. He'd never been one for dopey gags—or he should rephrase that—he'd never been one for dopey gags where he was the recipient of the gag.

He'd made it through three of these excruciating "appointments" so far. Or maybe those who had to listen to him screech endured three of these excruciating "appointments" so far. Only seven more to go. That was if Harper's coworker didn't get his way and reserve a gorilla telegram for his wife.

One could only hope that whoever answered the phone at the florist informed the real estate agent that all of the slots were filled for the day.

Kade unlocked Trace's truck and was about to slide in with the remaining balloons for the next stop when he heard a shriek from the clothing store adjacent to the real estate office.

"Help! That woman is stealing!" A female clerk in her thirties, hands waving in the air, pointed to a frizzy-haired redhead with an oversized purple purse in her hand, fleeing down the sidewalk.

"Help! Somebody call the police. That lady just stole a whole bunch of clothes!"

She was looking right at him.

And, well, he was a member of law enforcement. It was his duty to track down and arrest criminals who stole from clothing stores.

Even if he was dressed as a gorilla.

"Ma'am, go back inside and call the police."

He didn't wait to see if the clothing store employee did as he told her, but instead, he launched into a run. Hindered by the awkward gorilla costume and the thin rubber feet through which he felt nearly every rock and crack in the sidewalk, made him grateful this was a one-time deal.

Because of the holiday, several people milled about on the sidewalk. The thief brushed past them and weaved between onlookers. It wasn't so easy for Kade. Moving efficiently in a gorilla costume was a challenge, especially since it was a little tight and restricted his movement. "Excuse me, excuse me." Most people failed to promptly move out of the way and instead stared at him, their jaws slack.

He would stare too. A gorilla in a cowboy hat and red vest wasn't something you saw every day in Lake Radford.

The thief entered a small mom-and-pop grocery store on the corner. Kade followed her inside. She dashed down a narrow aisle, and he turned sideways and squeezed in between a display of cereal and a stand with numerous tubs of oats.

She reached with her free hand and knocked several boxes of granola bars off the shelf and into his path. He skidded to a stop, stepped over the snacks as best he could, and pursued her through the store.

A woman with a jug of milk in her hand screamed and tossed the gallon jug at him. A baby in a shopping cart wailed when he passed by. And an elderly man with a cane attempted to trip him. "Quit causing trouble, young man," he growled.

Kade forged ahead, hoping the saleswoman at the clothing store had called the police. It might take two of them to apprehend this crook. She zipped through the "Employees Only" double doors and into the musty storage area. An employee attempting to wield a cart full of yogurt containers stalled in front of him, and Kade jumped to the side before proceeding after the thief as she escaped through the emergency exit.

Never, not once, had he ever allowed a criminal to go free on his watch. Not in his early days as a patrol officer, and not now.

He pushed his legs as fast as humanly possible in the restrictive gorilla costume. A man on an electric bike narrowly missed him.

"Watch where you're going!"

Easy for him to say. He didn't have limited peripheral vision due to a heavy mask.

A mask he could remove, except that the ladies at the florist shop—albeit somewhat gleefully—had ensured it was snugly fit on his shoulders. Likely, he'd need assistance removing it.

The criminal ducked into the Lake Radford Museum next to the mom-and-pop store.

"Police! Stop right there!"

The woman did not listen. She nearly knocked some artifacts from the shelf as she brushed past with her stolen goods. A group of ten or twelve elementary school children stood near some old saddles and a rickety stagecoach while the museum curator told them about the first settlers in the area. Kade yelled again for the woman to stop as she played hide and seek, first the stagecoach, then as she lodged her hefty self behind a covered wagon.

The children's voices chorused with numerous questions, only half of which Kade heard in his rush to apprehend the thief.

"Who is that guy?"

"Are we going to watch a play?"

"Why would a policeman dress like a monkey?"

"Why is he after that lady?"

"Did they have gorillas on the Oregon Trail?"

Finally, he cornered the thief upstairs, where she attempted to hide behind a stuffed buffalo exhibit. "Hold it right there. Police!"

She attempted to bat at him with her oversized bag. That was the good thing about sporting a gorilla mask. It protected your eyes and nose. She whacked him on the head before he grabbed the bag and spouted off her Miranda rights. Unfortunately, he didn't have his handcuffs, but he could keep her contained until help arrived.

Officer Uchida, a smirk on her face, stepped forward less than five minutes later to cuff the woman. "Looking good today, Detective."

"Yeah, yeah, just haul her away."

Uchida laughed. "Not sure you'll be able to keep this shenanigan a secret." She nodded toward a young woman with a camera.

"Detective Lassiter? I'm Tanisha from *The Lake Radford Daily*. When you're finished, can I get an interview?"

TWENTY

The thief hollered and argued the entire time she was being arrested. Tanisha from the newspaper was relentless with her questions, including a very poignant one directed at the criminal. "How does it feel to be arrested by a gorilla?" she asked.

He'd hand it to her. She was adept at lightening the mood.

The thief had some things to say in response to Tanisha's inquiry, including the typical, "I did nothing wrong!" and "He broke my fingernail when he arrested me."

Neither of which was true.

Uchida rolled her eyes but said nothing before she and Baldwin tucked the handcuffed woman into the police car and hauled her away to the station.

Bystanders had crowded around on the sidewalk, having probably never seen such a debacle, especially with a police officer dressed as a gorilla. Too bad he couldn't have stayed incognito. By this point, Kade had—with the assistance of a snickering Uchida—removed his gorilla head mask. He caught a glimpse of himself in the nearby furniture store window. His sweaty hair stuck up at odd ends. Good thing it would be memorialized through Tanisha and the cameraman's incessant picture-taking duties. Tanisha asked a few more questions, some of which he couldn't answer because this was currently an open investigation.

The clothing store employee had finally calmed down, and she told Tanisha it was estimated the thief had attempted to steal about $500 worth of clothing. That was either a lot of clothes, or the items were expensive. Regardless, the thief would be charged with misdemeanor theft, among other things, if the $500 amount was correct.

Kade often wondered about people's motives. The red-headed thief didn't look poverty-stricken. Quite the opposite in her faux brown leather jacket, unless she'd stolen that too. He didn't recognize her, but then, being somewhat new to the community hadn't enabled him to memorize the faces of the frequent offenders—which, from what Uchida had insinuated—the thief was a habitual offender.

He tucked the gorilla head under his arm and plunked the cowboy hat back on his head. Not that he was prone to vanity, but at least it would hide his messy and sweaty hair. He still had to deliver seven more singing gorilla telegrams, not to mention if the ladies at the shop had any more orders. He cringed. Adriana owed him. *Trace* owed him.

Big time.

After all the chaos, he was about to wander toward Trace's truck when a familiar face caught his eye. Harper stood not far away, chatting with some bystanders. She looked up at just that moment, and their eyes connected. If she didn't realize it was him before, she would know now for sure.

So much for making a good impression.

She waved at him then and started in his direction. He met her halfway in front of the museum.

"Wow, that was some arrest."

"Yeah, bet you never saw a gorilla run that fast." He chuckled, attempting to ease the embarrassment.

"As a matter of fact, I don't think I've ever seen a gorilla run at all." She laughed.

And he liked the sound of it.

Kade rubbed the back of his neck. "Well, at least we got another thief temporarily off the street." His stomach growled. What time was it anyway? It seemed like he'd been playing dress-up for days. A thought flickered through his mind. "Care to grab a bite to eat at Sheila's?"

The way her eyebrows rose into her hairline told him she was shocked at his inquiry. But she wasn't as shocked as he was. Where had that question even come from, anyway? He could easily drive through Olsen's and grab a burger, or better, and healthier still, stop by his house and warm up some leftovers. "I mean, if you have a minute. I have to go deliver some more of these, so it would probably just be better for me personally to grab something at the Olsen's drive-thru."

Now he was rambling. If one of his suspects did that, he'd peg it as nervousness. He didn't want her to think he was asking her out—not when hers was an active case—but the more he backpedaled on his words, the more moronic he sounded.

"Sure, I'd love to. I was just needing a break from working on marketing stuff for some ads."

"Speaking of the paper, today's capture is going to be an interesting article when it comes out tomorrow."

She laughed. "Yes, but Lake Radford needs some excitement every now and again."

He felt sorry for her because she'd had enough excitement to last for years with the guy who was harassing her. "I need to discuss a few things with you about your case."

Kade's crowded brain scrambled to conjure up a few questions he could ask that he hadn't already asked. Or maybe he could just give her some updates. Were there updates?

"Let me just grab my purse, and I'll meet you right back here." Her brow creased. "Assuming you're going dressed like that?"

He peered down at the fluffy black costume and smoothed a hand over the vest. "I was thinking about it. Would you be all right with that?"

It wasn't his intention to embarrass her, but if he needed to deliver the rest of the singing gorilla telegrams, running home to change wasn't conducive to being efficient.

"Oh, yes." She smiled, and he found it difficult to tear his gaze away from her face. "All right, give me just a minute, and I'll meet you right back here," she said again.

Before he could say another word, she pivoted and walked the few steps to the real estate agency.

Unexpectedly, two kids from the museum field trip approached him and asked for his autograph.

Maybe this was his fifteen minutes of fame.

He winced when he thought of how Trace and his coworkers would goad him to no end about his gorilla criminal-capturing adventure.

***

Harper snatched her purse from her office, told Loretta she'd be back after lunch, and hurried down the sidewalk to where Kade stood. Her heart thumped in her chest a little faster than usual, but not entirely due to her brisk walking. She hadn't anticipated Kade asking her out to lunch. But it wasn't a date—it was to discuss the case—and because he was starving. She had heard his stomach growl, proving that very point. Besides, she needed to have lunch at some point herself. And what better time than before continuing to write the ad info for her listings before they were due at the paper?

People continued to mill about, and a few were talking to Kade when she approached. She noticed his brown hair in complete disarray before he'd clapped the worn cowboy hat on his head. Detective Kade Lassiter was a good-looking guy, no doubt about that. But his personality was what really drew her to him. And now, as she prepared to join him for lunch, a peculiar nervousness settled within her.

They strolled to the corner where the white stoplight icon told them it was safe to walk. As they crossed the street, several cars beeped their horns.

"I feel like a celebrity," he said with a chuckle.

"You are somewhat of one after nabbing that woman who thought she could get away with stealing clothes."

"She was actually pretty adept at getting away at first. I chased her down the sidewalk, into a grocery store, out of said grocery store, and into the museum where I arrested her." He made sure he was on the outside of the street as they continued to Sheila's.

The gesture warmed Harper's heart. It was a challenge to find men who still practiced chivalry in today's world. As a matter of fact, in her experience, it could be considered rare.

Just another thing to appreciate about him.

On the topic of chivalry—he held open the door for her and followed her inside Sheila's. The delicious aroma of lunch tickled Harper's nose. A mixture of hamburgers, tater tots, and something sweet like cookies lingered in the air. There was something about it that reminded her of Grandma's house when Harper was a little girl. The employees had decorated Sheila's full-on for Valentine's Day, complete with pink and red streamers at the entrance. Cut-out white, pink, and red hearts had been taped all over the glass dessert display case. It appeared the owner had even provided her waitresses with special clothing for today's holiday, as they all wore red button-up shirts rather than the usual uniform.

The hostess, a woman named Jade, who was three or four years behind Harper in school, greeted them. "Harper, so nice to see you. Table for two?" Her eye darted the length of Kade, stopping at the gorilla head mask under his arm. "Is it Halloween, or did I miss something?"

That was exactly how Harper remembered Jade—witty and inquisitive.

"No, I am actually delivering some singing gorilla telegrams for the florist shop today."

"Are you serious? I have seen those online and wondered about them. I had no idea we even had such a thing here in humble Lake Radford." She tapped her chin. "You know who would love something like that? My aunt. She's in a nursing home, and it would mean so much. Do you think you could stop by and sing her a little jingle? And take her some balloons?"

"You would have to call the flower shop and arrange that with them."

"Oh, awesome! I will do that."

Harper heard Kade groan. The poor guy probably thought his delivery duties would never end.

Jade led them to a booth tucked in the back corner. More streamers had been hung corner to corner in the dining area, as well as taped to the ceiling fan. Sheila had gone all out.

"Someone will be with you in just a few minutes to take your order," Jade said before walking away to greet the next customer.

The noisy din of the restaurant proved how popular it was. Every age group visited the acclaimed eatery that had, according to Grandma, been founded back in the fifties.

Within minutes, a waitress whom Harper didn't recognize delivered two menus and water with lemon slices.

Kade downed his water in nearly one swallow. When he finished, he took a deep breath. "Being in that gorilla costume made me thirsty."

"I'm sure. Good thing it's not the middle of summer."

"Exactly."

"How did you get roped into doing that? Is it something for an undercover case? Or can you tell me?"

"I wish it were for an undercover case. Adriana, who owns the florist shop, is Detective Trace Tucker's cousin. She's pregnant and being induced. Because she was shorthanded, guess who got nominated to help out?"

Just another reason to like him. Anyone who would step up and wear a gorilla costume for his coworker's cousin was exceptional in her mind. "That was nice of you."

He groaned. "As I previously mentioned, I have seven more places to go. That is, if your coworker and the hostess here haven't secured spots on the schedule as well. If so, I might be delivering flowers and balloons late into the evening."

"Just think of all of the joy you're bringing on this holiday."

He winced. "That's true at least. Making a difference one tiny way at a time."

Harper pondered the irony of his statement. His career demanded that he help keep criminals off the street, solve cases, and make a difference for the betterment of his community. Yet here he was also making a difference by bringing happiness to people on Valentine's Day.

The waitress jotted down their orders, and Harper took a sip of water. "You mentioned you had some news about the case?"

Kade hesitated. "I'm going to be re-interviewing the Cox property neighbors in the hopes that maybe someone might have remembered something about who was on the property that day you were showing it. Maybe they truly did see a vehicle they didn't recognize in the vicinity. Sometimes it takes more than one interview, and unfortunately, witnesses don't always call on their own accord. Or they may have an idea about why someone wouldn't want you to sell the property. If we can find out who was there that day, it might shed some light on the other circumstances surrounding this case."

He must be convinced it wasn't Mr. Fontenot. "The only problem is that there are no nearby neighbors. That's one of the charms of the listing. While it's close to town and even in the city limits, it's rural."

"I found that out during the first round of interviews, but it never hurts to ask. It's surprising how sometimes people see or know something, but don't mention it unless they're specifically asked or, in this case, asked again. Have you had any more dealings with Clark Montayne?"

"I have to deal with him every day. He steals my parking spot and causes other petty and juvenile conflicts, such as stealing my ideas and presenting them to the boss, and, more concerning, removing my food from the staff refrigerator so it spoils."

"Sounds like harassment and that he's creating a hostile work environment. Have you talked to your boss?"

How many times had Harper prayed about handling this situation the correct way? "I have to be honest and say that Clark does intimidate me. I've prayed about whether or not to tell Paulette—my boss—but haven't done so for a few reasons. One, Clark is her best agent and brings in the most revenue. She thinks highly of him. On Clark removing my food from the fridge, he could easily defend that saying there wasn't room for his food or that it was an accident." Although even as she said the words, she knew they sounded ridiculous in her own ears. There was plenty of room in the fridge for smaller items, and her fruit bowls and baggies didn't take up much space. That and since it had happened twice, it couldn't be an accident both times. "He could deny it as well, and truthfully, it could have been an honest mistake by someone else."

All of her excuses amounted to one thing: Harper didn't care much for conflict and attempted to avoid it when necessary. Perhaps if she just left well enough alone, Clark would get tired of pestering her and move on. And what if he was the one behind the recent incident?

She could only pray and hope that would be the case. "I think when it comes to Clark, he's just attempting to intimidate and annoy me because he sees me as competition, although I've never come close to bringing in the commissions he does. If I do sell the Cox property, that will give me an edge, but I'll still not be on par with him. He's known for being the top agent in the county with a reputation for those with high-dollar homes and properties to sell."

From the way his brows furrowed and he stroked his clean-shaven chin, Kade wasn't convinced.

"I know he's not the guy in the hoodie and the guy who pulled a knife on me the other day."

"No, he's not, but he did have a conversation with the guy who pulled a knife on you and mugged you."

Kade had mentioned before when apprising her of her case over the phone that he had Clark on surveillance cameras speaking to Mr. Fontenot. What had Clark been doing that evening when he'd spoken to the man? Had it been as he mentioned? Just giving the guy a few bucks? Or was it something else?

As if to read her mind, Kade said, "I still think it seems as if he's connected somehow." His phone buzzed. "Excuse me. I need to take this."

While Kade spoke on the phone, Harper asked the waitress for a refill of her lemon water. He disconnected soon after the waitress brought the pitcher to the table.

"New information."

"Oh?"

"I was skeptical that it was Fontenot who was prowling around your house that night. This is proof."

"Proof?"

"The footprint impressions found in the snow indicated a size twelve boot with someone weighing approximately 150 pounds. Fontenot is a size nine and probably 130 soaking wet."

"But if it wasn't Mr. Fontenot, who was it?"

"That's what I aim to find out. But rest assured, Fontenot will do some serious time for his actions."

While that relieved her about Mr. Fontenot, it also meant that someone else was out there stalking her.

TWENTY-ONE

The cop was hanging around Harper far too often.

Some people might have been fooled by the detective's disguise, but not him. He just happened to be in town as the whole scene with the woman trying to steal clothes unfolded. People were idiotic to think they could avoid getting caught when they crammed several clothing items into a purse.

In the middle of the day, no less.

The cop in his gorilla costume chased the woman through a couple of stores. He'd stood by and watched, along with several others.

Boring town. Had daily events really necessitated some monkey cop apprehending a low-life thief just so there'd be some news to report?

He'd almost left until he realized Harper and the gorilla were going to Sheila's for lunch. So enamored with each other, they hadn't even noticed *him* noticing them. Nor had they observed him following them into the restaurant.

He hated this time of year. Hated all the hearts and decorations. Overkill would be the word he'd use for the decorations at Sheila's. If he hadn't been curious about why the two decided to eat there, he would have avoided the place and instead gone home for lunch.

Then the incompetent waitress seated him at a front booth, while Harper and the cop were led to the back corner. So much for listening in on their conversation.

And attempting to ascertain whether or not the cop had any suspects in Harper's case besides some homeless guy.

He chuckled to himself. Not even Motta, with his lack of brainpower due to his drug addiction, had been arrested—or probably even suspected.

It boded well for him that Lake Radford boasted a lack of intelligence when it came to law enforcement.

He saw a party of eight from a circular booth near where Harper and the cop sat leave and traipse through the restaurant, the baby in the mom's arms crying. Why people brought their kids to restaurants was beyond him. Didn't they realize not everyone was fond of children?

It was tempting to request being relocated to the circular table, but that would for sure draw attention to him. He could lie and say he was waiting for others in his party, but when they didn't show, he'd be moved to a smaller booth to accommodate some large family.

Harper looked up. Had she seen him? Wouldn't matter if she did. No one would suspect him.

He took a bite of his steak and chewed slowly. Even from his vantage point now, he could see the two of them chatting as if old friends.

People like her irked him, causing trouble the way she had. Life was going along just fine, and then she had to interfere. But such a move would be to her detriment. If she didn't stop her attempts to sell the Cox property, he'd have to take more drastic measures. After all, he hated betrayers, and she had betrayed him by listing the place for sale. She could have declined the owners' request to sell.

Speaking of the owners...he punched in the names Jeff and Vanna Cox into the search engine for the hundredth time. He shook his head. What was he thinking? That this internet search would be different? That it would show a number for the problem-causing couple that *was* in service? If he could locate them, then a hasty call might solve the issue altogether when he threatened them if they didn't delist the property.

But no such luck. The same number shown on the screen of his burner phone. Who in their right mind would sell the acreage anyway? Of course, he shouldn't be too surprised. They were sitting on a gold mine.

Miserly people.

He harrumphed, drawing a peculiar glance from some meddlesome woman in the booth next to him. Likely, the owners wouldn't have even wanted to list it if it weren't for Harper encouraging them to do so. Things were slow right now in real estate, and Harper Amerson was just like every agent—a greedy vulture.

Greedy people infuriated him. Always had. For a brief moment, he stepped back in time. He'd been the poor kid who got free lunch at school. His high-water pants and outdated shirts were an embarrassment, as were the too-small shoes he'd been forced to wedge his feet into. He blamed his worthless parents for their poverty. Dad never could hold down a job—his alcohol habit slurped up any funds after bills. Mom was always nagging at him. Even now, he could hear his mother's nauseating tone ringing in his ears. Rarely a day passed when his parents weren't at each other's throats about something.

And he'd had to sit there and listen to it all.

Good thing he didn't have to deal with them anymore. Dad had died from complications from diabetes, and his mom succumbed to cancer eight years ago.

He didn't miss either of them.

Now he had a well-paying job, owned a decent place, and did whatever he pleased. Life wasn't all that bad with the exception of Harper Amerson attempting to sell the Cox property.

Acreage where his deadly secret was located.

And must remain hidden.

If only he'd buried the body elsewhere. But it was convenient at the time. Now, who knew if that would be the exact location where some new homeowner would decide to build a house and do a little excavating, or even some landscaping? They'd probably want to install a pool. It wouldn't do for the heavy equipment operator to stumble across his betrayer's decaying bones. Of course, it wouldn't be the first time a body was found during a construction job.

He attempted to convince himself several times over that just because someone purchased it didn't mean they would ever build on it. Look at the current owners—the acreage with its mountain views and pond was one of the most coveted in the county, if not the state. But Jeff and Vanna Cox had never possessed the ambition to move out of their dumpy little townhouse and move up in the world.

What's to say the new buyers would want to build there?

What was to say the people who purchased it would ever do any thorough excavating and dig up something they shouldn't? Some might say he was paranoid, and maybe he was. Yet, he preferred to be proactive, and no one could be too careful these days.

The waitress interrupted him and asked if he'd like more coffee. He barely tamped down his simmering irritation that she interrupted his contemplations. He scowled at her before affirming her question. She poured the coffee into his cup with a shaky hand.

Pride filled him. He liked having that effect on people every now and again. It was too difficult to constantly be living under a "nice" façade day after day at his job.

Harper Amerson and the cop were laughing about something. He narrowed his eyes as he watched them from a distance. They could laugh all they wanted now.

He balled his fists beneath the table. The worst part of it all? Harper wasn't deterred. And she wasn't listening to the threats. His warnings had fallen on deaf ears.

Because he was a patient and tolerant man, he'd give her a few more chances to get the hint. And if she didn't? It would be time to ramp up his game. If something happened to her before she sold the property, then everyone would get the hint, and the only one who would be laughing would be him.

TWENTY-TWO

Harper was discussing with Loretta about how her parents had finally convinced her grandparents to move back to Lake Radford in a few months, and how she couldn't wait to see them, when she noticed Clark standing nearby. She wrapped up the conversation, and Loretta leaned forward. "You really need to tell Paulette about how he's been antagonizing you."

"I know. Kade—Detective Lassiter—mentioned the same thing. I just don't want to cause problems, and two, he is Paulette's best agent."

"Best agent or not, it's harassment."

"You're right. I'll go talk to her."

Harper found Paulette in her office. Offering a prayer heavenward for courage, she rapped on the door frame. "Do you have a minute?"

"Sure, Harper, come on in."

"Do you mind if I close the door?"

Worry knotted Paulette's brow. "No, that's fine."

Harper shut the door and then took a seat in front of Paulette's desk. "Is something wrong?" her boss asked.

"Yes, I need to talk to you about Clark." Harper wrung her hands. "I've been putting this off, but I think it's necessary."

"Is something wrong with Clark?"

Harper proceeded to share with her boss about the fruit and how it was important since she had hypoglycemia to be able to graze during the day, and the importance of needing food.

"Yes, I remember you saying you had hypoglycemia," agreed Paulette. "Are you sure it was him?"

"Fairly sure." She told Paulette about the parking spot, the glares, and the other general ways that Clark contributed to a hostile work environment. "I don't want to cause trouble, and I know Clark is an award-winning agent and has the most commissions…" she looked over to see Clark passing by Paulette's office. He slowed his pace, and his glare bored into her before he continued on. "I love my job, and I am so grateful to work for you, but it's been a challenge lately with him."

"I understand."

"And I don't really want you to talk to him because I'm worried about retribution."

"That's understandable. I'll be honest, Harper, I've never had a situation like this before."

Harper was about to tell Paulette about the recent ongoings about the Cox property, but decided against it. While Paulette possessed integrity and was supportive of her agents, if she felt as though Harper was more trouble than she was worth, would she determine to part ways with her?

"Neither have I. I guess I just, at this point, wanted you to be aware."

They brainstormed a suitable outcome before Harper left her boss's office and returned to her own. Although how she would be able to get her head back into the game with some upcoming appointments was beyond her.

Had she done the right thing by telling Paulette?

She walked down the hall to her office, rehashing the conversation in her mind when her cell phone rang, and a number she didn't recognize flashed across the screen. As long as it was local, she'd answer it because she didn't want to take the chance of it being someone hoping to look at one of her listings. Especially since she provided her cell on her business cards as well as the office number.

"Harper Amerson."

"Harper?" The voice, a gravely and guttural one she didn't recognize, sounded on the other end.

"Yes?"

"How are you today?"

"I'm fine, and you?" Something unsettling niggled in her stomach.

"Fine. Just fine."

"Can I help you with something?"

"Yes, you can. I'm interested in a property."

Something about the fake-sounding monotone voice gave her pause. If she were asked to show him the property, she'd be sure to take another agent with her. Preferably someone like Enrique or Ean. "What is the address?"

"The Cox property."

"Oh, yes, that one is somewhat new to the market."

"Do you have grandparents, Harper?"

"I don't know what that has to do with..."

"A grandpa who recently had a stroke, perhaps?"

"How did you know?"

"I know a lot of things, Harper."

The call was sending red flags at a rapid pace. "Who is this?"

"You can just call me a concerned citizen."

It was past time to end the call. "Thank you for your time. Good—"

"Don't hang up, Harper." The voice spoke slowly and enunciated each word clearly. "Do. Not. Hang. Up." A pause, then, "You listen to me, Harper Amerson, and you listen well. You need to back off."

"Back off?" Her knees felt like jelly, and she settled herself into her chair.

"Back off from selling the Cox property."

Perhaps she could ask some questions and ascertain who the person was and link him to the other troubling instances she'd recently experienced. *Lord, give me the words to ask.* "Are you worried about losing your view?"

"My view?"

To her regret, her voice shook. "Yes. I know some neighbors are worried the new owners will build a sizable home and block their view of the mountains."

"No, I don't care about the view."

"Are you angry with Jeff and Vanna for selling?"

"What?" He emitted several curse words. "No, I'm not angry with Jeff and Vanna for selling."

"Then why can't I sell the Cox property?"

"Look, lady, I'm not playing your game."

Was the vendetta only against her? "If I don't sell the property, someone else will."

More oaths, then frigid words that were so unfeeling and harsh that fear rippled through her as though the person stood in front of her.

"If you don't delist the property immediately, I'll see to it that your precious grandparents never make it back to Lake Radford."

Harper dropped her cell phone, and it clattered onto her desk as her cold and clammy hands trembled. She fought the rising panic as it surged through her.

How had whoever it was on the phone known about her grandparents returning to Lake Radford?

Her heart pounded with such force that her breath came in gasps before her body went numb.

This was no longer just about her.

Some people were such comedians. Case in point: Chief Spence.

"You asked for me, Chief?" Kade wandered into Chief's office.

"Kade, how goes it?"

"Good."

"Have a seat."

Kade did so, and Chief leaned forward and clasped his hands on the desk. He congratulated Kade on solving the most recent cases before asking for updates on Harper's and the Dumaine case.

"Keep up the good work. I went over and visited Trace the other day. Seems he's a little antsy."

Kade nodded. "That he is. I think we could give him some video footage or something to do. The hours are long when you're laid up."

"He could read or watch TV. I've heard there are still options for watching old game shows and westerns on some channels."

Kade wasn't sure Trace would be open to watching old game shows or westerns. "Probably not his style, Chief."

"Oh, that's right. I'm dealing with the younger generation. Then maybe he could watch something on his phone or listen to an audiobook."

"Could be. I know he's caught up on his favorite movies, and he's had quite a few visitors, so that helps."

"All right, well, I'll contemplate some way we can put him to work while he's recovering. He's an exceptional detective."

"He is, sir, and what better way to have his full attention than now?"

Chief chuckled. "Good point. Speaking of exceptional detectives, I heard you caught a shoplifter on your day off in a gorilla costume, no less."

Kade felt the heat climb up his face. "Yes, I did."

"Not my business to know what my employees are up to on their days off, but I did want to commend you with a little reward."

"A reward?"

Chief reached beneath his desk and retrieved a wrapped box. "For going the extra mile." He nodded at Kade. "You can open right now."

"All right." Kade tore at the Christmas wrapping paper.

"Excuse the wrap. The wife had it left over from Christmas presents."

Kade lifted the lid of the box and removed a sheet of protective brown paper to reveal a framed picture. Of himself. In the gorilla costume. "Uh...thank you?"

"I was sure to cut it out of the paper. Tanisha did a thorough job of covering the story, and the picture, well, it's one of your best."

"Yeah..." Kade removed the frame and studied it. The picture of him from the paper showed a sweaty and exhausted-looking man holding a gorilla mask under one arm. He was making a goofy expression, likely answering Tanisha's questions.

"Feel free to hang it up in your office."

Kade wasn't so sure about that. There was only so much ribbing he could handle, and the framed article would invite more of it for sure. Still, it was an arrest he'd likely never forget.

He'd just returned to his office when his cell rang. Harper's number flashed on the screen. "Detective Lassiter."

"Hi, Kade, this is Harper. Are you in your office?"

"I am. Is everything all right?"

"Could I meet you there in a few minutes?"

"I'll be here."

Had her stalker contacted her again? Kade met Harper in the lobby less than ten minutes later and led her back to his desk. He listened as she explained about the call, likely one with an altered voice made from a burner phone. Kade took down the number, but his gut told him the phone was long gone. One thing about Harper's words stuck out to him immediately. "You mentioned your grandparents."

"Yes." Her voice trembled.

"Who knew that they were returning to Lake Radford?"

"I haven't been keeping it a secret, as a matter of fact, I've been asking people to pray for God's will about the matter. Of course, Mom, Dad, and I want them to move back, but we don't want them to feel forced." Her stiff shoulders told of the burdens weighing on them. She held a shaky hand across her mouth. "I'm sorry, probably TMI, but as for those I've told, it's been my best friend, Kennedy, people at church, coworkers, friends at the gym, and my neighbor, Mrs. Satterwhite, to name a few."

"I'll see if I can find out anything with this number, but I'm not sure since it's likely a burner phone. You didn't recognize the voice?"

"No. It sounded fake. Almost robotic, but harsh and cold."

"I'm confident it was altered."

"I can't believe this is happening. I told him that if I removed the listing, another agent would pick it up. Does he think that he can scare everyone into not selling this property? And for what reason?"

"That's what I aim to find out."

TWENTY-THREE

If only he could give himself a pat on the back. That had gone much better than he'd anticipated. He could hear the fear in her voice. Good. Maybe she'd delist the property.

Who knew these newfangled apps could alter one's voice so well? And neither she nor the cop would ever figure out who placed the call. Not with him using a burner phone. A burner phone that had just met its demise at the bottom of Lake Radford.

He chuckled to himself. Some things in life were just too easy. Now, if Harper would just heed his advice. He had no doubt in his mind that he could harm her and her family if need be, but honestly, he really didn't like messes.

Overhearing her conversation had been pure luck. If he hadn't, he never would have known that her grandparents were returning, let alone that she had grandparents at all.

But one thing she'd said had given him pause. If Harper removed the listing, would another agent take it? What then?

He kicked the tire of his car. That was a problem he hadn't really thought through.

However, just as rapidly as the potential hindrance entered his mind, he shoved it aside. If someone else decided to list the property, then he'd just do the same thing to them.

A notification on his other cell phone sounded, and he grunted as he peered down at the misspelled words.

The druggie's text reeked of desperation.

He fought the frustration that filled him as he read the words.

Do you have any more jobs for me?

No, not right now.

Motta's trigger finger was really getting the best of him because his reply text came within milliseconds.

But I need anuther pill.

The druggie was such an addict. It wasn't like he was a pharmacist handing out painkillers all the time. Such things had to be earned, and that was only if he actually had positions open for jobs. Which he did not.

Unless...

I might have something.

Rilly? When can we meet?

He rolled his eyes and set his beer on the table. It was ten o'clock. He wasn't going back out tonight, too cold, and he'd just gotten home.

How about tomorrow?

But I can't wait till tomarow.

Well, you're just going to have to.

The dots blinked on his phone screen, indicating Motta was typing something. The guy had barely two brain cells to rub together, so it wasn't like it was going to be a novel.

I rilly can't wait. I rilly need a pill.

There were very few people in this world he would go out of his way for. As a matter of fact, he couldn't even think of any. And certainly not the druggie. He put his thumbs to work and texted a reply.

I'll meet you tomorrow at the vacant building at 4:00 p.m., not a second before.

A couple of minutes passed. No text from Motta. Was the guy throwing a tantrum or had he just not had a chance to type a reply? Either way, he wasn't going to sit around and wait. There were things to be done. Plans to be made.

Motta finally replied an hour later. It was a bunch of jumbled words together, likely indicating he'd been into his habits again. He had no use for people who abused drugs and did unlawful things.

The following day at four p.m., he took a break and met Motta at the vacant building. He'd wanted to drive his truck today, but likely Motta would get confused, so instead, he drove his car. He'd only brought along one pill. This wasn't a huge job, and more of just a diversion to irritate Harper more than anything else. However, he was anxious to see how it would unfold. If he weren't so serious about achieving his goal, antagonizing her just because might be pretty fun.

Motta slipped out of the shadows, walked up to the vehicle, and rapped on the door.

He sat there as the seconds ticked by, watching the druggie shiver in the cold, his breath fogging up the passenger side window. The guy really needed to get a different coat. His hoodie was not warm enough for Lake Radford winters. If he were a nice guy, he'd find something in the lost and found, give it to him to wear. He'd seen several jackets in the lost and found at the mom-and-pop grocery store on Main. But he wasn't a nice guy, and if truth be told, Motta was almost more trouble than he was worth. The druggie continued to rap on the window. He knew better than to yell through the window to have him unlock the door. If the cops got wind that Motta was doing anything illegal, the courts would revoke his probation so fast that Motta's head would spin. That was beneficial because the guy did his best then to stay under the radar. Finally, he clicked the button, unlocked the door, and the druggie slipped in.

"What took you so long to unlock the door?"

"I wasn't in any rush."

The druggie scowled at him. "It wasn't like it was cold out there or anything."

"Warmer than it has been."

"Where are my pills?"

Wouldn't Motta be disturbed when he discovered he was only getting one today? He withdrew the little baggy from his jacket pocket and held it out to Motta with an open palm. Motta tried to grab it, but he pulled it away. That was the good thing about people who didn't constantly do drugs. They actually had quick reflexes.

Motta did not.

"Why's there only one in there?" he asked, his unibrow furrowing.

"Yep, only one, this is a one-pill job."

"I can't just have one." Motta's voice grew shrill with terror.

"Not my problem. Either you take it, or you don't. There are many others who'll do the job if you can't."

Motta flung himself against the seat and folded his arms across his body. "Maybe this isn't worth it," he mumbled.

If the druggie thought he was going to gain the upper hand in this situation, he needed to think again. "Then get out of the car." Had to be firm with the druggie.

Motta panicked and crossed his arms and flailed about. "No. I changed my mind. I'll take the pill," he said, and he uttered a few oaths, ending his sentence with, "better than nothing, I guess."

But he wasn't going to give him the pain pill just yet. "I have a simple job for you."

The druggie just stared at him, his eyes unblinking.

"I want you to go to Harper's neighborhood this Sunday and keep an eye on it for a while."

"Hey, man, one pill ain't enough payment to spend my entire day watching some chick's neighborhood."

"Then get out."

Motta rocked back and forth against the seat, his dirty, greasy hair sticking to his seat. Like he had time to clean up after him.

"Knock it off, Motta. You're going to go to Harper's neighborhood Sunday morning and watch for when she returns home from church."

"And why am I doing this?"

The guy asked too many questions. "You want the job, don't you?"

"Yeah, okay. So I watch her. Do you want me to walk around her house again and try to get in like last time?"

The rise of excitement in Motta's tone made him gag. "No, you're not going to her house because she has cameras now."

"Cameras?"

He'd noticed them last time he'd driven slowly by her home. He instantly spied a camera on the porch. If she had one, she likely had more. No sense in setting the druggie up for failure. Idiot would probably share too much with the cops if he were caught.

"Yeah, so don't go to her yard."

"But how am I gonna see her?"

"Every Sunday, when the weather allows it, she walks the neighbor's dog around the block. You'll be hiding just at the end of the street, around the corner behind some shrubs and bushes. That house is vacant, so no one will see you."

"How do you know all this stuff about her walking the dog and vacant houses and stuff?" Motta's awe didn't impress him.

"Because it's part of my job to know this stuff. Now, when she gets past the shrubs and trees, you're going to jump out and scare her, maybe attempt to grab the dog or something."

"Can I keep the dog? They don't allow us to have them at the motel, but maybe I could keep it somewhere else. I've always wanted a dog."

"No, you can't keep the dog."

"Wait. Is it a mean dog? What if it bites me?"

Motta was such a wimp. The guy shot up drugs and had track marks all over his arms, but he was afraid of a little dog? "Then after you scare her and pretend to grab the dog, you're going to say something to her."

"What am I gonna say?"

"'Back off from selling the Cox property.'"

"Back off from what?"

He repeated it three more times and made Motta say it back to him.

The druggie's eyebrows dipped. "What's the point of this again?"

"After you have completed the task, give her a shove, then run back here and text me. I will meet you back here, and you can have the pain pill."

"Shove her?"

The thought of Harper flailing backward gave him much satisfaction. "Yes. Shove her hard so she falls, and don't forget to say the words."

"And I have to run back here."

"Yes."

"But that's a far way to walk. She lives way on the other side of town."

"Yes, and you walk all over the place, so what's the problem?"

"And I can't wait that long for the pill." His voice was a long, whining drone that grated on his nerves.

"Be sure to wear your ski mask so she can't see your face, and wear gloves too."

"What if I don't have any gloves?"

"Find some." Then he nearly shoved the druggie out of his vehicle. "That's all," he said.

The druggie stumbled out into the cold afternoon, his arms wrapped around himself as he staggered back to the dive he called home.

He put the car in drive and mulled over his current plan and the plans for the future.

Just keep it up, Harper. Keep attempting to sell that property. This may seem like just scare tactics so far, but keep pushing me, and you'll find out what happens to those who betray me.

TWENTY-FOUR

Each Sunday after church, weather permitting, Harper took Coco for a walk around the neighborhood. Someday, she hoped to get her own dog, but for now, babysitting the sweet miniature chocolate poodle would do. It was a way to get her doggy-fix and to help Mrs. Satterwhite as well. The elderly woman did enjoy a slow meander around the neighborhood, but wasn't too fond of anything below forty degrees.

Harper ate a bowl of cucumbers, one of her favorite fruits, paired with sunflower seeds for protein to stave off any hypoglycemia until she ate lunch. She then changed from her church clothes into weather- appropriate exercise wear and pulled on tennies before closing the door and locking it behind her. She waved as a patrol car drove by, once again grateful to Kade for soliciting the help of his coworkers to surveil her neighborhood. And immense gratitude at the cameras Griff had installed.

Both made her feel much safer in the wake of some lunatic's schemes.

Still, she needed to be hypervigilant. She stepped back into the house and grabbed some pepper spray and clipped it onto her waistband. Three more months until the next women's shooting course was offered, and Harper had already signed up.

Mrs. Satterwhite didn't know about Harper's stalker, and Harper didn't wish to scare the precious elderly woman, but she had mentioned to her to always be sure to lock her doors because Lake Radford had changed in recent years.

"I've never locked my doors," Mrs. Satterwhite argued. "And never once have I ever had a break-in."

"I know, but the town has grown much larger and is significantly different from when you were growing up, and even since I was a child."

Mrs. Satterwhite's eyes had widened, and she fiddled with the hem on the sleeve of her shin-length green moo-moo dress. "But even in our neighborhood?"

Especially in our neighborhood. "It has changed everywhere, unfortunately."

"All right. Well, I will do my best to remember that."

Thankfully, Mrs. Satterwhite hadn't even noticed Griff installing the cameras or the patrolling of the neighborhood, or Harper would have had to explain that as well. "Coco, are you ready for our walk?"

Coco propped her paws on Harper's pantleg and yipped.

"I so appreciate you doing this, Harper."

"Not a problem at all. I enjoy spending time with my adopted niece."

Mrs. Satterwhite scooped up Coco, and the dog nuzzled against her. "Now you be a good girl for Aunt Harper." She then proceeded to stuff Coco into a red knit sweater and a matching knit hat with a white puffy ball on the top of it.

"We'll be back soon," said Harper, as she maneuvered an excited Coco out of the door on her leash.

The thirty-nine-degree sunny weather with a slight breeze greeted Harper and Coco as they moseyed down the sidewalk past Harper's house and around the corner. No one was out and about today, and Harper took several additional glances, keeping her head on a swivel and being hyperaware of her surroundings.

The sidewalk curved around a tree-lined property, and Coco increased her speed. Just as they reached the end of the expansive yard, a man jumped out in front of Harper and attempted to snatch Coco.

A very familiar man.

Harper froze for a brief second before tugging on the leash, beckoning Coco to her. "Get away!"

But the man in the black hoodie, ski mask, and navy-blue gloves ignored her. He swooped down and lifted Coco. The dog barked, her shrill yelp echoing in the quiet neighborhood.

Would anyone hear her? Where was the patrol car? Her belly cramped in fear as her body went cold with dread. This was the man who'd chased her. The one who'd been on her deck. Of that she was sure.

Lord, please help me. Help Coco.

She needed to run, needed to call 911 so they could arrest this guy, but she couldn't leave Coco in his clutches. "Give her back!"

The poodle squirmed in his arms, and the man tightened his hold on her. "Now you listen here, lady." The man's beady hazel eyes peered at her through the slits in his mask.

Harper took a step backward.

"You better not keep selling the Cox property." He pointed a gloved finger at her. "Better just back off. You got it?"

"Give me the dog!"

The man lunged toward her, and Harper screamed. She backed away, preparing to run, but her frozen legs argued and remained firmly planted. Harper kicked the man in the knee and aimed for his nose with her fist. Fortunately for her, he had a slow reaction time, but unfortunately for her, he raised an arm and shoved her hard. She stumbled backward, her feet going out from beneath her as she fell to the hard cement and smacked her elbow. Her assailant threw Coco at her before darting in the opposite direction.

Kade saw Harper's number flash on his screen and answered it on the first ring. "Harper, are you all right?"

"Kade, it was him."

"What? Where are you?"

She gave him the address.

"I'm on my way."

"I'll meet you at my house. I have to drop Coco off first."

"Who's Coco?"

"My neighbor's dog. I'll explain it all when you get here."

"But you're all right?"

"Yes." But her shaky tone didn't convince him. If only the station weren't clear across town. He couldn't get there fast enough, but at least she wasn't still in danger.

Kade pressed on the gas of his service vehicle, surged around the corners a little faster than he ought, and pulled into the space in front of Harper's house just as she hobbled from the neighbor's home. "Harper!"

"I'm fine. Just a little shaken and maybe a scrape or a bruise or two."

He assisted her to the porch where she unlocked her door, and he followed her inside.

"I'm so grateful Mrs. Satterwhite didn't ask a bunch of questions. She was satisfied with my answer that I had tripped."

"But you didn't."

"No."

He aided her to the couch and sat in the chair across from it. "Tell me what happened."

His pulse picked up, and his neck muscles tightened when she shared about the man who'd accosted her and attempted to steal the neighbor's dog. "And you're sure it's the same man?"

"Yes, almost one-hundred percent certain. And this time I got a look at his eyes. Hazel, small, and beady."

"And not Fontenot, since he's still in jail. Did this man say anything?"

"Yes. He threatened me that I better stop attempting to sell the Cox property."

"I wonder what has this guy so obsessed with that property. Was it the voice of the same man who called you?" Although Kade was fairly sure that voice had been altered.

"No."

He requested an APB with Harper's description of the man. "Do you need to go to urgent care?"

"No." Her voice broke.

And more than anything, he wanted to pull her into his arms and comfort her. But he couldn't cross those lines when hers was an active case he was investigating. So instead, he placed what he hoped was a reassuring hand on her arm. "There's something about the Cox property being for sale that is provoking this individual."

"I know, but I can't figure out what. During that phone call, I asked him about the view or if he was angry at Jeff or Vanna Cox."

"I remember that."

"I just can't understand why he would be targeting me."

"We will catch this guy, Harper. That's a promise."

Kade only hoped it wouldn't be too late. The stalking case where he'd failed again flooded his mind, and with effort, he shoved it aside.

God was faithful. He would help Kade with this investigation. *Please, Lord, before it's too late.*

TWENTY-FIVE

He put down his binoculars and drove away, this time in his truck so the druggie wouldn't recognize him if he saw him sneaking around. He didn't stop until he reached the crowded parking lot at the farm and ranch store. Then he marveled at his innovative idea.

The druggie had done better than he ever thought he would. He'd managed to not only take the dog for a few seconds but also successfully shove and say something to Harper.

He'd frightened her.

Mission accomplished.

Good thing Motta had on a face mask, or else he really would have scared Harper with his meth mouth and foul breath.

Motta must have hightailed back to the motel, either that or he was texting along the way, because his asinine request came through a little too quickly.

Can I have my pill now?

He could almost hear Motta's whiny voice as he read the words. Motta was not a patient man. But he could wait a few more minutes.

Did anyone see you?

Yeah, Harper did.

No kidding, lamebrain. Motta was such a moron. **I mean, were there any police around or any other neighbors?** He'd heard that a cop was patrolling the area, although from his view, he hadn't seen any.

There was a pause, and he envisioned Motta scratching his lice-infested head while he pondered the question.

I don't think so.

Good.

Can I get my pill now?

I'll meet you at the usual spot in half an hour.

Half an hour? I've had to wait a long time.

He didn't care in the least how long the druggie had to wait. He still had to drive home and switch vehicles. Motta had never seen his truck and never would. Were he asked about the car, that wouldn't be as big a deal because there were several of those around town. His pride and joy truck? Not so much.

Wait half an hour or forget it.

Okay. I'll wait. I'm still wokking anyways.

Motta's sloppy spelling drove him crazy. Doubtful the idiot even knew what a wok was.

He drove to his house, donned his disguise, traded his truck for his comfortable car, then drove to the meeting place. Motta was already there, shivering in the shadows, before shuffling toward the car and rapping on the window.

He rolled it down about an inch. "Can I help you?"

"Yeah, you know you can. It's me, man."

He laughed, amused by his own wit, and unlocked the door. Motta climbed in and rubbed his hands together in front of the heater. "It's getting cold out there." Motta shivered for extra effect.

Meeting with the druggie was such a waste of his time. It was just to his benefit that he'd found the loser that day when he'd first asked him to do his bidding. He opened his hand where he held the squished baggy with the lone pill. Motta snatched it from his hand, nearly drawing blood with his sharp, yellowed fingernail.

He studied the druggie. Would the druggie be able to identify him or describe him to the police, even though he always wore a disguise when meeting with him? The vacant look in Motta's eyes answered his question. The man could barely function, let alone recognize anybody. It was amazing that he even found Harper's neighborhood, and even more amazing that he actually recognized the woman he'd been hired to stalk.

"Do you have more jobs for me?"

"Maybe. We'll see."

"But I've been a good employee."

Motta knew nothing about being a good employee. "Whatever. Look, I need to go. I'll be in touch."

"I'll need another pill."

"Find it somewhere else while you're waiting for another text from me."

Motta mumbled something beneath his breath before exiting the car.

As he drove away a few minutes later, a sense of satisfaction filled his chest. While today might have been nothing more than a way to scare Harper, it was all fitting into his carefully plotted plan.

TWENTY-SIX

Zephyr Malles was charged with reckless driving, given a fine, and ordered by the judge to perform community service. Kade desired to do all he could to help the kid turn his life around.

If Zephyr was willing.

Kade invited him to church, and although his mother immediately declined to attend, Zephyr agreed. Perhaps it had been the mention of the potluck afterward.

Regardless, hopefully something the pastor said would resonate.

Zephyr sat through the sermon, arms folded across his chest and a glower on his face. He perked up a bit during the potluck when all of the old ladies serving the food welcomed him as though he were their own grandson.

Kade had never seen such a skinny kid pack away so many helpings of cheesy potato casserole, macaroni coleslaw, fried chicken, and apple crumble.

So when Kade mentioned the men's lunch, scheduled for this coming Saturday, Zephyr didn't even hesitate when agreeing to attend, especially after Kade informed him there would be all-you-can-eat pizza.

When Saturday arrived, Kade picked Zephyr up at noon. The teen still folded his arms and said less than five words on the way to the church. Kade had prayed that somehow

God would help this floundering kid make good choices in his life—choices that would deter him from a life of crime, because that seemed to be where the kid was headed.

Kade had discovered the reckless driving hadn't been Zephyr's only brush with the law. As a juvenile, he'd been caught stealing twice and had used his artistic abilities to ensure the concrete bridge on the pathway was covered in graffiti, along with help from Talon and Orion, who'd had their own interactions with the law.

Kade had worked with troubled youth in Fairmont as well, and each time, he desired to help those struggling to find their way onto—or back onto—the right path. Not all of those he'd come into contact with had a troubled upbringing. Some came from solid homes, yet made poor decisions.

Zephyr's parents had never been married, and Zephyr had met his dad once when he was three years old, a time the teen didn't even remember. The lack of a father figure in his life had, undoubtedly and understandably, left the boy at a disadvantage.

His mom wanted nothing to do with what she called the "religious people". Kade prayed for her, too, that God would soften her heart. And because the Lord worked in mysterious ways, perhaps it might be Zephyr who would someday lead his own mom to Christ.

But that was Kade's optimism and belief that no one was beyond hope. Zephyr was still young and hadn't yet committed any major offenses. It would be by God's grace that the teen would choose to stay on the right side of the law.

"Ready for some pizza?"

Zephyr shrugged.

Kade had heard that teens uttered monosyllables when being spoken to, and Zephyr confirmed it.

They drove down Main Street, then turned onto Poplar Avenue, where the Lake Radford Community Church stood proudly at the end of the street. A red brick church with an oversized white cross above a rounded entranceway stood in the yard with multiple bushes, trees, and, in the summer, flowers that the women's Bible study would plant.

Kade had been glad to have found this church when he moved here. One that preached the truth from God's word and focused on fellowship and reaching others for Christ. While it wasn't perfect, and the church struggled with things just like any other church, it was the place where Kade fully believed he was meant to be.

"Here we are," he said, knowing that Zephyr would likely not even respond. But the teen shocked him.

"Are you sure it's all-you-can-eat pizza?"

"I'm sure, but you have to save some for the rest of us," Kade joked.

That elicited the tiniest of grins on Zephyr's face. "I hope they have supreme. That's my favorite."

Kade had known that from speaking with Zephyr's mom, and he ensured that had been one of the types ordered.

They walked in the door and were immediately greeted by several of Kade's friends, including Baldwin and one of the dispatchers named Nathan. The aroma of pizza floated in the air, and Kade's stomach growled. He could probably eat an entire box himself.

Baldwin raised a fist bump. "Good to see you, Zephyr."

With a lack of ambition but a slight straightening of his slumping shoulders, Zephyr fist-bumped him.

"Glad you could join us." Nathan pointed at his son, a stocky eighteen-year-old with black hair and glasses. "This is my son, Ryan."

"Yeah, I know him from school. Hey, Ryan."

"Zephyr, how's it going?"

Before long, the two started talking and meandered their way near the bulletin board.

"Thanks, Nathan. I'm trying to make him feel like he belongs."

Nathan nodded. "It's not easy going somewhere where you don't know anybody. Ryan said he's in a couple of classes with Zephyr, including a math class, and Zephyr probably won't pass it. Ryan and I talked at length about it, and Ryan said if Zephyr is open to it, he'd be happy to tutor him."

"Ryan's a good kid. Zephyr might just take him up on that."

They met in the youth room where the pastor was setting several boxes of pizza on the table.

Zephyr and Ryan entered a few seconds later. "My nose always leads me to food." Ryan chuckled.

"Yeah, mine too. I was hoping there would be supreme pizza here."

"You can have all the supreme you want. Canadian bacon is my favorite."

The pastor invited the men in to grab some pizza before the guest speaker spoke.

Kade stood behind Zephyr in line and watched the indecision flicker in the teen's eyes as to whether or not to pile his plate with only two slices or see how many he could fit on the flimsy paper plate.

Ryan piled two pieces of Canadian bacon on his plate and reached for a healthy serving of breadsticks. "We can always come back for more, but probably better make sure there's enough for everyone."

Zephyr grabbed several breadsticks and followed Ryan to a table where Nathan had already snagged a seat for him and Kade.

After a prayer blessing the meal, everyone started eating while the elder presented his talk about forgiveness—God's forgiveness, what Jesus did on the cross, forgiving others, and asking others for forgiveness.

Zephyr finished the last bite of his pizza, crossed his arms across his body, and slumped in his chair. Midway through the talk, he straightened his posture, leaned forward, and rested his hands on the table. Kade prayed something would resonate with the young man.

He'd always believed no one was beyond God's grace, and that was proven throughout God's Word.

After the elder finished his talk, he led a prayer. So far, Zephyr had not joined in any of the prayers at church or during the men's lunch. Instead, he sat there, eyes open, staring down at the table. He did the same now as the elder thanked the Lord for the day, for those in attendance, and asked that God would help the men to search their hearts about any forgiveness they needed to ask of God, needed to offer to others, or needed others to forgive them for.

Zephyr and Ryan polished off several more pieces of pizza each and stood around talking in a group of five other young men their age before Kade overheard Ryan tell Zephyr he hoped maybe he could hang around with him and his friends at school sometime.

"I don't think your friends would really accept me. I'm not a jock."

"Actually, I think they would. You've already met a couple of them here today."

Zephyr shrugged. "All right then, if you think so."

Ryan clapped him on the back. "Will you be here tomorrow at church?"

The seconds ticked by before Zephyr finally answered. "Yeah, I guess so."

Perhaps if Zephyr got in with the right crowd in the next few months of school before it ended, it would help him considerably.

After telling everyone goodbye, Kade and Zephyr hopped in Kade's truck and headed back to Zephyr's house.

"Did you get enough to eat?" Kade kept his gaze focused on the road.

"Yeah, I did. Maybe even too much. I told myself I'm never having supreme pizza again after eating…" he paused. "Eight pieces. But I think that might just be a temporary thing."

Kade chuckled. "If you're anything like me, you can't go without pizza for too long."

A quiet laugh rumbled through Zephyr. The first Kade had heard.

They drove in silence with Zephyr peering out at the passing scenery until just before Kade turned into the trailer park.

He cleared his throat. "I'm probably not supposed to have any contact with that lady we were following that day. What was her name?"

"Ms. Amerson."

"Ms. Amerson," Zephyr repeated. "But I was wondering if maybe she would be willing to talk to me for a few minutes."

"About?"

"I want to ask her if she'll forgive me."

It was all Kade could do not to allow his jaw to go slack as he removed his eyes from his surroundings and stared at Zephyr. Emotion swirled in the young man's eyes.

"I think that would be a great idea. Maybe at church."

Zephyr said nothing more pertaining to the topic. He opened the door. "Yeah, that would work. Bye."

"See you tomorrow at church?"

"Yeah. I'll take my mom's car. She's not working until later in the day."

Kade watched as Zephyr strolled to his house, unlocked the door, and entered without so much as a glance behind him.

As he drove away, Kade thanked God for the way He was already orchestrating change for the better in the young man's life.

TWENTY-SEVEN

Harper was counting down the days before Mom, Dad, Grandma, and Grandpa would be returning to Lake Radford. They would all fly here, and then two weeks later, the moving truck would bring all of her grandparents' possessions to Lake Radford. Mom had assured Grandma that she wouldn't miss out on anything except the new friends she had made and the warmer weather. Grandma had agreed and said she'd be okay about the friendship thing because she still had numerous friends in Lake Radford that she had known for decades. As far as the colder weather, she wasn't quite sure about that. When she and Grandpa had moved South, The Cottages had not yet been built. Harper had texted several pictures to share with her grandparents.

Grandma was already planning what she would plant in the provided pots. And The Cottages just installed security cameras and other safety measures, alleviating some of Harper's stress about her grandparents moving back, given the recent threats.

Surely, they'd catch whoever was stalking her before Grandma and Grandpa arrived. Surely.

Harper parked her SUV in the church parking lot, and as she walked inside, Kade caught her attention and asked if she could join him and Zephyr Malles in one of the vacant Bible study rooms.

She'd never met the teen who'd been part of the group of boys who'd followed her, but she assumed the awkward blond-haired boy who sat in one of the chairs, picking at his fingernails, was Zephyr.

"Zephyr?"

Zephyr looked up at her but didn't say anything. He instead looked at Kade, who nodded at him.

Kade mentioned that he had chosen to mentor Zephyr and that Zephyr was attending some church events. The boy was being raised by a single mother with no father in the picture. He probably wouldn't graduate because of some bad choices he'd made and that Zephyr had fallen in with the wrong crowd. But Kade also said that God was working in Zephyr's life.

It had been just over ten years since Harper had been in high school, but as hard as things could be back then—and she came from a strong Christian family and still struggled—she could only imagine how much more difficult it could be these days. Zephyr was fortunate that Kade wanted to help him and give him a second chance. She wondered for a moment if his friends had been offered that second chance, and if so, how they had responded.

Awkward seconds ticked by as other churchgoers passed by in the hallway, some of them peeking into the room.

Finally, Zephyr spoke. "I just wanted to say I'm sorry for that day we scared you."

Harper's eyes misted. Sincerity laced the boy's words. She was about to say she would forgive him when he spoke again.

"I was wondering if there was any way you could forgive me."

She took a seat in a chair across from him, and in that moment, she didn't see an eighteen-year-old boy, but a lost young soul in need of redemption.

"Yes, Zephyr, I forgive you."

"You do?"

"Yes."

"I'm not really sure why you would."

Harper prayed for the right words to say. "I have been forgiven for much in my life, especially by Jesus."

A skeptical expression crossed Zephyr's features, and he arched an eyebrow.

"We are all in need of forgiveness and grace."

They sat there for a few more minutes until an idea emerged. Harper would need to run it past Kade first, but it just might work. She scooted back her chair, stood, and asked Kade if she could meet him in the hall for a brief moment.

"Do you think it would be all right if I asked Zephyr if he would want to come help unload the moving van when my grandparents get here? I could offer all-you-can-eat pizza."

"He loves pizza even more than I do, and yes, I think it would be a great idea." He smiled that heart-stopping smile, and her own heart stuttered. She really, really liked him and would be glad when her case was solved for a variety of reasons, including perhaps exploring a relationship with him. "And, of course, I'll be there to help too."

"Thank you. I really appreciate that."

"No problem."

They stood for the next few seconds, gazes connected, before Kade cleared his throat. "Guess we should iron out the details before church starts. I think your idea is a good one, and Zephyr wants so badly to belong. I witnessed that firsthand at the men's lunch." Kade ushered her back inside the room, and Harper again took a seat across from the teen.

"My grandparents are moving back here in a couple of weeks, and we're going to need some help unloading and arranging everything in their new home. Would you be interested in helping? Kade will be there, and maybe you could invite Ryan."

Zephyr shrugged. "All right, I guess I can help you with that."

"That would be fantastic! And there will be all-you-can-eat pizza."

For the first time, Harper saw a huge grin light Zepher's face. "Then, yeah, I'm definitely in."

Kade appreciated Harper's grace toward Zephyr, but it wasn't unexpected. From what he knew of her, she was a godly woman who herself had tasted God's grace and generously meted it out to others. He sat down beside her, Kennedy, and Zephyr on his other side. He attempted to focus on announcements rather than on her but found it to be a struggle. When they'd stood in the hallway discussing Zephyr assisting her grandparents, he hadn't been able to take his eyes off her. Sure, he'd dated quite a bit when he lived in Fairmont and once or twice in Lake Radford, but there was something different about Harper Amerson.

Something that felt like it maybe could be more permanent.

But first, he needed to keep her safe from some crazy person attempting to stop her from selling the Cox property. Now he had to deal with not only the note, letter, and shots fired at the Cox property, but also a phone call and two assaults. Although it was looking more and more like Fontenot was unrelated to the events. More than likely, Fontenot had seen an opportunity while high on meth and had randomly mugged and threatened her. And Kade had confirmed the phone call had been made on a burner phone they hadn't yet been able to trace.

The music started, and another song, this time a hymn, flashed across the screen, and Kade pushed thoughts of work aside and instead focused on worship. Someone entered the row from the edge, and as Kade moved out of the way for them to pass, his fingers gently brushed Harper's.

Which caused that now-becoming-a-regular-thing-when-he-was-with-her zip of excitement to trill through him.

The sermon today was about God seeing the full picture, even when we don't understand why certain things happen. The pastor read from several Bible passages, and Kade thumbed through to each one and read along. A glance from the corner of his eye indicated Zephyr was listening intently. Kade prayed that something the pastor said would permeate Zephyr's heart. The boy wasn't yet interested in a Bible, but Kade prayed that time would come when the teen would desire to soak up all he could about God's Word.

The pastor spoke again about the full picture. Kade hadn't seen the full picture with the stalking victim in Fairmont. Not at first. He hadn't thought the occasional texts from the victim's ex-boyfriend were anything to be worried about.

When those texts escalated to nearly forty a day, he assisted her with getting a protection order. But it hadn't been enough. A crazed lunatic who was obsessed with the woman he'd dated for three months instead took her life. The image of the woman's lifeless body would forever haunt him.

He should have done more. Should have done all he could.

Kade swallowed through the lump in his throat. *Lord, I know I could have done better. I'm so sorry.*

A woman was dead because of him. A life snuffed out.

"God sees the full picture, and while we don't always understand, He knows. Knows all. Sees all. Forgives all. But one thing that is hard for us sometimes is to surrender all that pain to Him. All the pain we struggle with, including the pain from the things in life that we don't understand."

Kade had spoken at length to Dad about the situation. Had spoken with the department psychologist. Had talked with his pastor in Fairmont. Had prayed like he'd never prayed before. For the woman's family left behind, and for wisdom should he ever encounter a similar case.

Which he'd prayed he wouldn't.

He'd prayed for wisdom. For guidance. For relief from the guilt, even though Dad reassured him it wasn't his fault, that Kade had done the best he could. But Kade had strongly considered not continuing in his role in law enforcement.

God had other plans.

"Cry out to Him. Give Him every hurt and every sorrow and every question," the pastor was saying.

In the quiet of his heart, Kade did just that.

TWENTY-EIGHT

He wasn't Motta's employer. The guy needed to get a grip and find a real job. Druggies honestly made him sick.

Motta sat in his vehicle tapping on the dashboard to some unknown tune in his head. The guy's nervousness made him cringe. Pretty soon, he would no longer need the druggie's pathetic services. At least so far, Motta had been loyal to the cause.

If he hadn't been committed and compliant, there was another place Motta could reside.

He nearly chuckled at the thought, then ground his teeth. The Cox property better never sell.

"Look, man, I just need another hit." Motta's bloodshot eyes darted about, and he wiped his runny nose with the back of his sleeve. The guy's pathetic lack of personal hygiene nauseated him. Just the odor emanating from his person was enough for him to open the door and boot Motta from his vehicle. If he didn't need the loser's services one more time...

Perhaps one more scary episode for Harper before her coming demise would be beneficial. And besides, he wouldn't be to blame. If Motta was ever arrested for his "foolish" actions, the cops couldn't pin it on anyone but the druggie. He was surer of that than ever. He inwardly laughed. Motta could no more describe his appearance to law enforcement than run for

President of the United States. And the texts they'd find on Motta's phone? All from numerous burner phones long since abandoned and destroyed.

Not with his disguise, which changed regularly, and this time included a ski mask. Yes, he'd taken numerous precautions to hide and alter his appearance.

He looked over at Motta. His spastic movements and incoherent speech made him wonder what Motta's choice of drug was for the day. Of course, he doubted the guy only had one drug preference—likely, he was into the whole potpourri thing and mixed a lot of them.

He scowled. How people could be so idiotic was beyond him.

"I need something, man," repeated Motta. "Like a pill or two."

"I don't care what you need. "

Motta shrank back in offense, clearly insulted. "Look, I've done what you've told me to."

"Yeah, you have." He pretended to mull things over. Ah...the benefit of manipulation, and if he had to admit it, he was good at it. "All right, one more job, and then you're going to have to find somewhere else to get your pills."

Motta's chin trembled like a little kid who'd gotten caught with his hand in the cookie jar, and he blinked rapidly. "But where?"

"Not my problem."

He needed to get this done and over with so he could get to work. "You need to pay attention to my instructions."

"I always do." But just as quickly as Motta's over-the-top arrogance appeared, it disappeared. "Don't I?"

He wouldn't answer that. The guy's insecurities were pitiful. "I just need you to scare Harper Amerson one more time."

Motta settled down a bit, and a creepy grin crossed his face. "Ooh, that sounds like fun."

The druggie needed some serious mental help.

"So, what am I going to do, boss?"

It was the first time Motta had called him boss, and it would be the last. Before he could respond, Motta asked another of his ridiculous questions. "Can I use my gun again like I did that one time at that one place when I shot into the air?"

"The Cox property, and no, you can't use your gun this time."

Motta pouted. The last thing he needed Motta to do was accidentally shoot Harper with his stolen weapon. No, it would be him who had the satisfaction of final revenge with Harper Amerson. "I just need you to..." how to phrase this so the dimwitted Motta would comprehend it... "Maybe grab her or attack her in a parking lot—something like that or—"

"You mean like I shoved her last time?"

"No. This time you're going to grab her and attack her."

Motta started rocking back and forth, shaking the entire vehicle.

"Quit it!" He thrust a hand and sucker-punched Motta in the gut.

The druggie released a groan before he started trembling. "Can't do it at her house. Can't do it at her house." Motta shook his head slowly and repeated for a third time, "Can't do it at her house."

"No kidding, genius. We both know she has cameras and cops all around there."

"I can do it by that house in the neighborhood again."

"No, too much of a risk to have it happen in the same place again, and she hasn't taken that dog for a walk since you shoved her last time."

"Why not?" asked Motta.

He rolled his eyes. The guy was hopeless. "You probably can't do it at her place of business either."

"But then where?" Motta flinched at the sound of someone's car backfiring in the distance.

"That's for you to determine."

"I have to determine that?" Motta's voice rose an octave. "But how will I do that?"

"Stalk her. Find out where she's going. Have you not already been working on this case for several weeks?"

"Working on this case? I like that. It sounds like I'm someone important."

He wouldn't tell Motta that he was of least importance on the importance scale.

Motta kept yammering on. "But I don't have a car. I have to—" he peered down at his bouncing knee. "I have to walk everywhere."

"Yep, and good news for you, Harper doesn't go that many places. Work, home, church, to show properties..."

"Yeah, yeah, that's true. But how..."

He exhaled a weighty breath and rolled his shoulders to alleviate the tension. This was *not* his problem. "Look. You want the pills or not?"

"Pills? Yes."

"Good. Then find out where she's going, follow her, and do some damage."

"Like maybe break her arm or her leg?" An evil grin tugged at Motta's chapped lips, and his pupils dilated.

"Don't get all deranged on me."

"Deranged? What's that?"

He shook his head. He didn't have time for vocabulary lessons. "Just get the job done." Were it not that he himself wanted the satisfaction, he would "hire" Motta to do the endgame job.

But no, he wanted all of the gratification from that. He deserved it after all the stress Harper had put him through.

Motta picked at an unraveling hem on his filthy shirt. "Okay, so what do you want me to do?"

Did he really have to repeat his instructions? Make them more easily understood by someone constantly doped up? "I want you to scare her. Maybe grab her arm, shove her again, but this time harder, something like that. Throw her to the ground, hit her,...things like that. But you cannot hurt her too badly."

That will be my job.

"I get to choose what I do?"

Motta was such an opportunist.

"I don't care what it is as long as you don't hurt her too badly and as long as you take care of this within the next few days."

Time was running out before the end day.

"And how many pills do I get?"

He pulled the baggy from his pocket. "You'll get one now and two after you're done."

"One now?" Motta sat up straighter and pressed his bony shoulders against the car seat. "You've never paid me in advance."

"Yeah, well, consider it a bonus."

"All right, I'll do it. But you're sure after this, I'm done?" A wistfulness edged his words.

He couldn't wait to be finished with Motta. The guy tested his patience like no one ever had before. Well, except maybe a coworker. "I'm sure." He handed Motta one of the pills, then, figuratively speaking, kicked him from the vehicle. The sooner he was done with this guy, the better. He hated the thought that he even had to consort with such low-life people.

He started the vehicle and veered out from behind the vacant building. Harper had been given numerous chances to relent in selling the Cox Property, and more importantly, to persuade the owners not to sell.

But she'd failed.

Miserably.

Soon, Harper. Soon, this will be all over.

TWENTY-NINE

Harper left the offices at The Cottages. The lightness in her heart invigorated her steps. The Cottages were the perfect place for her grandparents to experience independence but also have help nearby if needed. They would own the one-bedroom, one-bath cottage she'd put a down payment on. Four blocks beyond The Cottages sign, the Lake Radford Senior Citizen Center hosted daily events, excursions, and life enrichment programs. A doctor's clinic was situated just kitty-corner in case Grandma and Grandpa needed medical care. In between, canopies of trees, picnic tables, and winding walking paths promised plentiful time in the summer sunshine. And the best part? The security system.

The best of both worlds, as the saying goes.

Granted, Grandma would have preferred a huge backyard where she could plant all of her flowers and collect a host of items like wheelbarrows and bathtubs in which to plant said flowers. But The Cottages did boast a compact 5,000 square foot lot where their house stood and a generous common area beyond that with trees, flower gardens, and a community vegetable garden plot, along with an adjacent park. If Grandma still desired to plant seedlings in her own yard, such could easily be accomplished with pots as well as the existing wooden troughs placed along the west side by the former owner.

Harper tilted her head to the sunset-colored sky. *Thank You, Lord, for letting Grandma and Grandpa acquiesce and agree to move back here. Thank You for letting Grandpa be doing so much better. Please help us to get them here safely and let them be happy here just as they were before they moved South.*

Grandma, ever the social butterfly, would delight in once again partaking in various ministries at church, and no doubt she'd pick up where she left off in her book club and Friday night bingo. Grandpa, while more introverted, had been an appreciated addition at the men's Bible study and, if he fully recovered, could still go fishing.

It would be good to have them close again. And between Harper and her parents, they would all be able to ensure that Grandma and Grandpa's needs were met.

She had stayed longer than she'd anticipated speaking with the manager of The Cottages. The woman lived onsite, her house doubling as the office. Harper couldn't wait to tell Kennedy that she discovered that Lake Radford Senior Citizens Center was looking to fill a position next month for a senior activity coordinator. Kennedy would be perfect for the job.

All in all, things were going well. Especially since she hadn't had any run-ins with her stalker for the past couple of days, and no more assaults, phone calls, notes, or letters.

She could only hope he'd given up harassing her and that Kade would find and arrest him soon.

Harper zipped up her lightweight jacket and headed toward her SUV. Soon, the days would be longer, and spring would be here. She could hardly wait. Next week would be March. Yes, there were still a few months before consistent warm weather arrived in her Rocky Mountain town, and snowstorms would still happen for three more months, but she looked forward to the gradual change in weather.

Her SUV was the only car in the parking lot, and she conducted a quick sweep of her surroundings. It was a safe area—although so was the fitness center, the realty office parking lot, and her own neighborhood, and she'd experienced concerns in those places. But the various cameras on the light pole in the parking lot and on each cottage reassured her.

Harper reached into the outside pocket of her purse and extracted her keys. She was about to hit the unlock button when, from out of nowhere, a man rushed toward her, pushing her hard to the ground.

Her purse and keys flew from her hands and scattered on the asphalt.

Stunned, she attempted to get her bearings about her.

She knew her assailant. His black hoodie was secured tightly with a drawstring; however, this time he wore no face mask.

But now wasn't the time to attempt to memorize his facial features, even if she would need that information later.

Later.

She had to get away first.

He stood, and Harper struggled to her feet and forced her legs to cooperate. She half-limped, half ran from him.

He yelled something, then rushed her again. Her head snapped back, and the impact of the fall sent a ripple of pain through her back. She screamed.

Her first inclination was to roll into a fetal position and guard her head as he lurched for her a third time, fists pummeling. But her fight or flight response kicked in, and she floundered to her feet just as his fist connected with her stomach. He shoved her a third time. Her elbow hit the side of her SUV, and she cried out in pain.

Praying for strength, she reached up and, with a balled fist, attempted to connect with his nose. He turned his head, and instead, she clocked him in the left ear. He wobbled backwards slightly, giving her time to escape.

Attempting to ignore the pain that surged through nearly every part of her body, Harper scanned the area, looking for her keys. He noticed her intent and scrambled in the same direction.

Harper wouldn't leave her back exposed. So with astounding agility, she slid around, then crouched quickly, swiped her keys off the ground, and floundered to the driver's side of the SUV, her hand hovering over the unlock button.

He seesawed toward her and yanked her arm, jerking her toward him. Before she could react, he trapped her in a headlock, knocking her keys from her hand. Panic rushed through her as her heart raced in her chest. Pain seared where his forearm pressed.

Was anyone watching the cameras right now? Was the manager of The Cottages calling 911? She attempted to scream again, hoping—praying—someone would hear her. But his arm pressed against her throat, making doing so impossible. Would he cut off her breathing completely?

Lord, please help me!

She hadn't seen anyone in the park, and all of the businesses in the nearby vicinity were closed. The residents of The Cottages were likely inside watching TV.

The man, while thin, was stronger than her, but she would not relent in her fight. She caught a whiff of his foul breath, marijuana mixed with alcohol, overwhelming body odor, and some other stench she couldn't identify.

Think, Harper, think!

Her hands were unoccupied, and she could use those to free herself. With one hand, she reached up and pinched his tricep as hard as she could. She twisted her fingers while digging in deep with her fingernails to claw him. He winced and loosened his grip. With her other hand, she aimed for the back of his knee and, while not connecting perfectly, did manage to hit it hard enough with her fist to cause him to falter. She kneed him as hard as she could in the groin. He emitted numerous oaths as he folded in half from the pain.

Harper bolted again toward her car, unlocking it as she ran. Her hand shaking, she clicked the button several times. The sound of the door unlocking sounded in the otherwise quiet air, and she reached for the door handle. Her assailant stood upright, and limping, and made a beeline for the passenger side. She climbed inside, clicked the lock button, and inserted her key into the ignition. The man pounded on her window and yanked on her door handle. She shifted the car into drive and peeled away from the parking spot.

Tears blinding her vision, she drove directly to the police station while glancing constantly in the rearview mirror to see if he was pursuing her. No one was behind her until she turned onto Main Street, and a gray car pulled in behind her. She exhaled the breath she'd been holding when she realized it was not the man. Her head, neck, and back ached, and her elbow reduced full movement in her arm. She hadn't even healed fully from the last attack.

It was only then that she remembered that she'd left her purse and cell phone behind. Those things could be replaced. At least she had escaped with her life.

"Thank You, Jesus, for keeping me safe." Her shallow breathing came out in gasps.

Less than ten minutes later, she pulled into the police department. She exited her vehicle and stumbled to the door.

THIRTY

Kade exited the PD, ready to leave for the day, when he saw a familiar SUV zip into the PD parking lot.

"Harper?" He hurried over to her vehicle just as she opened the door and slid out. "Harper, are you all right?"

But even before she answered, he knew she wasn't. She collapsed against him, and he steadied her. "Harper?"

"I was just attacked at The Cottages."

"What?" Fury burned inside of him. Just how far would this man take his obsession?

Still holding on to her, Kade stepped back and looked into her eyes. He couldn't see much detail in the dark beneath the streetlights, but he could see that her hair was disheveled. She wobbled, and he offered his arm. She gripped it, and they slowly walked the short distance to the door of the station. Questions bombarded his mind.

He opted to lead her to the wheelchair-accessible ramp rather than the stairs. Her sluggish progress concerned him, but she continued to move one foot in front of the other.

Once in the light of the waiting room, Kade could clearly see that she'd been physically assaulted. That was bad enough, but so help him if... "Did he—only the physical assault?" As if that weren't enough.

"Yes."

He exhaled a hefty breath of relief. "We need to get you to the hospital."

"No, I'm all right."

She was clearly *not* all right. "Harper…"

Her eyes glistened. "I just want this guy caught."

"Believe me, I do too. Was it the same guy?"

"Yes."

Kade balled his fists at his side. Whoever did this to her…with effort, he reigned in his temper. Justice would be served. They just had to apprehend the man first. "Did you hit your head?"

Harper's gaze connected with his, and she nodded. Mascara streaks trailed down her face, and the ponytail holder was barely hanging by a thread at the bottom of her long, dark hair. "Yes."

She fell against him again, and he instinctively wrapped his arms around her. His mind went all sorts of places regarding what could have happened to her. His throat lurched with a hard swallow. He was beginning to care very much for this woman.

Kade patted her hair and rested his chin on her head. He closed his eyes, offering a prayer of thankfulness that couldn't even begin to express his gratitude. He inhaled the aroma of strawberry shampoo and marveled at how well she fit into his arms. If only he could hold her forever. Keep her safe.

But for now, with him working her active case, he couldn't allow himself to fall for her.

Too late, Lassiter.

It was too late. At present, his main objective was to find out who it was who continued to stalk and harass her. Kade reluctantly took a step back. "Let's get you to the hospital to be checked out, if for nothing else to make sure you don't have a concussion." He paused and searched her eyes, noting the indecision in their depths. "Harper, you don't have to prove your resilience to me. I already know you're brave, capable, and strong."

She bit her lip. "Thank you," she whispered.

"I'll drive you to the hospital."

Harper slowly nodded. "All right."

"Give me just a minute." Kade met with dispatch, described the assailant, and asked that two patrol cars be sent immediately to The Cottages. He'd get the camera footage later. Then he drove his truck to the front door before assisting Harper to the passenger side. He activated the heated seats, then dashed to his side.

She leaned back in the seat and closed her eyes. The pain etched in her face reminded him why he'd chosen the career he had.

No one should be able to treat someone the way this man had treated her. What if she'd not escaped? What if he'd kidnapped her...or worse?

Kade proceeded through the downtown area and took the shortest route up the hill to the local hospital. "I'll get your statement once we get you settled. Dispatch is sending two officers to the scene."

"I also left my phone and purse there, too." She shivered, despite the warm seats and the blaring heater.

He pulled to the side of the road and removed his jacket. "Here. Put this on."

With trembling hands, she removed the seatbelt, and Kade assisted her with tugging on his coat.

He would catch this guy.

The sooner the better.

Thankfully, Harper hadn't suffered a concussion but only bumps, bruises, and a strain in her arm. He sat with her after the doctor left and took some notes about what had happened.

"Did you see the man who did this?"

"Yes, it was the guy in the black hoodie, only this time I saw his entire face." She shuddered. "I couldn't see as well as I would have liked because it was starting to get dark, but I did notice that he had hazel eyes, a wiry brown goatee, bad teeth, and a long oval face. He was thin and smelled of alcohol, marijuana, body odor, and something else I couldn't quite determine."

He wanted to reach for her hand and tell her everything was going to be okay. But he knew he needed to remain professional. "So, he attacked you just out of nowhere?"

"Yes. He rushed me just as I was about to get into my car."

Kade wrote a note to himself to inspect the footage from the surveillance cameras around the area. Thank goodness there were plenty in that vicinity.

After several more questions, he came to the final one. "Do you have somewhere you can stay tonight?"

"I just want to go home."

"I understand, but I prefer you stay somewhere else tonight and probably for the next few days until we figure out who this guy is and hopefully apprehend him."

Her gaze met his. "What happens if it takes longer than just a few days?"

"How about you stay somewhere for two days, and then if we haven't caught him, then we'll reassess the situation."

She slowly nodded. The sadness and fear in her eyes bothered him. She was strong, brave, independent, and capable. But having to deal with all she had in recent days would rattle anyone.

"Maybe my parents' house? They're not here, they're in Florida for a few more weeks."

"No one's home?"

"No. But their house is in a rural setting about three miles from town."

Kade processed the pros and cons of her suggestion. "While that would be somewhere where our stalker probably wouldn't think about you being, it's also more secluded and would take us longer to get there if there was a problem. What about staying with Kennedy?"

"I just don't want to put her at risk."

"I'll have a patrol car watching her place."

Finally, she relented.

Harper hated bothering Kennedy at this hour. Her friend had always been one to go to bed early and rise early, and she was likely already asleep. Harper chuckled to herself, recalling how slumber parties were not as fun for Kennedy, who turned into a pumpkin at nine.

She closed her eyes and leaned back against the comfortable seat. At least none of her injuries were serious, and all would heal with time, rest, ice packs, and pain relievers. She was grateful she didn't have a concussion, although she figured she'd be having nightmares for some time after dealing with the attack.

Her body ached, her muscles were weary, and her thoughts were consumed by the man who was set on harming her.

Kade pulled up to Kennedy's home on Lakeview Drive. The newer red brick condo with its white railing surrounding a small rectangular porch and the window grids with shutters offered a classic appearance that differed from the more modern varieties often found in Lake Radford. It had only been by God's grace that the adorable 900-square-foot townhouse had come on the market just in time for Kennedy's return to Lake Radford. Snagging a home on Lakeview Drive, with its popularity due to the convenient location and adjacent park with a walking path, wasn't an easy feat.

Kade put the truck in park just as his phone rang with a ringtone from a popular Christian music artist.

"Lassiter. Really? Great. Thank you." He clicked off and turned to face Harper. "They found your cell phone and purse. Your cell seems fine, but your purse was opened. Maybe tomorrow, you can come down to the station and see what's missing."

"I'm thankful they weren't stolen." Harper's throat tightened, and she again relived the frightening moments of just hours before.

Kade reached across the console and placed his hand on hers. "We'll find out who did this. I promise."

She knew he wouldn't make such a vow if he wasn't sure he could keep it. "Thank you. It could have been so much worse."

"Yes, it could have." He squeezed her hand. "Let's get you inside." Kade removed his hand, and the second he did, she missed the comfort and warmth of it.

He then exited his vehicle and walked around to her side. She opened the door, and he assisted her from the truck. Once again, she was reminded of his chivalry, such an uncommon thing in today's culture. He offered his hand, and she took it and noted his strong, yet tender touch. He reached into the back seat and grabbed her overnight bag.

Kennedy's house was dark, and Harper wasn't even sure she was home, let alone awake, as she hadn't spoken to her today. They walked down the sidewalk and up the stairs to Kennedy's front door. Kade raised a hand to knock, and within seconds, the porch light flicked on. Kennedy opened the door, dressed in her red plaid jammie bottoms and a matching red oversized t-shirt. "Harper? Is everything okay?"

"Would it be all right if I stayed here tonight?"

"Absolutely." Kennedy stepped aside, and Harper and Kade entered the warm house. Kennedy shut the door behind them. "What on earth happened? Don't tell me it was that creepy guy again?"

"Unfortunately, yes."

Kennedy gestured to the couch, and Harper and Kade took a seat while she folded her leg beneath her and plopped into the antique chair adjacent to it. "You absolutely can stay here tonight and for as long as you need to. Can I get you anything?"

"I'm all right at the moment." Her voice shook when she answered. It had been a long day and even a longer evening waiting at the ER, answering Kade's questions for the statement, and dealing with the aftermath of being assaulted in a parking lot. She explained to Kennedy all that had happened before thanking Kade for his help.

He stood to leave. "I'm going to check the perimeter before I go, just to be safe. Please call me immediately if you need me, or if you happen to see anything suspicious."

"I will." She appreciated so much his concern for her. Then she remembered she was still wearing his jacket. She wondered how he'd not been cold in just his thin shirt that stretched across his muscular chest and broad shoulders.

Not that she was noticing.

Okay, she was. Even in her exhausted state, she had noticed.

She removed the jacket and handed it to him.

"Feel free to keep it. I can always get it later." Before she could argue, Kade continued. "I'll check in on you tomorrow. Thank you, Kennedy."

Concern etched in Kennedy's forehead, and her brow furrowed. "You could have been killed. I am so thankful you are okay."

"I am too. I don't even want to think about what would have happened if he had been able to get in the car."

"I just can't believe this kind of stuff is happening in Lake Radford. It has always been such a safe town, but lately it's been insane about the crimes. First, that burglary at Dumaines, and now all this stuff with you."

"I think there's always been some level of crime, it's just different when it hits close to home."

Kennedy put her hand on Harper's arm. "Have you called your mom yet?"

"No. I didn't want to worry her, and she's two hours ahead and likely already in bed. Speaking of which, I'm sorry I awakened you."

"Yes, but I would have been upset if you hadn't stopped by here when you needed me. You know I'm always here for you."

"Thank you."

"Speaking of Kade, I think he likes you."

Harper felt the heat rise in her cheeks. There would be no use in denying anything when it came to Kennedy, as she was the most observant person Harper knew. "He is a great guy. Caring, smart, funny, good at what he does, handsome, and most importantly, he's a Christian."

"Too bad you didn't meet him under different circumstances."

"I can't tell you how many times I have thought of that very same thing."

Kennedy yawned, and Harper was reminded that she needed to allow her friend to get some sleep. "I do have one exciting thing to tell you, although I probably shouldn't say anything because you might not be able to sleep after I do."

"What you've already told me wasn't exciting enough?"

Harper laughed, grateful for a reprieve from the frightening evening. "No, I think you'll like this news."

"Don't keep me in suspense."

"The Senior Citizen Center is looking to hire a senior activity coordinator. I think you'd be great for the job."

"Really? That would be fantastic. Is it full-time?

"It is." Harper gave Kennedy the details.

"You're right. I won't be able to sleep tonight. I have been needing a full-time job since I moved back, and I love working with the elderly population. This would be perfect."

"That's what I thought, too."

As Kennedy helped Harper get situated in the guest room, she thanked the Lord several times for keeping her safe again tonight and prayed they would catch the responsible person once and for all.

THIRTY-ONE

Finally. A break in the Dumaine burglary case.

Kade was nearly cross-eyed from spending so much time viewing surveillance video. Not that he hadn't examined it before—more than once—but he wanted to ensure he wasn't missing anything.

He begged his eyes not to glaze over. A person minding their own business, sitting in their car that evening, had filmed the entire thing and handed it over with the promise they'd be kept anonymous. It showed the men casing the place.

They walked several times up and down the alley. Then, executing their carefully planned scheme, two men opted to be on "lookout" while the others forced their way through the back door of the business and were subsequently joined by the two on "lookout".

The men were all dressed in dark sweatpants, shirts, and puffy black vests, with face masks and backpacks. A couple of them boasted sheathed knives and holstered guns on their waists. Were it not true that such a crime happened in Kade's small town, he might have thought it was something out of a movie.

The bystander had filmed them entering the store, then ten minutes later, exiting it, stolen goods in hand.

He zoomed in on the characteristics of the men. He could not identify them from their covered faces, but he did take note that two were exceptionally lean, one was tall, and one was overly rotund.

Kade sat back in his chair and closed his eyes for a minute to give his vision a rest. A minute later, he leaned forward again, clicked on the video to continue playing it, and stroked his chin.

He would catch these guys. Would see that Dumaine's was restored as best as it could be.

Kade threaded a hand through his hair. One of the things he did not like about his job was having to see the immense disappointment, fear, and discouragement in the eyes of robbery victims. Thankfully, no one had been there when the theft occurred. Who knew what the men would have done if someone had caught them in the act?

While it may seem like a slow-moving drudgery of a film for Kade, the men had carried out their plan with efficiency. He thought of all the damage the men had caused.

Such an unnecessary act of maliciousness.

The anonymous person hadn't filmed them inside Dumaine's, but the damage itself was proof. Stolen baseball cards, sweatshirts, and necklaces, water poured on the cash register, a display case shoved over, a broken window, and water left running in the bathroom with a plugged sink.

Mrs. Dumaine had sobbed when she told him of how they'd worked so hard to build the business to what it was, only to see it destroyed in a matter of minutes.

Now, to identify and locate the men.

He stood and stretched his legs. He should call it a day after clocking in so many hours, but he wasn't ready to give up just yet. People depended on him, and he'd never been one to want to let anyone down.

As much as it depended on him, anyway.

Harper's face flashed through his mind. If he solved no other crime, including the Dumaine case, while on the force this year, he would solve the crime that had impacted her so negatively.

It was becoming personal.

Baldwin poked his head in a few minutes later. "Lassiter, you should see who we just arrested."

Kade needed a break anyway. "The guy who's been after Harper Amerson?"

"I wish. No, but it's a rather interesting case. Remember the woman whose credit card was stolen?"

"Yes."

"We may have caught the perps."

A few minutes later, Kade was apprised of an update on another current case where two women in their early thirties had stolen a credit card from an elderly woman whom one of the young women provided home health care to. The women had allegedly gone on quite a rampage through town and bought all kinds of things, from clothes to phones to shoes and even a new flat screen TV. All with the elderly woman's credit card. Not only that, but they took it upon themselves to order several items from online retailers. When the elderly woman's daughter sought to purchase some of her vitamin supplements online, she noticed the credit card was gone.

Kade welcomed the diversion from his investigation and knew he would be involved in investigating the credit card fraud at the local level. They would also be turning it over to the Secret Service, which was responsible for investigating such types of fraud under its "device fraud" jurisdiction.

But it wasn't until the next day that he saw just how this credit card case coincided with the burglary at Dumaine's.

<hr>

Getting probable cause for a search warrant for both of the women's cell phones proved easy. But what was interesting were the interactions via text between the women and two of the alleged burglars from the Dumaine case. One of whom wasted no words in describing a huge windfall he and his friends had come upon after selling some collectible baseball cards.

"Bingo," Kade muttered aloud.

If only all cases were this easy to catch a break on, especially Harper's.

If Kade was right about his assumption, and more than likely was, whoever it was who had texted the woman didn't just happen upon baseball cards to sell. Upon further searching, the other woman's cell phone indicated she and one of the robbers were dating. He scanned the text messages from the latter.

Remember that dumpy place on Main we robbed a couple weeks ago?

Dumaine's?

Yeah. We sold all the baseball cards to a Fairmont pawn shop. Guy never suspected a thing. We're heading to Cali.

The next text detailed the time and place for the women to meet them. In this case, the visitor's center parking lot just off Exit 12. This was followed by a young man holding some of the baseball cards and grinning.

There was nothing more, so it was likely the Dumaine thieves didn't know the women had been arrested.

Time to plan a meeting and subsequent arrest at the visitor center parking lot.

Kade finally saw an end in sight to solving the Dumaine burglary.

Now, if he could do the same in Harper's case.

THIRTY-TWO

The sting at the visitor's center parking lot had been successful, and the Dumaine case would now progress through the justice system.

Kade viewed the footage of the incident that happened in the parking lot at The Cottages. Pride swelled in him at how well Harper had defended herself against the madman. But more than that, he'd offered his hundredth prayer thanking the Lord for keeping her safe when things could have gone so much worse. He didn't want to imagine what could have happened had she been seriously injured or the man had carjacked her vehicle with her in it.

He wasn't a rookie. He'd seen a lot of things working first as a patrolman in Fairmont, then as a detective, both in Fairmont and now in Lake Radford.

Kade enlarged the grainy images. Even with the decreased quality, the guy looked familiar.

More than familiar.

The team had found fingerprints on the passenger side door. If Kade was correct in his assumption—and he would bet the gorilla costume that he was—those fingerprints would belong to one Alan Motta.

The man proved easy to find. His last known address was the Shabby Motel on the north end. He'd already been arrested several times, even in Kade's tenure, mainly for drug possession and theft, but also once for assault and once for shoplifting a box of cigarettes. The guy was on probation and had no ties to the community. No job and no vehicle registered in his name.

Why would he target Harper?

Was it a random situation?

Or had he seen her somewhere and had become obsessed with her?

When Kade returned Harper's purse and phone, he asked her if she'd ever heard of a man named Alan Motta and showed her a picture of the man, whom she recognized as her attacker. But she'd never before heard of or seen him until the harassment started.

Kade strode into the interview room after Motta was arrested, irritation pummeling through him.

The man had already been Mirandized and hadn't yet lawyered up—a good sign.

Motta sat in the interview room, hands on the table and fingers tapping incessantly. Normally, Kade could deal with tapping, but Motta's non-rhythmic and spastic drumming was akin to someone scratching their nails on a chalkboard.

Kade closed the door, ensured the video cameras were running, and set his notebook and pen on the table. "Mr. Motta."

"I don't wanna go back to jail." The tapping continued, only faster. "Can't go back to jail." Motta's panicked comment echoed in the room, and his leg shook so badly it rocked the entire conference room table.

The forty-four-year-old man sported stray brown hairs sprouting on his chin and upper lip. Greasy brown hair hung over his forehead, and a nauseating odor, something akin to urine, body odor, and vape, emanated from his person.

"My name is Detective Kade Lassiter, and I have some questions for you."

Motta twitched as if startled before bobbing his head quickly. "Okay, but I don't wanna go back to jail."

Kade ignored his repeated words. "Do you know a woman by the name Harper Amerson?"

Motta ceased tapping his fingers for all of five seconds and stared up at the ceiling. "Yeah. Yeah, I think so."

"Were you at The Cottages parking lot two nights ago at about 6:30 p.m.?"

"The Cottages?"

"Yes, the senior citizen residential area over by the clinic."

"Oh, that place."

Silence except for Motta's beating on the table again with his crusted fingernails and the ticking of the second hand on the clock on the wall.

Kade waited.

Finally, Motta answered. "Yeah. Yeah, I know that place. Old people live over there." He peered down at his hands and gave a clipped nod. "Yeah, I was there."

"And did you see Harper Amerson?"

The guilt was written all over Motta's face. He bit his lip as his posture slumped. "I did see her. She was walking. Over by that one park with all them trees."

"Did you talk to her when you saw her?"

"No, I don't think so. I didn't talk to her at all. Am I going to have to go back to jail? I didn't like it there." He paled. "It was really dirty, and I didn't like the food. And the people there weren't very nice."

Kade had absolutely no pity for the man. If Motta didn't want to return to jail, he shouldn't have broken his probation by potentially committing another crime. But that would be for a judge and jury to determine. Kade's job was just to find out if he'd been the one who attacked Harper.

"Did you talk to Harper Amerson?" he asked again.

"No, I didn't talk to her. I didn't even say one word."

"Did you walk by her?"

"Did I walk by her? Yeah, I kinda walked by her."

"Can you tell me what happened that night when you walked by her?"

Sweat glistened on Motta's creased forehead as he scratched at his face. "I pushed her."

"You pushed her?"

"Yes, and she kneed me and pinched my arm." As if it was happening all over again, Motta winced, a scowl covering his grimy features.

"What else happened?"

"I tried to get in her car. But I wasn't going to hurt her. I just wanted to scare her. It isn't my job to hurt her really bad or kill her. Just to scare her."

His job?

"Have you ever sent Harper Amerson any letters?"

"Letters? No, I don't send letters." He offered a nervous chuckle. "Who sends letters anymore? Besides, I don't even like to write."

"Have you ever followed Ms. Amerson while outside the fitness center?"

"Long time ago. But she went back into the building."

"Have you ever visited the Cox property?"

"How do you know this stuff?" Motta muttered an oath beneath his breath. "Yeah, I've been to the Cox property."

Kade scribbled some notes. "What did you do when you were there?"

"Walked around...and stuff. But I don't want to have to go there again. It was a really long walk to get there, and the day was cold. I don't get paid enough to go to the Cox property."

Paid enough? Something else to discuss in a separate line of questioning in a few minutes. "What kind of stuff did you do there?"

Motta blanched. "Shot my gun and stuff."

Why did that not surprise Kade? "Did you ever follow Ms. Amerson while at the Cox property?"

Motta's pupils dilated. "Don't know if I *followed* her, but I did see her there, and I scared her." He paused for a second and emitted a high-pitched laugh. Just as quickly, he sobered. "She was there with some people."

"Do you know where Ms. Amerson lives?"

Motta averted his gaze, so Kade repeated the question.

"Yeah, I know where she lives. It's over there on Washington Avenue. Blue house with a carport."

"And have you ever been to her house?"

Motta again muttered a curse beneath his breath. "I might've been."

"What did you do when you were at her house?"

"Walked around. Nothing bad."

With a little luck, Kade might have most of this case solved and wrapped up soon.

"Look, man. I didn't do nothing bad to her. I was only supposed to scare her and hurt her a little bit. That's what the boss told me."

Yes, back to the boss. Motta's additional revelation invited further questioning.

"Does the name Clark Montayne ring a bell?"

"Clark who?"

"Clark Montayne."

"I ain't never heard of him."

While Kade wouldn't consider Motta the most honest man, his answer seemed genuine regarding Montayne. "Did you ever scare Ms. Amerson while she was walking a dog?"

"Yeah, I might have."

"Did you ever call her?"

"Call her? No. I don't know her number." Motta fidgeted and scraped a fingernail against something stuck to the table.

"Who is your boss?"

"My boss?"

"Yes, the one who told you to go to the fitness center, Harper Amerson's house, the Cox property, her neighborhood, and the parking lot at The Cottages."

"I don't know who he is."

"But you do have a boss?"

Motta started drumming on the table again. "Yep, I sure do."

"And is his name Clark Montayne?"

"Don't know a Clark Montayne."

"Can you tell me what your boss looks like? What color of hair? What color of eyes?"

Motta sank low into his seat, removed his hands from the table, and placed them in his lap. "Is this where I can ask for a lawyer?"

"You are certainly within your rights to ask for a lawyer. Would you like one?"

Motta ducked his chin. "No, I don't want one. Didn't much like my last lawyer." He sighed. "Ain't supposed to tell any stuff about the boss. I don't want him mad at me. Besides, he never gave me his name." Motta began chewing on a hangnail.

"Look, Motta, you're in a lot of trouble here, but if you work with me, I can put in a good word for you."

"And I don't gotta go back to jail?' For the first time, the man's eyes lit.

"That's up to a judge, not me. But I will put in a good word and tell them that you cooperated if you help me."

Motta reached up and scratched his head. "Like I said, I don't know his name. I just met him in the parking lot."

"What parking lot?"

"And you said if I cooperated, you would put in a word for me, right?"

"Yes, I will."

"It's just at that vacant building down there by the Shabby Motel."

Kade knew exactly which one he was talking about. "What does your boss look like?"

"I don't know. Sometimes he wears a ski mask or something else on his face, and most of the time it's dark."

"What type of vehicle?"

"It's a car. A nice, black one. I don't know what kind. I just climb in there and sit and talk to him to get out of the cold. He pays me to do what he tells me to and not ask questions."

If Motta was accurate about the car, Montayne owned a nice, black car. Of course, Motta's definition of "nice" could be subjective.

"What does he pay you to do these jobs?"

Motta picked at a scab on the back of his hand. The seconds ticked by.

"Mr. Motta, what does he pay you?"

"I ain't saying no more words 'cause I don't want to go to jail."

"All right then. Would you like to get a lawyer?"

Indecision flashed across Motta's face. "I do things for him for some pills."

"Pills?"

"Yeah, pain pills I need them because I have lots of pain."

"Is there anything else you can tell me about the boss?"

"Don't think so. Just that he said this was my last job to scare the chick in the parking lot and to hurt her, but don't kill her because that's all I'm supposed to do."

A chill traveled down Kade's spine. While they'd caught Alan Motta, and he'd be off the streets for a while—if not permanently—Harper was still in trouble.

And Kade would do whatever it took to protect her.

THIRTY-THREE

Kade carried the pizza box and bag of breadsticks to the front door and knocked. He was again grateful for the cameras Griff had installed for Harper. He'd hated having her spend the money, but it was better than the alternative. With that and the regular patrols through her neighborhood, he rested a little easier.

She opened the door and ushered him inside, then took the pizza and set it on the counter. He had checked her house and yard after her recent attack and hadn't really examined Harper's house. This time, he surveyed the clean and welcoming atmosphere. The cream-colored couch and matching chair with a coffee table in the center faced an electric fireplace. A mantle hosted several photographs, and above it, a rectangle-shaped mirror with a gold frame. To the right, a built-in bookshelf held several books and a few collectibles.

He shrugged off his coat and hung it on the hook by the door. "Nice place."

"Thank you. I love this little house. It has taken me a bit to accumulate the furnishings, but overall I really like how it's turned out."

Everything about it reminded him of her. Warm, classy, and stylish.

Harper opened the pizza box, and the tantalizing aroma of pizza filled the air. "Would you grab a couple of plates and cups right over there in that cupboard?" She pointed to one of the oak cupboards above the countertop. Kade retrieved two plates and two cups and set them next to the open pizza box. Harper grabbed a spatula and loaded two pieces of Canadian bacon on his plate and a slice of cheese for her from the half-and-half pizza.

"I couldn't resist getting some breadsticks too."

"Oh, I love the breadsticks. Almost more than the pizza." Her smile drew him in. After this was all over, he hoped to ask her out on an actual date rather than a "meeting" under the guise of updating her on the progress of her case. He realized he was staring and diverted his attention to his plate, where he'd positioned a couple of breadsticks in addition to the pizza.

They wandered over to the comfortable four-person farmhouse table. Kade said grace, and they started eating and engaging in comfortable conversation. Thankfully, she was feeling much better after the attack, although he worried about the pain Motta had inflicted on her.

Kade could definitely get used to this. While far too soon to even consider such thoughts, he wouldn't mind one bit coming home after a hard day of work and spending the evening with Harper.

After they finished eating, they took a seat on the couch in front of the fireplace. Warm air blew through the vents, and the fake flames created a peaceful ambiance. To be here with her meant that whoever it was after her wouldn't have access to her. That in itself comforted him. Kade had purposely waited to tell her about the details of the case until after dinner. No sense in bringing up the fact that they hadn't yet apprehended the guy who'd hired Alan Motta to attack her.

"You mentioned you had some new details about the case?" Her eyes searched his face, and he wished he had more information than he did.

"As I mentioned previously, we apprehended Alan Motta, whom we believe is responsible for attacking you both times, chasing you at the fitness center, and firing shots at the Cox property. However, we haven't been able to locate who's calling the shots. Motta is just a pawn."

"Are you sure he's not the main one harassing me?"

"He's not. We took a handwriting sample from him, and it doesn't match the writing on the envelope. He also struggles with holding scissors, so he couldn't have been the one to cut out all those letters, and he denies calling you. He referenced a boss when I was interviewing him. Also, the casings from the Cox property were from a 9mm. We secured a warrant and searched Motta's room at the Shabby Hotel and located a stolen 9mm."

"What about Clark Montayne?"

"He's lawyered up, but we brought both him and Motta into the same room. It was clear they didn't know each other. Whoever hired Motta likely also sent the letter, wrote the note, and called you from a burner phone."

Harper propped her socked feet onto the coffee table beside his. "I've suspected Clark is just a difficult coworker rather than a criminal, although I spoke again with Paulette, and she had promised to give him a warning."

"That's good to hear."

"I do hate being accompanied everywhere I go. I for sure won't take freedom for granted ever again."

"I understand, but I don't want you to go anywhere alone. The cameras Griff installed are good, as is the patrol car. We've secured coverage not only with drives through the neighborhood, but are also scheduling someone to be here across the street, off and on, at various times of the day."

"And my coworkers, Loretta, Ean, Enrique, and Jamila, are making sure we all arrive at the office at the same time and park in the same lot so we can walk in together, which means Clark will have to only use one spot for his fancy car."

"Also good to know."

Kade hated that she had to be so cautious. It was no way to live. "And Kennedy is going with you whenever you go to the gym, correct?"

"Most times, yes. Tomorrow, the Blumenstock family from church is accompanying me, both going there and leaving."

Kade reached for her hand and held it in his. "If I weren't working a case, I'd accompany you there and back." He paused. "I feel like we're getting closer to solving this."

She smiled at him, and for a minute, he grappled to keep his mind on the case rather than on her. "I do appreciate all your hard work on this case. And speaking of cases, congratulations on solving the Dumaine burglary."

"Thanks."

"I read a few details in the online edition of the paper." They discussed it for a few more minutes before Kade changed the topic to something *other* than work.

That was one thing he appreciated about Harper. How easy she was to talk to. They discussed their families, including his dad's MS, and her grandparents' planned return. The warmth of the fireplace and the lowered lights created a romantic atmosphere. Not that he was a romantic guy—all right, maybe he was when it came to a certain woman named Harper Amerson.

He was drawn to her strong faith, personality, sense of humor, intellect, and, of course, how pretty she was. He looked forward to getting to know her on a personal basis, rather than protecting her from a crazed lunatic. Kade gently squeezed her hand, mindful of not crossing that line until he'd solved the case, which he *would* solve. "Once this is all over, I might have to ask you out."

"I might just have to accept."

That was good enough for him.

***

Harper told the Blumenstock family she'd see them after the game, then proceeded to the cardio room while they went to the gym.

"You're in a rush. Special plans for tonight?" Clark accompanied his mocking tone with a fake smile that failed to reach his eyes. He strutted beside her in a tight white workout shirt, its form-fitting suction accentuating his muscular physique—and his vanity. He held his head high as though the world should bow down in his presence.

"No, not really." As a matter of fact, she'd be taking it slower tonight because she was still healing from the attack. Besides, Harper wanted to hurry so she could be ready to leave at the same time as the Blumenstocks after their ten-year-old daughter's basketball game. While she'd not told them the reason for asking for them to accompany her, she knew Mr. Blumenstock would likely understand since he was a protective father.

Harper would be grateful when they caught whoever this person was who was bent on harassing her. Never had she had to worry about something as mundane as going to the gym.

"Or so you say." Clark looked at her askance. "Going to go for a run today?"

"Yes, that's the plan." So challenging to make niceties with someone like Clark Montayne. Why was he making small talk when he hardly ever spoke to her? She sped up her pace, but could still hear Clark behind her, his breath causing the hairs on the back of her neck to stand on end.

She shifted the duffel bag to her other arm. She first stopped into the locker room to change from her work attire to a pair of black running shorts and a pink tank top before again lugging her duffle down the hall and to the main cardio area.

When she reached the line of treadmills, she snagged her favorite one and noted that there weren't as many people in the gym today. Likely, many were at the basketball tournaments, or they decided not to come out on such a frigid night.

Clark hopped on the treadmill beside her. Of all of the ones he could choose, why had he chosen one in such close proximity?

Definitely not like him.

Especially since he'd never hidden the fact that he despised her. Even more since the police had questioned him about his involvement in her harassment.

Harper carried one of the unused large round fans from the strength training area, plugged it in, and tilted it toward her.

Digging through the zippered area in her gym bag, she found her wireless earbuds and popped them into her ears. She tapped play on the "run" playlist on her phone, and her favorite

Christian workout song filled her ears. Even so, a peculiar anxiety rippled through her.

She loaded the workout onto her fitness tracker, logged it as a run, and hit the start button.

The treadmill flashed its lights at her until she hit the "quick start" button and started off with her typical warm-up of walking, incrementally increasing the speed over the next ten minutes until she was ready to launch into a full-blown run. Clark did the same, although his lengthy stride far surpassed hers. Sometimes Harper would pretend to be racing the person beside her on the adjacent treadmill. The competitive edge improved her running time and distance, but she had no intention of racing Clark.

The realization that he had chosen the treadmill next to her entered her mind again.

There really was no understanding him.

Harper attempted to lose herself in her music and the euphoric high of the run, but she could feel Clark's gaze upon her the entire time. Even if he wasn't staring at her full-on, she knew he watched her from his side eye.

What was going on?

Some people fell for his charisma. She never had. *Focus on your run, Harper. That's why you're here.* Or better yet, focus on the handsome Kade Lassiter. She thought again of how he'd reached for her hand while on the couch and then again as he prepared to leave. She recalled how everything about them clicked and how easy he was to talk to. How she wished he would have kissed her as they stood at the door and she bid him goodbye.

She'd been hoping he felt the same for her as she was beginning to feel for him, and his question about dating after this was all said and done confirmed it. If only they had that freedom right now.

It was far too soon to even contemplate such thoughts, but honestly, Kade Lassiter might just be "the one".

Harper increased her speed, and soon her body acclimated to the increase in heart rate. While taking it easier due to the lingering pain, she still ran her five miles, steadily glancing at her tracker several times to check the time. She didn't want to delay the Blumenstocks since they were going out of their way to see that she got safely home. They lived clear on the other side of town, a mile outside of city limits.

She lifted her phone from the treadmill cubby and checked to ensure they hadn't texted her.

Then she resumed, attempting to forget the past several weeks and instead focus on improving her health. And thinking about a certain detective.

THIRTY-FOUR

Tonight was the night.

He'd made sure to share with those around him his plans, even gym members. Most of the regulars knew him anyway. They all offered their condolences. At first, he thought it would be challenging to keep a straight face—to act nonchalant while spewing lies, but practice over the years, along with *really* believing what he was saying—made him all the more convincing.

He checked his watch. About an hour to go, and then things would start moving quickly. The only thing he had left to do was make sure that his pawns were in place. That shouldn't be too hard. People were so gullible.

And nobody suspected anyway.

"I'm going to see my mother, who's in the hospital in Fairmont. So we'll be closing up earlier than usual, with permission from the fitness center CEO, of course." He offered one of his most dazzling smiles. Of everyone, Mr. Genuardi had been one of the easiest to convince when he'd broached the subject with him.

"*Absolutely,*" the CEO said in response to his inquiry. "*Are you sure you want to come to work at all? You could just take the day off. That would put you in Fairmont sooner.*"

Oh, he was sure. He'd broached the subject with his boss earlier today. *"Thank you, Mr. Genuardi. I appreciate that, but I take my job very seriously and wouldn't want to let anyone down or cause any inconvenience."*

"You do whatever you need to do. We consider you a valued employee."

And now it was time to persuade his coworkers.

"I'm so sorry to hear that," said Marilyn when he told her and Bettina about his mother.

"Thank you." He paused for effect and exhaled a shaky sigh. "She hasn't been doing well with her heart issues. I've actually been pretty worried about her."

Bettina folded her arms and stared at him. "Am I still going to get paid the full amount, even though I have to go home early? I mean, it's not my fault."

The self-centered girl was chronically on his nerves. If he had his way, she would've been fired long ago. Here she was complaining about not getting paid for all of her hours when half the time she called in sick. When she was there, she did a lousy job. Customers were ignored, she rarely smiled, and most of the work fell on Marilyn. Bettina spent an inordinate amount of time scrolling on her phone and lazing around. Once when Enzo mentioned something about it, she lashed out at him and told him point-blank that he wasn't her boss and that she was on her break.

As if her breaks lasted for hours on end.

Enzo moved on and tended to his own duties. The difference between the two Gen Z workers was obvious. Enzo worked hard. Bettina lacked any work ethic.

But whether or not Bettina possessed a work ethic meant nothing to him. He was neither her boss nor her supervisor and had no say in whether she remained employed.

Bettina's eyes, heavily covered in makeup, bulged. "Yo. Did you hear me?"

Her voice clawed at him like fingernails on a chalkboard. Despite that fact, he would retain his calm, kind, and approachable demeanor.

Such was necessary.

"You can work that out with your supervisor," he told her.

"Yeah, okay. Whatever."

He wasn't expecting Bettina to be compassionate about his mother's heart condition, but then that's how young people were these days. They didn't really care about others or their struggles.

Marilyn wobbled over and rested a hand on his arm. He resisted the urge to flick it off. "Well, I want you to know I will be praying for her." Marilyn drove him just as crazy as Bettina did, only in a different way. She was too motherly, too gushing, and just plain *too much.* Not everyone needed someone to nurture them, especially someone who wasn't even related. And the prayers? No, thank you. He didn't believe in God or want anything to do with the imaginary man in the sky.

But he couldn't act like he wasn't grateful. He had to play the part. Had to continue honing his craft.

"Thank you, Marilyn. Your prayers and kindness mean a lot to me."

"Of course."

Just when he thought she'd move on and quit with the platitudes, she continued, much to his annoyance. "I can't imagine how hard that must be, watching your mom go through all of this. Has she been sick for some time?"

"Yes, she has had a couple of heart attacks and then with this recent development..." He hadn't even missed a beat in answering her nosy question. He hung his head and dramatically swallowed before raising a finger to his left eye. No grown man would normally get teary-eyed except one who was extremely concerned about his dear mother. "We're close, and if I were to lose her, I'm not sure what I would do."

That elicited more unwanted compassion in Marilyn's wrinkled face. He needed to stop now, or it would start to get fake. His coworkers were so naïve. If only they knew his mom had died of cancer years ago.

"Just know I'm praying for you. Is there anything I can do to help so you can get out of here sooner and close the place? I heard it may even snow again overnight."

He couldn't care less about the weather forecast.

Well, that wasn't entirely true.

Something about the dismal late-winter weather invigorated him. Especially when there was a job to be done. Of course, he still had to figure out a way to retain one particular gym member even as everyone else left.

"Two hours by freeway really isn't so far," he said. "I could wait until tomorrow, but I really just want to get there tonight, just in case…" He allowed his shoulders to drop as if defeated. "I appreciate your offer to help, Marilyn. I think I have it all under control, but if you and Bettina could handle everything on your end, that would be great. I'll start letting people know they need to wrap up their workouts."

Enzo strode back up to the front desk, and he told him about his plans as well. "Ah, man, I'm sorry to hear that. My dad had a heart attack a few years ago, and it was rough. You got this, man." He offered him a fist bump. Enzo was a nice kid, and he knew that the young man would be kind about kicking people out early. "I hope the basketball game winds down soon."

"It should be," said Bettina. "Who needs to play a game like that for so long anyway?" She rolled her eyes and ran a hand through her colored hair. It was likely the girl had never played a game or any type of sport in her life. Well, an active game. He looked at her chubby body and plump hands as she scrolled through her social media account. Someone really needed to tell her to focus on her job during work hours.

Chatting with fellow employees and members, he continued down the long, winding, shiny, white tile floor. Yeah, he didn't mind his job, but what really irritated him was when someone scuffed up the floor after he took all that time to shine it to the perfect sheen. One particularly lengthy black mark edged around the corner by the racquetball courts. It was even worse than the gyms where people played basketball, and their scuff marks were all over his clean floors. The anger rose within him. At least he would be taking care of one stressful matter tonight. A significant matter.

He strolled into the gym to check the scoreboard, and asked one of the parents how things were going. "Our team is winning," said the proud dad.

He inwardly scowled. Parents were so ridiculous about their kids and their sports. He was thankful he'd never had kids and had never even married. It was better that way. He offered his best false grin. "Good to hear."

A family consisting of a mother, father, a young son, and a pale-faced daughter rushed past him. "Everything all right?" he asked.

"She's not feeling well. We're going to have to take her home," answered the dad.

Just then, the girl retched. "Ew! She just barfed," said the little boy, pointing to a pile of liquid in the corner by the bleachers.

The dad swooped up his daughter and said he'd be carrying her to the car. The mom offered to clean up the mess.

It was all he could do not to glower at the little girl. He'd just cleaned these floors earlier, and now the mess and stench of barf? He was never going to get out of here on time to see his dear mother if things like this kept happening. "Don't worry about it," he told the mom. "I'll take care of it."

She blinked. "Are you sure?"

"Yes. Don't worry about it."

They thanked him and continued down the hall toward the front entrance. Meanwhile, he went into the janitor's closet and grabbed the mop bucket. It was things like this that made him hate his job. When they'd offered him a substantial raise to combine both janitorial and maintenance work, he'd thought it was an acceptable idea. After all, he got paid reasonably well, but now, as he swiped up the foul odor of vomit with his string mop, he was thinking he needed another wage increase.

The crowds of people had moved away from the area, but it hadn't stopped them from being completely involved in the game. A game for fifth-grade girls. Go figure. Who cared about basketball at that age? He finished mopping up the vomit, put out some cones and a yellow caution sign, emptied the mop bucket, and stuffed it and the mop back inside the janitor's closet.

He checked his watch. Time seemed to be moving slowly. Too slowly.

THIRTY-FIVE

The countdown timer for the cooldown on the treadmill was at one minute. Harper slowed her pace and stretched her shoulders and arms. Clark looked over at her and smirked. "Giving up so soon," he asked.

"I'm done for the day," she answered, not that he needed any response at all. When the beep indicating that the treadmill had stopped sounded, she climbed off, wiped down her machine, then plucked out her earbuds and walked over to the wall to stretch her calves, quads, and hamstrings. A hastier stretch than usual, much to her disappointment, because the last thing she needed was an injury. But she needed to hurry, just in case the basketball game had already ended. A cursory glance at her phone indicated the Blumenstocks hadn't texted her to tell her the game had ended.

Enzo was wandering around talking to the members in the gym. "Hey, Harper, in case you haven't heard, the gym is closing in fifteen minutes. Jasper's mom is in the hospital, so we need to have everyone leave sooner than usual."

"Oh, no. I'm so sorry to hear about Jasper's mom. I'll be sure to pray for her."

"Yeah, Jasper's a great guy. And since he's the one who closes the place, the CEO allowed us to close early."

Harper set her phone on one of the benches nearby and continued stretching. She didn't know much about Jasper, but she hoped all would go well with his mom. She also prayed for traveling mercies because it was already thirty degrees outside, with temperatures expected to fall.

Had the basketball game ended yet? She rushed into the locker room. Once there, she changed back into her black leggings and tall brown boots and buttoned up her navy coat. She kept her knit hat out for when she went outside, and then zipped up her duffel bag and flung it over her shoulder before heading to the gym, where the basketball tournament was taking place.

Folks passed her going in the opposite direction, some of whom she knew from church and work. She waved and got sidelined by one of the ladies in her women's Bible study, before continuing on. She peered into the gym. Only a handful of people remained, mainly moms and littles who were taking a while to get their shoes and coats on. She then poked her head inside the women's bathroom and perused both directions down the hall, but didn't see the Blumenstock family. Perhaps they were waiting for her at the front desk. Harper hastened her speed, her brown boots tap-tapping on the white tile floor. When she got to the front desk, she asked Bettina if she had seen the family.

"How should I know who the Blumenstocks are?" She shoved her phone into her back pocket. "Besides that, we're closing early, so you need to leave."

Marilyn emerged from the conference room at the front of the building. "Marilyn, have you seen the Blumenstock family?"

"No, I haven't."

"If you see them, can you let them know I'll be back by gym one?"

"I'll let them know, Harper, but we're closing early tonight, so you might want to just wait for them up front."

Harper hoisted her duffel onto one of the round tables in the foyer area, where people typically liked to congregate and chat before their workouts. Maybe she should text the Blumenstocks, although her last text had gone unread. She rifled through her duffel looking for her phone. It wasn't in the main area, wasn't in the small zippered area, and wasn't tucked in the side pocket. She tossed aside a stale granola bar, her water bottle, and her sweaty workout clothes.

Her phone was nowhere to be found.

In her rush to find her cell, the container of glucose pills toppled onto the floor and spilled. She crouched down and picked up the two glucose pills that fell, stuffing them into the pocket of her coat. She would throw them away later. For now, she needed to find her phone

Harper stepped up to the front desk again, where Bettina was tapping her long black fingernails on the counter. "What now?"

"Have you had any phones turned in to the lost and found?"

With an exaggerated sigh, Bettina forced herself to tug open the bin and heft it onto the counter in front of Harper. With exaggerated movements causing many of the items to fall over the side, she rummaged through the disorganized items, throwing hats, gloves, filthy socks, an old shoe, and several water bottles to the side. "Don't see it."

"All right, I'm going to run back to the treadmill and see if it's there."

"You'd better hurry. Jasper needs to leave, and he's serious about closing up early."

Harper ran down the halls, her duffel bag slamming against her right thigh as she did so. She first entered the locker room. An efficient perusal of the countertops, the bathroom stalls, and the lockers told her her phone was not in there. Where could it be? How would she contact the Blumenstocks or know if they'd contacted her? She swept the area with an efficient perusal before exiting.

She entered the main cardio room and saw Jasper and Clark talking. Perhaps Jasper had seen her phone. "Have either of you seen my phone?"

"I'm sorry, but I haven't," said Jasper. "Did you check the locker room?"

Worry consumed her. The Blumenstocks had been so kind to offer to walk out with her and follow her home. "Yes, I did. I've checked everywhere. I followed my path back here to all the places I've been."

Clark cocked his head to one side. "Maybe you should be more responsible." He shook his head, and sweat from his curly black hair dripped onto the floor. She resisted the urge to cringe. Jasper narrowed his eyes at Clark. Poor guy had to clean that up.

"I'll keep an eye out for it," said Jasper. "Did you check the lost and found?"

She nodded.

"We're closing the gym soon, so unfortunately, you might have to come back tomorrow." His gaze held an indiscernible expression, one that Harper couldn't quite ascertain. Likely, he had a lot on his mind, especially with the fact that his mother wasn't doing well.

"All right. By the way, I was so sorry to hear about your mom. I'm praying for her and for you."

Jasper offered a clipped nod. "Thank you. That means a lot."

Clark snickered. "Like prayers do any good."

She wouldn't get into it with him about prayers. One time, she'd actually tried to discuss with Clark the things of the Lord to no avail. The man was extremely difficult to pray for, but she'd done her best to do as the Bible said and pray for her enemies.

Harper wandered over to where she had stretched and the weight machine nearby. She recalled setting her phone there, but it wasn't there now. Jasper and Clark continued to chat before Jasper caught her eye. He excused himself and started looking around as well. Perhaps he would find it.

Within a couple of minutes, the cardio room had completely cleared. She thought of one other place where it could be. Had it fallen out of her bag when she was down at the gym or when she poked her head inside the bathroom at the far end?

Rushing, she zipped in that direction. When she found nothing, she returned to the front desk, peered out the window, but did not see the family's minivan parked next to her SUV. They must have given up on her and already left. Had something come up?

Harper would check the gym one more time, and then she would leave. If nothing else, she was sure that Jasper would walk her to her SUV. As far as heading home without someone following her, well, she'd just have to deal with that. Hopefully, the officer was still making his rounds and would be in her neighborhood in case something went awry. Marilyn waved at her as she and Bettina stepped out into the night. Bettina rolled her eyes as she followed the older woman. Enzo waved and escorted the two out the door. Perhaps Harper should just walk out with them. That would be a lot safer than walking out by herself. Or maybe she could see if Jasper could walk out with her.

She saw him heading up toward the front desk. "Jasper, would you mind walking out with me?"

"Sure. By the way, I think I may have seen a phone near the bicep curl machine in the weight room. I would have grabbed it, but I ended up having to help someone who got sick.

"By the bicep curl machine?"

"Yeah, I'll be back there in a minute if you need me to help you, but I have to take care of some matters. And yes, I will be happy to escort you to your car."

She jogged toward the weight room. Bizarre that her phone would be by the bicep curl machine, as that was on the other side, where she'd not been. But if someone had found it and was maybe on their way to taking it to the lost and found at the front desk, they could have accidentally left it there.

When she meandered down the halls, there was no one left in the building. She didn't want to keep Jasper waiting, so she bolted into the weight room and scrutinized the area around the bicep curl machine. If she didn't see it within a few seconds, she would just leave. A cell phone wasn't that important, and she really would prefer someone walk her out, especially since it was already getting so late.

The problem was that if anything happened and she needed to call Kade, she wouldn't be able to do so.

THIRTY-SIX

The time was drawing near. Everything had easily fallen into place, and he'd discovered a way to get her alone in the gym. He took out a large bag of garbage, flipped open the lid of the dumpster, and threw it in. He'd buried the phone inside after turning it off, and it was doubtful anyone would find it easily, especially since tomorrow was trash pickup day. In his perfect world, he would have discarded it elsewhere, but he was a little short on time. He returned to the gym through the back entrance adjacent to where he had parked. Excitement tingled through him. It was the same excitement he'd experienced that day when he'd had to eliminate the betrayer. Warmth radiated through his body, and the pleasant drumming of his heartbeat pounded in his chest.

He locked the door behind him. He'd be back out in a little while.

He efficiently dismantled the cameras in the observation room. He'd rehearsed what he would say should the police ask him why the cameras suddenly no longer worked. The things were flighty anyway and had a propensity to have mechanical problems. Just another reason for the board not to be so frugal in purchasing necessary items. But that didn't bother him at this stage. As a matter of fact, it worked well for his purposes.

Clark met him upstairs by the indoor track. "You're sure this is what I have to do just to get some information?"

He sized up the younger man. No wonder Harper didn't like him. Clark was arrogant and thought he was better than everyone else. If he hadn't needed Clark's assistance, then he'd have nothing to do with him.

"Look, I'm not even supposed to be giving out information from the computer. If you want to know just about everything you could know about the blonde on the elliptical, then you're going to need to help me out here."

"All I have to do is just vacuum that rug by the side entrance?"

"Yep, that's it. And you do it for ten minutes."

"Ten minutes? That's an awful long time to be vacuuming a rug."

"You just ran for an hour, and you can't even vacuum for ten minutes?"

The fiery glare on Clark's face told him all he needed to know. Apparently, the way to get something done with this man was to offend him, which he had easily done. Clark obviously didn't like the insinuation that he was a wimp. Which he was.

He wielded the upright vacuum from the janitor's closet, unwound the cord, and plugged it into the nearest outlet. "Here you go. If you can handle it."

Clark scowled. "Just remember, you promised me the information.

"Oh, you'll get it, and believe me, you'll be glad you did this. We ask all kinds of questions when people decide to become members here. Keep vacuuming until I find you."

He didn't wait for Clark to argue. For this whole plan to work, he needed no hiccups.

Now to nab Harper. It helped that she had asked him to escort her out of the building. That meant she would be looking for him and would be open to any suggestions he might have. Suggestions like a little detour before he closed up the building and followed her to her car.

His neck muscles tightened. This had better work. There was a lot at stake.

THIRTY-SEVEN

Harper noticed Jasper near the janitor's closet. Should she still ask him to walk her out to her car, or should she just rush out there herself, climb in, and head home? But Kade's voice rang in her ears, *"Make sure you have someone with you."*

He would have been here tonight himself had he not been dealing with a big case.

Jasper's voice interrupted her inner musings. "Did you find your phone?"

"No."

"I wonder what happened to it?"

"I'm not sure. I'm going to go ahead and leave. Do you have a second to walk me out?"

"Sure. I have to stop in the janitor's closet real quick and grab something. It'll only take me a second."

She stood in the doorway and watched as he entered the long, narrow room. He proceeded to the far end. Suddenly, she heard what sounded like a loud crash. "Jasper, are you all right?

He moaned. "No, I think I just wrenched my back."

She entered the room, past shelves full of toilet paper, cleaning supplies, and equipment wipes. Past a mop bucket, a sink, and a wheeled cleaning cart. Past a stack of rags, several large, round green garbage cans, and a desk littered with a computer and a stack of papers.

The smell of bleach permeated the air.

"Jasper, are you all right?"

Harper found him bent over a chair, his right hand on his lower back. "I think I strained it."

"Do you need me to call an ambulance?"

"No, I'll probably be all right." But he didn't look all right, his face was contorted, and he had squeezed his eyes shut. Jasper attempted to straighten but then quickly hunched back over and groaned. "I was just lifting my toolbox—something I do all the time," he muttered.

Harper glanced behind her. "Perhaps there's still somebody in the gym who could come and help. Do you want me to see if anyone is still here?"

"No, I think everyone has left."

But then she heard the roar of something that sounded like a vacuum. "I think I hear someone out there. Is there anyone else on the janitorial staff here tonight?"

He shook his head and grunted. "The pain is excruciating. I think I might have to sit down for a minute."

"I can see myself out after I make sure you're all right."

"No, I'll see you out. It's not safe for you to be walking out there this time of night, and some of the lights have been known to go out."

Harper rolled the chair from the desk to him, grasped a firm hold on his left arm, and carefully settled him into the chair.

"Is that better?"

Jasper nodded. "Much. Thank you."

"I'm going to go find the person vacuuming and see if they can come help."

"Maybe that would be a wise idea."

Glad he'd finally relented, Harper slipped through the narrow closet when suddenly a hand flew over her mouth, and another hand wrapped around her waist and dragged her backward. The unexpected movement took her by surprise. Jasper?

She kicked and attempted to rip free from the tight hold. The vacuum continued to roar in the distance. His hand, smelling of disinfectant, tightened over her mouth, and nails dug deep into her cheeks. She thrust her arms back and lifted a leg to kick him in the kneecap. He cursed but retained his footing as he continued to drag her farther into the janitor's closet. Finally, he let go of her mouth, and she screamed. But as swiftly as that happened, she felt something hit her in the head.

Everything went black.

THIRTY-EIGHT

Jasper shoved her into the smaller 3'x3' closet and slammed the door. From the outside, he locked it and pocketed the key. She'd be out for a little while, giving him time to do what he needed to do.

And even if she did wake up, she'd awaken in cramped darkness. He exited the janitor's closet and found Clark still vacuuming the rug. Clark snarled at him and flipped off the switch. "This is ridiculous. I've been vacuuming this thing for eight minutes. I think I'm done now."

The man was an irritant. The sooner Jasper was rid of him, the better. "Yeah, looks good. Maybe you ought to consider hiring on."

Clark sent a glare full of daggers, and a vein pulsed in his forehead. "Like I would ever work here."

Of course, working as a janitor and maintenance man is far beneath you, isn't it? But Jasper kept his thoughts to himself. The last thing he needed was for Clark to think something was amiss, and that Jasper's perfectly honed calm persona was out of character. He knew there would come a time when the cops would question Clark. The better Jasper could control the outcome of that questioning, the better.

"Why did I have to vacuum this anyway?"

Clark may make good money selling properties, but the man was an imbecile. "I can't tell you how much I appreciate you doing that for me. I wasn't sure how I was going to get everything done in time." Jasper wound up the cord and pushed the upright vacuum over to the corner, where he'd put it away later. "I need to get out of here so I can go visit my mom. Thank you for your help."

Clark shook his head. "Whatever. I just want to know about the blonde chick on the elliptical." Jasper motioned for him to follow, and they walked up to the front desk, where the computers had already been turned off. Jasper fired one up and clicked on the members' button. "Her name is Julane Whisel. She's twenty-eight years old." Jasper recited the woman's address.

Clark peered over Jasper's shoulder. "I can read."

Jasper resisted the urge to roll his eyes. "She works as a teller, is single, and has no known health issues."

"Just find out where it says her phone number."

Jasper scrolled a little more and rattled off the number. "I hate to cut this short, but I do need to get on the road to Fairmont." He turned off the computer and followed Clark to the door, opened it, and ushered him out before locking it behind him. He stood there for a moment watching as Clark traipsed down the sidewalk and to his fancy car. There were only three vehicles in the parking lot. Clark's car, Harper's SUV, and another unknown vehicle Jasper did not recognize—a dumpier, low-to-the-ground, dark colored car with a dent in the bumper. Likely someone parked here then hopped in with someone else. Jasper didn't care. He just needed to do something about Harper's SUV.

He returned to the janitor's closet and pressed his ear against the door. There was no sound. Good, she was still unconscious. He rifled through her duffel bag until he found her car key, grabbed his coat, and pulled on a pair of latex gloves. He checked once more in the surveillance room to be sure the cameras were offline, snagged a stack of towels from the front desk, and dashed outside.

The cold slammed into him. A blustery night was perfect for his plan. He hit the unlock button, adjusted the towels on the seat, and climbed inside Harper's vehicle. Jasper drove it two blocks away to a deserted dentist's office and parked it there, then locked the keys in Harper's vehicle. The cops deserved to work for their pay. Then Jasper hoofed it back to the fitness center. From all appearances, he was just a regular fifty-nine-year-old man with some injuries, but no one really knew that he was quite fit for a man his age. He worked out whenever he got the chance, which was often since he had a free membership and his own set of keys to the gym. Dedicating his life to his employer had established loyalty that came with perks.

His stomach rumbled, reminding him he hadn't eaten for several hours. Perhaps a trip through Olsen's would quell his appetite. An added benefit in case he needed an alibi.

When he reached the fitness center, he veered around back, climbed into his extended cab truck, and drove the short distance to his favorite fast-food drive-thru.

"Welcome to Olsen's. How may I help you?" He recognized the chipper voice. It belonged to one of the teenage girls who frequented the fitness center.

"A hamburger, hold the mayo, a large fry, and a medium root beer."

She told him the amount and to drive to the first window, where he greeted the teen.

"Hi, Jasper. How are you tonight?"

"I'm not sure if you've heard about my mom. She's in the hospital in Fairmont. I'm leaving now to go see her." He paused and forced fake emotion to clog his throat. "She might not make it."

The girl looked like she might cry. "I'm so sorry to hear that. I had no idea."

"It was just so unexpected." He allowed his gaze to flicker to the street in front of him as if he couldn't even bear to think about his poor mother and her ailments. "I'd really appreciate your prayers."

"Sure, you got it. She handed him first the cup of root beer, then a bag of food. "Well, I would say have a good night, but you have quite a drive ahead of you."

He allowed himself a minute smile. "Yes. Sure hope the interstate is clear." He bid her farewell, then drove back to the fitness center. Yet another person tricked into believing he would be on the road rather than staying in town.

THIRTY-NINE

Her head throbbed with quite possibly the worst headache she'd ever endured. Harper attempted to sit up, but there wasn't much room in the confined quarters. She blinked, willing herself to be able to see something—anything—in the pitch-black room. Where was she? How had she gotten here? A sliver of light beneath the door did nothing to add to the visibility.

Then it all came back to her. She had been checking on Jasper because he'd hurt his back. The sound of a vacuum outside the door and down the hall. Jasper assuring her he would be fine and would walk her out to her car. Then someone attacking her from behind.

But not just someone. Jasper.

She reached up and rubbed her temples. *Lord, please help me.*

What would happen to her? "Help!" She repeated it numerous times, then leaned against the door.

No sound.

Her stomach grumbled, and a wave of nausea fell over her. But not just nausea because of the predicament in which she found herself. But also that little warning signal that her blood sugar was dipping. Her arms shook, and lightheadedness fell over her. Or was it because she'd been hit so hard on the head?

Seven more times she screamed, accompanying her yells with pounding on the door.

Would anyone come for her?

She bowed her head, folded her hands, and prayed. Psalm 23 flooded her mind, and she recited the words aloud. "Even though I walk through the valley of the shadow of death, I will fear no evil, for you are with me; your rod and your staff, they comfort me."

Harper wouldn't give up. While the chances of escaping were slim, what *could* happen if Jasper returned was far worse. She struggled to her feet, her forehead connecting with the corner of something. A shelf, perhaps? She winced and reached up to wipe something wet on her forehead. Had the corner drawn blood?

If Jasper didn't return and the worst that could happen was being locked in a closet until someone arrived tomorrow morning, she could live with that. The hairs on the back of her neck stood on end.

Anyone who would hit her over the head and lock her in a closet likely had nefarious plans.

Harper felt around for the doorknob and turned it, or attempted to. It was locked. Fear struck anew within her. She was trapped. Ignoring the dizziness, she pounded on the door and yelled again. Still no answer. Where was Jasper? What were his plans? She had no phone, no way to call for help, and no one knew where she was. But she did have one thing in her arsenal. Her fitness tracker watch. Or at least, as long as there was battery. Now she seriously regretted not hooking up the ability to text and call from it. She'd always seen it as cumbersome and unnecessary, and didn't want to be attached to having to talk on the phone and text 24/7.

However, someone *could* locate her if she logged in an exercise, especially walking or jogging, and the GPS indicated where she was.

But only if the police thought of that.

Suddenly, hopelessness smothered her, and she fought for a breath in the cramped confines of the closet. "Lord, I don't know what to do. Please let somebody find me, and please don't let Jasper take me anywhere else. And please give me peace."

Her stomach rumbled again, and her anxiety ramped up a notch. Normally, she didn't have to worry too much about anxiety, but whenever she was having a blood sugar dip, it seemed to increase tenfold.

She banged on the door again and yelled. Perhaps there was something in here that she could use to knock down the door. She dropped to her knees and felt around in the crowded closet. Nothing on the floor, but what if there was something on one of the shelves? In complete darkness, she reached up and felt on each of the shelves, careful to avoid the corner where she'd smacked her head previously. It seemed only things like toilet paper or some sort of cloths were on the shelves. Nothing that could help her break down the door.

But she wasn't giving up.

She was strong, worked out nearly every day with either cardio or weights. Mustering all the strength she had and fighting the challenge to even be able to have enough room to raise her knee, she took a kick at the door. It came off as painfully ineffective. She kicked and pounded it several more times. Had it jarred slightly? She then listened for any sign of anyone outside on the other side.

Fatigue set in, and she knew her heartbeat had become irregular. She needed something to eat. When she'd been diagnosed with hypoglycemia years ago and instructed to carry glucose pills and graze throughout the day, she'd never imagined being unprepared and unable to do so.

Harper slowly lowered herself to the floor. Sweat dripped down the back of her neck, and she was about to wiggle out of her coat when the door flung open.

Jasper drove around to the back of the building. It would be so easy from this location to remove Harper from the closet and into the truck via the back door. That was the nice thing about working there for so long—he knew all the little cubbyholes, all the places to hide, and all the entrances and exits. As a matter of fact, it was doubtful anyone knew the place as well as he did. He chuckled. This was going so much easier than he could have ever imagined. Scanning the empty parking lot and the adjacent street to ensure no one was around, Jasper climbed out of his truck, unlocked the back door to the fitness center, and slipped inside.

First plan? He would sit at his desk and eat his food. In front of her. Before he carried out part two of his plan. Jasper was surprised she wasn't pounding on the door or making some sort of commotion. Maybe she was still unconscious.

The aroma of hamburgers and french fries permeated the air. His own stomach grumbled and begged that he might sit down and have a bite right now. But no, he would exercise patience. He had other things to do first.

Jasper reached into his pocket and retrieved the set of keys. He unlocked the door to find her crouched in the closet. A wound on the side of her head was slightly bleeding. He hadn't done that. Wonder what she'd been up to while he was away.

She looked up at him, then stood. Her arms flailed as she attempted to hit, pinch, and kick him, but he caught her by the wrist and pulled his knife from his pocket. He should have brought in his gun from the truck. But he would use that later.

The blade shimmered in the light, and he held it to her neck. "I wouldn't try that."

Harper eyed the knife, then him, then her surroundings. He'd already shut the door and locked it—she wouldn't be escaping that way. The petrified look of fear lurking in her wide-eyed glance gave him such satisfaction.

"Oh, the things I have planned for you, Harper," he said.

"Why are you doing this?"

Jasper needed to put a gag in her mouth. He didn't need her attempting to converse with him. "You should know why," he snarled.

Still holding the knife to her neck, he backed her back into the closet and slammed the door and locked it again. He needed to retrieve the duct tape and handkerchief. The food beckoned him from the desk, and with effort, he ignored the urge to put everything else aside and eat.

He located the duct tape in the desk drawer as well as the soiled handkerchief from the lost and found. If he knew Harper, she wouldn't give up without a fight. Well, she wouldn't be winning this one.

He only had two hands, so holding the knife on her while he bound her would prove to be challenging. Not that he would let that stop him.

Jasper opened the closet door, and Harper attempted a repeat, along with screaming, although she seemed more lackluster—tired—this time.

Harper screamed several times, and Jasper shoved her to the floor and first attempted to tie her feet together. "Let me go!" She rolled over and kicked him as hard as she could, squarely in the jaw. He winced but recovered quickly. She began to crawl away, and he grabbed her ankle, squeezing it as hard as he could until he heard something pop. Harper shrieked and kicked at him with her other leg, this time landing it on the side of his head.

He wrestled her onto her back, immobilized her legs, bound her wrists, then moved to her legs. "Quit fighting me, Harper!" She didn't even have the decency to recoil from him. Well, they'd see who won in the end.

Jasper leaned Harper against the wall. Her head lulled to one side, and she was shaking. Sweat glistened on her forehead. Good, maybe she would temporarily stop being such a pain. Huffing, he went to the desk and plunked down on the rolling chair. He opened the bag and withdrew the hamburger. He held it to his nose and inhaled the delicious scent. He unwrapped it, then walked over to where Harper sat against the wall. He waved the food beneath her nose. "Doesn't that smell good?" She attempted to turn her head away, but he followed her movement with the hamburger clutched tightly in his hands.

After a few seconds, he rose, grabbed the box of french fries, and did the same thing. "Too bad you won't be having any." He heard her stomach rumbling in response, causing a blissful stream of joy to ripple through him at her agony.

"So, what is it like to have hypoglycemia, and when was the last time you ate?" He balled his right fist as if a microphone. "Maybe we'll just interview you about this because I've always wondered." Not that he truly had, but his spirits lifted at her discomfort. With her being so weak, she'd been much easier to overtake. Perhaps he could just let nature take its course, and he wouldn't have to do what he was planning to do to fatally incapacitate her.

Then again, what pleasure was there in that? He grabbed his entire meal and sat down on the floor beside her and took a bite of the hamburger, smacking his lips on purpose and allowing the food to satisfy his hunger. Had he ever enjoyed a meal so much before in his life? "This sure is good. Have you ever eaten at Olsen's before? They have the best food in town." He periodically waved the hamburger in front of her face, although it took all of his control not to wolf it down in a few meager bites. But watching her distress was worth his restraint. He did the same with the fries. She closed her eyes as if that would remove the aroma from her mind.

He laughed. "No matter how hard you try, you can't escape this, Harper. Not the food and not what is about to happen to you."

Had she just shuddered, or was it his hopeful imagination?

Jasper waved it one last time in front of her before taking the final bite of the hamburger. She looked at him through wary eyes. The cut on her forehead had started to scab.

"Ah, poor Harper. Probably didn't have enough to eat, especially with engaging in such a demanding workout. Or was it not so demanding since you're still recovering from an *episode* near The Cottages?" He'd researched hypoglycemia. Such was necessary for his end goal.

Harper would regret ever letting him know of her condition.

FORTY

Dizziness nearly overtook her. If Harper didn't get something to eat soon, she would lose consciousness. If only she had reduced her workout time. If only she'd eaten more. If only she hadn't gone back to look for her phone.

Harper never anticipated being held captive by the "friendly" and "accommodating" janitor.

Jasper waved the hamburger under her nose again, and her stomach growled. It was almost too much to handle, inhaling the scent of food, any food, let alone something like a hamburger from Olsen's when she was so hungry. He took a French fry and waved it in front of her before downing it in one bite. He reached up and roughly pulled the handkerchief from her mouth, and she sucked in an enormous gulp of air. The abhorrent taste of the handkerchief, with who knew what was on it, made her gag.

"Tell me, Harper, are you happy you're selling the Cox property?"

"That's what this is about?"

His mouth bunched into a bitter pucker. "Of course, that's what this is about. If you had just decided not to sell it, you wouldn't be in this predicament."

Harper attempted to reconcile what he'd said about the Cox property. Her mind seemed so fuzzy, and she was having a hard time concentrating. She swallowed the knot of emotion surfacing in her throat. Fear shook her, and combined with the hypoglycemia, rendered her shaky.

She cleared her throat, still tasting the handkerchief remnants.

Lord, please give me wisdom. Help me ask the questions I should.

Answers to which Kade would need later.

"Why would you care about the Cox property?"

"I have my reasons. Secrets, really." Jasper stared at her for several heartbeats, his eyes never blinking, almost as if he didn't really see her sitting there. Dare she prod?

"Secrets? You mean like you wanted to purchase it?"

At that, the cords in his neck strained, and red flushed his face. "No, I don't want to purchase it. Why would you think that?"

She attempted a shrug.

"Like I said, secrets."

Harper figured probing deeper would only infuriate him, so she changed the direction of her questioning. "I can see if somebody else will sign as the listing agent. Maybe Clark?" What would have happened if Clark were the selling agent rather than her? Would he be the one having this conversation with Jasper instead?

Jasper wadded up the hamburger wrapper and stuffed it inside the French fry box before tossing it to the right of him. "Too late now," he said.

"I'm sure he would take it. He's always looking for new properties."

He squeezed her upper arm in a tight clench, his own hand shaking as he did so. "I told you it's too late for that," he seethed between gritted teeth. His face was mere inches from hers, and this was the first time she'd noticed certain aspects of his appearance. Things like his hook-like nose sporting a tiny black mole just to the side of it, the way two of his bottom teeth jutted forward. Or the dark, cat-like, shark-gray eyes. His breath filled her nostrils, a mix of onions and mustard, and she fought the urge to retch.

Enunciating slowly and clearly, Jasper spoke. "No. One. Needs to be selling the Cox property. And I will put an end to this."

Harper's heart constricted. If that meant what she thought it did, that didn't bode well for her. "But how will your plan prevent the property from being sold? Even if I'm not here, another agent will take the property and sell it."

"They might try to, but there are other ways around this." He leaned back and lifted a hand to his gray hair. "I'll just find out where the owners live."

Her breath caught. Jeff and Vanna and their sweet son, who battled cancer...they didn't need harassment or worse from Jasper on top of everything else.

"Maybe we can talk about this." But the second she said it, she knew her request was futile. But she had no idea just how furious it would make Jasper. He reached up and slapped her hard on the side of the face. She winced as her head jerked to the side.

"We will *not* talk about this. What's done is done, and no one will find him there!"

Who was the "him" Jasper was referring to? And was he shaking due to nervousness or anger, or both? Her eyes smarted from the slap, and she willed herself to stay strong. *God is my refuge and strength. A very present help in trouble.*

The room spun, her heart rate increased, and her vision blurred. She needed something to eat. Right now.

Jasper rose and withdrew keys from his pocket. "Now you wait here. I'll be right back." Then he chortled a deep, evil laugh. "Not that you'll be going anywhere anyway."

Where was he going, and how soon would he be back? Would she have time to break free from the bonds? Surely the cameras would capture what was going on and would be useful after she called 911. That was if she could. Her vision blurred again, and she was about to try to remove the duct tape from her hands when she remembered the two glucose pills in her pocket she'd stuffed in there after her glucose tablet container had opened, and the pills had tumbled to the floor. She had meant to throw them in the trash, but thankfully, she hadn't.

Harper attempted to reach inside her pocket with her hands bound and retrieve a pill. With her hands bound, she leaned back the best she could, lamenting that her pocket was deep. With one pinky, she held the tablet in place. While with the other one, she scooted it up the length of her pocket. She heard something and stopped. Was he coming back? If she didn't get the glucose pill, she wouldn't stay conscious long enough to find out. Trembling, she attempted to put it in her mouth when it fell onto the floor. She leaned slightly to the right and attempted to grasp it. It slipped again before she finally got hold of it and lifted it to her mouth.

Good thing she was flexible.

Harper savored the citrus flavor on her tongue and allowed it to melt into her mouth. Allowed the sugar do its job.

Thank You, Jesus!

She repeated the task for the second and final glucose pill. This time it had somehow gotten stuck in one of the folds of the fabric, and she worked to release it before slowly and methodically putting it on her tongue. It would be a few seconds or even minutes before she stabilized, and would two glucose pills even be enough? Perhaps not with how hungry she was and how many calories she had expended. She rested her head back against the wall and took a deep breath, knowing it would be futile to yell as no one else was in the gym, but in a few seconds, she would again attempt to get the duct tape off of her hands and then her feet.

Harper begged the Lord to guide her.

She'd often wondered how people got through difficult times without faith. While she didn't know the outcome of this situation, she knew Who walked alongside her through it.

Harper had just raised her hands above her head in an effort to bring them down and break the duct tape when Jasper emerged through the door.

"What are you trying to do?" He stomped toward her and again squeezed her upper arm as hard as he could, his jagged nails piercing her skin. He reached for the handkerchief. "Time for this to go back in." His hands shook as he replaced the foul handkerchief in her mouth as a gag. "We're just about ready to go."

Go where? She knew if he got her out of the family fitness center, her chances of survival slimmed dramatically. There had to be a way to get away.

She groaned something, attempting to speak beneath the bandana.

He yanked it out of her mouth again. "What is it?"

Jasper didn't replace the handkerchief, but he did reach up and pinched one of her cheeks and twisted as hard as he could, bringing tears to her eyes. "Don't even try to escape. You will not succeed." He opened the back door that led into the alleyway, dragged her to her feet she teetered due to her ankles being bound. She tried to hit him with her bound hands, but Jasper, who was surprisingly strong, hoisted her onto the back seat of his older model extended cab truck. Her head hit the armrest on the opposite door, and pain radiated through her skull.

Jasper climbed in, started the truck, put it into reverse, and slowly pulled out onto the street.

The truck smelled of fast food and body odor. She gazed up to see the lights of the town and tried to memorize where they were going. As long as he didn't apply a blindfold, she might have a chance.

Jasper blared the radio and began tapping his fingers and thumbs on the steering wheel in a rhythmic beat to the screeching of some unrecognizable rock song. A canned woman's voice interrupted the last few strains of the tune. "1970s rock and roll, all day, every day."

The glucose pills kicked in, and a surge of energy overcame her.

She could do this. She could.

Lord, make me strong.

She flattened herself as much as possible. Now was the time to attempt to break free. How much of her could he see in his rearview mirror? Harper squinted in the darkness of the truck. They came to an intersection, the stoplights temporarily illuminating the cab. She inspected the duct tape that he'd wrapped around her wrists. Looking for the seam, she slowly and quietly reached it to her mouth and picked at the tape with her teeth.

It was only by the Lord's mercy that Jasper had not replaced the handkerchief. Were there people around who would hear if she screamed? She didn't see any lights of other vehicles, but then there could be cars nearby that were not as tall as Jasper's truck. Dare she try to raise her legs and press them against the window? It was doubtful anybody would be able to see through the black tint. No, there had to be another way she would have to break free from her constraints.

Jasper muted the radio just as the sound of ripping tape echoed in the cab. He suddenly stopped the vehicle, and Harper lurched to the right, nearly rolling off the seat. He turned around to face her, his eyes darting to her wrists.

FORTY-ONE

Kade sat at his computer. He rubbed his temples and blinked his eyes, forcing them to focus on the computer screen. It had been a long day, and he looked forward to when Trace would be back on the job after his accident. This jurisdiction definitely needed more than just him and Gossett, and he missed his friend and partner.

He glanced at his half-eaten sub sandwich. The thought of the cold, dried-out meal did nothing for his appetite. That's how it was for him once he set his mind on something—his focus was rigid and steadfast until he came to the conclusion he was seeking. Tenacity, that's what he preferred to call it. He meandered to the coffee pot and poured the remains of the weak brew into his mug. He needed to log in at least a couple more hours before his day was over.

Kade glanced at his watch—9:02 p.m. He stifled the yawn, eased back into his chair, and scanned the contents of the open manila folder for the new case that had just landed on his desk.

The ringing of his phone, indicating an internal call from dispatch, interrupted his thoughts. "Lassiter."

"Kade, this is Nathan. I just received a phone call from a Mr. Blumenstock on the 911 line. It's about Harper Amerson. He's asking for you."

"Patch him through." Worry gnawed at Kade as he lifted the phone headset. "Detective Lassiter."

"Hello, Detective. My family and I were at the fitness center for our daughter's basketball game this evening and had agreed to accompany Harper home." Mr. Blumenstock's words tumbled one right after the other, and Kade pressed the phone against his ear in an effort to better comprehend the man's rambling.

Harper had informed him about the Blumenstocks. "All right."

"Yes, sir, but there was a problem."

Kade's heartbeat twinged up a notch. "Yes?"

"We were at the basketball game when our daughter got sick. She vomited on the gym floor, and we had to rush out of there in a hurry. I'm ashamed to say that Harper was not at the top of our concerns."

"Did you get in touch with her and tell her that you were leaving early?"

"Yes. After we arrived home and got our daughter settled, I hopped into the van and drove back to the fitness center. The doors were already locked, and people had gone home for the day, but Harper's SUV was still in the parking lot. I pounded on the door, but nobody answered. Also, I tried to call and text her several times, but she never responded."

Kade's chest clenched. Something wasn't right. He was already standing and tugging on his coat while he held the phone in the crook of his neck. "The last time you saw her was at the fitness center?"

"Yes. We walked in just ahead of her, and I'm assuming she went to the cardio room while my family and I went to the gym for the basketball tournaments."

"All right, thank you. If you hear from her, would you please let me know?" Kade rattled off his number and had barely hung up from the call when he was already out the door and unlocking the door of his service vehicle. Depending upon what he found, he may need backup.

He called Harper's cell, but it went directly to voicemail. Next, he drove to her house, but her vehicle was not in the carport, and all of the lights were off. He spun a quick U-turn and proceeded down the side streets to the Lake Radford Family Fitness Center.

The half of the sub sandwich he'd eaten didn't sit well in his stomach. It wasn't like Harper to not let someone know what was going on, especially in light of recent events. He would need to call Kennedy next.

He pulled into the parking lot, but Harper's SUV was nowhere to be found. He knocked on the fitness center's door, but there was no answer. He called Harper's number again, and again it went to voicemail. Kade then dialed Kennedy's number, which Harper had given to him as an emergency number and introduced himself when her friend answered.

"Have you by any chance heard from Harper?"

"No, I haven't. Is something wrong?" He could hear the concern in her voice.

He explained the situation and heard Kennedy's sharp inhalation of breath. "Do you have any idea where she might be?" he asked.

"No, I haven't seen her since yesterday. I've been home sick with a bad strain of the flu and wasn't able to go to the gym with her tonight." Kennedy gave him the number of Harper's boss in case there had been a late showing.

"If Harper contacts you or shows up at your house, have her call me immediately." He rattled off his number, disconnected, then notified dispatch to send an alert about a possible missing woman.

The problem was, he wasn't even sure where to look.

He called the owner of Lake Radford Realty and Rentals, but a woman named Paulette confirmed there had been no late showings. She agreed to drive to the office and see if Harper had been there. Fifteen minutes later, the woman informed Kade that Harper had not been at the office since that afternoon.

Kade prayed for wisdom, then returned to the gym's parking lot. By now, with an alert sent out, others would be looking for her as well. He cruised around the corner, going slowly down each side street. Perhaps she had broken down. And then a couple of blocks away at a dentist's office, he spied what looked like her SUV. He ran the license plate number, and sure enough, it was registered to her.

He rushed back to his vehicle, and a thought came to him. He recalled Harper saying at the 5K barbecue that she logged in all of her workouts into her fitness tracker and about how she'd preferred the information be on her laptop rather than the cell phone app.

He punched in Kennedy's number, and she answered on the first ring. Her breathless voice sounded over the line. "Did you find her?"

"Not yet. Do you have a key to Harper's house?"

"Yes, I do."

"I'm coming to get it. I need to access her laptop and the information for her fitness tracker.

"Oh, yes, she logs everything in," said Kennedy

He disconnected and was at her house six blocks away within minutes. He ran up the steps, and she held open the door and handed it to him. "Please let me know the second you find her." He agreed to do so, then sprinted back to his car and headed toward Harper's house. Maybe he would find her there, maybe she just had an errand to run, although he doubted she would be that foolish in running an errand so late at night.

But he could hope.

And pray.

That she was safe and nothing nefarious had happened.

Exigent circumstances existed, so thankfully, he didn't need a warrant. Who knew how long that would take?

Once at Harper's house, he went directly to the table in the living room where she kept her laptop. He opened it and fired it up. He wasn't really exactly sure he would be able to access what he needed, but he was going to try. And hopefully, it would tell him what he needed to know.

Lord, please help us find her!

He clicked on the fitness tracker desktop app. Thankfully, she didn't have it password-protected.

Her dashboard popped up. It showed that she had run 5.14 miles earlier that evening, along with her time. He clicked around and found how many floors she had climbed today and how many days of exercise this week. Then he clicked over to the map that showed the GPS and where she had run. Then a "walk" which started an hour ago and was continuing. He enlarged the map and zoomed in on the location. She had left the fitness center and traveled down several streets, including Alberta Avenue, which connected to the road that went to the Cox property.

"Good girl, Harper," he said under his breath. She was still allowing the watch to track her location.

Kade got on his cell phone and called for backup, then hustled out the door and into his vehicle.

He hoped he wasn't too late.

FORTY-TWO

Had he heard the sound of tape ripping? She put her hands down in front of her and held her breath. And prayed.

Jasper said nothing but waited as tenuous seconds ticked by before he again turned up the radio and began tapping on his steering wheel. She again raised her wrists to her mouth and continued her plan. The skin on her wrists tingled from the adhesive and ached from the stationery position in which she'd had to hold them for so long.

Now for her feet. That would take more doing and would likely be louder, but she doubted he'd be able to hear it due to the music, his drumming, and the roar of the engine. But would he see her knees when she brought them up to her chest so she could reach the tape and unwind it? Likely so.

Would there be a better time to achieve her goal? Or should she act now and deal with the consequences of him possibly hearing her, stopping the vehicle, and rebinding her?

Lord...please, please give me wisdom. You say in the Book of James that You give wisdom to all who ask. Please give me wisdom.

She carefully and methodically situated herself onto her side. Jasper muted the radio again. He put the truck in park, and it jerked, rolling Harper to the floor. Was she too late? Had they already reached Jasper's destination?

He killed the engine and flung open the door, allowing a flood of cold air to enter the truck. He jumped out of the cab, jerked the back driver's side door open, and roughly lifted her from the floor. Harper held her hands together, praying he wouldn't notice the tape had been torn. "You'd better not try anything, Harper," he growled before he backhanded her across the mouth.

She winced and tasted blood. *Lord, please let me have more time. Please protect me.*

Would he gag her again? At least now she had her hands for the tape around her ankles. Her legs and entire body trembled, but she did her best to keep her hands firmly together.

Jasper's flared nostrils, loud breathing, and reddened face shown in the shadows of the dome light. Finally, satisfied she wasn't going to run away, he slammed the door, took his place in the driver's seat, and fired up the truck once again.

Harper lifted her knees all the way up to her chest so she could reach her ankles. She'd heard many times that the Lord's fingerprints were all over someone's life. And she knew that nothing happened without His knowledge and without a purpose. Such was the case for her taking gymnastics for several years as a child. While she hadn't always enjoyed waking up early to go to the lessons, she was now grateful to Mom and insisted she go to the class. Had she not, she would not be as flexible as she was and able to remove the bindings from her ankles.

Jasper increased the speed of the vehicle, and she ascertained they were leaving the downtown and residential areas. Where were they? Martin Street? Alberta Avenue?

Lord, please go before me.

She couldn't see much in the darkness, but the area seemed vaguely familiar, even from her location in the truck.

He started to sing along with the music, his off-key voice terrorizing her eardrums.

Jasper slowed the truck, turned a corner, and she heard gravel beneath the tires. Perfect between that and his singing, she could now remove the tape from her ankles, hopefully without him hearing her. As quietly as possible, her trembling and nearly numb fingers unraveled the duct tape round and round as slowly and quietly as possible. The truck hit a pothole, and she bounced on the seat.

The tape had stuck well to her tall, brown boots, and the unraveling was no easy task.

The truck screeched to a stop. She gazed out the window into complete darkness. A low fog surrounded the area. Where were they?

Jasper flung open the door. "Time for you to meet your demise, Harper Amerson."

He banked on her being bound, which worked in her favor. With the hardest kick she could manage, her right foot connected with his face. She followed it with a second kick. Blood spurted from his nose, and he stumbled backwards, the oaths flying from his mouth and stinging her ears.

Harper rushed past him. The surroundings looked familiar—she was on the very back end of the Cox property.

Her ankles throbbed from being bound so tightly, and her legs protested. Her feet slid in the muddy weeds as she bolted away from him. Jasper's huffing and puffing sounded in her ears, and she stepped up the pace. The cold air lapped at her face, and she struggled to see where she was going due to the fog and darkness. A branch snapped behind her. Her foot hit a rock, and she tumbled to the ground.

The pain radiated through Harper's entire leg, and her head throbbed. The fall tore her pants at the knee. Her weak legs made it a struggle to stand. Jasper's heavy breathing alerted her that he was nearby. When had he become a runner? For as long as she'd known him, which was a couple of years, he hadn't seemed like the athletic type.

Harper limped, prayed for endurance to run this race well, then pushed herself, her breath coming out in a vapor in front of her in the cold weather. His hand swiped at her arm, and she teetered before escaping his grasp. Jasper may have the benefit of dinner on his side, but she had something better. The Lord.

No stars and no moon, just a dark and foggy night. No guidance on her next steps as her eyes strained to see two steps ahead of her. Harper's boots brushed along the damp weeds. In a night like this with its high humidity and stark cloud cover, a person could freeze. Thankfully, she had her coat and hat.

Somewhere along the way, there was a path that the Coxes had mowed last year through the brush that led to the entrance to the property. She just had to find it. Or she could turn around and head the way they'd come. But in the gloominess, she couldn't even see Jasper's truck. Harper kept running, feeling the chilly and murky fog on her skin.

The pond came into view, and while she couldn't ascertain it in the night, she knew zigzagged clumps of ice remained from the especially frigid winter. She darted around the edge to her destination—the entrance to the Cox property.

Every part of her ached, from her head to her face, wrists, ankles, and her arm where Jasper had dug his fingernails into her tender flesh. Reality jolted her. When she did reach the road—and she aimed to—where would she go? There were no nearby neighbors.

Harper's foot landed in a hole likely from a rodent, and her ankle tweaked. Wincing, she hastened on. She'd always considered the pond a selling point, but now, it was a detriment. Harper would need to take a wide berth to get around it. She veered to the right when she felt a shove behind her, causing her to stagger before she crashed, hitting the hard earth below.

Jasper grabbed her by the arm. "Thought you would get away, did you?"

She *would* get away. And she *would* fight back. Harper patted the ground beside her, searching for something that could be used as a weapon. She lifted a rock and swung it at his ear. Jasper fell backward, allotting her time to struggle to her feet. But he recovered and grabbed a handful of her hair. He jerked her head back, stalling her briefly as they wrestled at the edge of the pond. She attempted to scoot away from the perimeter, knowing the icy pond was a death sentence with the threat of hypothermia.

Harper crawled, dodging Jasper's reach. Wet earth soaked through her pants. He advanced and shoved her. She floundered and stumbled into the pond, and the water sloshed up to just above her ankles. Thankfully, she maintained her balance and rushed back out of the water, her frozen feet slowing her movements. Jasper muttered a string of curse words, but she had one thing on her mind. To reach the truck, where she would at least have shelter and lock herself away from his aggressive attempts to kill her. Perhaps there, she'd find his phone and could call for help.

Was that another rock on the ground? She bent, lifted it, and threw it at Jasper. From his mutterings, it must have hit him.

The dreary night spun around her as she struggled to gain her bearings. Which way was the truck? Harper began to shiver uncontrollably. Why was everything so confusing? *"Even though I walk through the valley of the shadow of death, I will fear no evil, for you are with me; your rod and your staff, they comfort me."* She clung to the verse even as drowsiness set in. She lifted her gaze to the cloudy sky above. "Lord, you have brought me this far. Please help me find my way to the truck."

She could die out here, and no one would find her for days, if not longer. Nobody knew she was here. Nobody knew Jasper had kidnapped her. Harper forced the reality aside. She would keep her eyes on the One who had given His life for her on the cross.

An owl hooted, and a coyote howled. The roar of an engine sounded nearby, or maybe it was just her imagination. Headlights bobbed in the distance. Harper waved her arms and shouted "help" several times.

A bright light flashed her way, and she screamed for help again.

"Harper!"

"Yes. Over here!"

A flashlight bobbed up and down in the dark through the trees. She recognized the voice, or maybe she was just imagining things. Strong arms wrapped around her before lifting her.

Or maybe she was just dreaming. She closed her eyes, and everything went dark.

FORTY-THREE

"Harper! Stay with me, Harper!" Ironic that he'd been wanting to hold her in his arms, but not under these circumstances.

Kade removed his coat, covered her with it, then, launching into a run, he endeavored to dodge the unseen obstacles in his path as he veered back to the service vehicle. Gossett had his back, and in the distance, the whine of a siren echoed in the air, confirming his call for backup had been answered. He thanked the Lord profusely before finally reaching his own car, grappling for the door, and placing Harper inside before starting it up and putting the heater on full blast.

"Kade..." she croaked, her voice edged in pain.

"Don't try to talk." *Just please...please be all right.*

She had to be all right.

He prayed again, his throat constricting at the thought of all she'd been through.

"It was...it was Jasper."

"Jasper? From the fitness center?"

"Yes."

"Don't worry. We'll get him."

Jasper Ceruitti, a man who hadn't even been on Kade's radar, but Kade knew that as the investigation proceeded, the pieces would begin to fit together.

But they had to find him first.

And even more importantly, Harper had to survive the hypothermia that had set in.

He balled his hands at his sides. He'd come so close to losing her. Could still lose her. Was it possible to care for someone the way he was beginning to care for her? He slid back into the car and held Harper in his arms, attempting to warm her.

What if he hadn't reached her in time? What if this turned out like the case in Fairmont? What if he lost the woman he'd hoped to have a future with? There was only one antidote for the fear that pierced his heart. Kade lifted his eyes to the One who could calm the trepidation. The One who was faithful.

Beneath his car's dome light, he saw a crusted scab, a swollen eye, and several scratches marred her beautiful face. She was so pale, her body shaking as she shivered. What had she been through at the hands of an unhinged psychopath? Kade leaned over and planted a kiss on her forehead. "Harper, you're going to be all right."

He climbed into the driver's side of his service vehicle, and Gossett settled into the passenger side. The heat, now blowing full bore, would hopefully warm Harper. He glanced behind him where he'd set her in the backseat. Her head lolled to one side, her breathing slow but steady. He again prayed that she would be all right and that she would heal completely from this latest assault. He'd stay inside the service vehicle and guard Harper until backup and the ambulance arrived. After that? He'd make it his personal mission to track down Cerruti.

Kade and Gossett kept their heads on a swivel. Why did it seem like the other units and the ambulance were taking their precious time to arrive? While he knew that wasn't the case and the roads were icy, he still wished they'd hurry.

The breaking of glass on the rear window caused him to duck. "Get down!" he shouted, just as another bullet was fired and pinged the left fender. Kade pulled his weapon, rolled down his window, and returned fire, just as three more shots rang out.

From the corner of his eye, he caught a glimpse of movement near a grove of trees, and he flicked on his bright lights, catching Jasper Cerruti in the spotlight.

"Shots fired," Kade yelled into his radio. "I repeat, shots fired."

In his rearview mirror, he saw the other units skidding on the ice and the ambulance hanging back.

Kade aimed at the grove and fired again, maintaining his position. A cursory glance at Gossett told him she was prepared for anything.

"Put your weapon down!" he shouted through the window.

"She betrayed me, and betrayal has consequences!"

"Put the weapon down, Cerruti!"

But instead of heeding Kade's words, Cerruti ran toward the service vehicle, firing more shots. Thankfully, he had poor aim. Kade fired his as well, and Cerruti fell to the ground, the threat temporarily eliminated.

Kade and Gossett jumped from the car and held their guns on the man as fellow officers flooded the scene. "It's over, Cerruti."

Cerruti cursed.

Officers gave the all-clear to the ambulance, and Kade directed the EMTs to the back of his service vehicle, where they tended to Harper and loaded her into the back of the ambulance. Another had been called for Cerruti, who kept screaming incoherent nonsense about betrayal.

Kade climbed into the back with Harper. There was no way he was leaving her side.

EPILOGUE

After lunch at Sheila's, Harper and Kade wandered down Main Street, window shopping. A lot had changed in the three months since Jasper Cerutti attempted to take Harper's life. God had spared her, and she never allowed a day to pass when she didn't express her gratitude.

Things returned to normal, along with some surprising new developments. Grandma and Grandpa eagerly moved into The Cottages, and Grandma reconnected with all of her old friends. It was as if she and Grandpa had never left. Grandpa was doing well after his stroke and had taken up one of his favorite pastimes—fishing.

Several of the men from church, including the elders, Kade, Dad, and Kade's best friend, Trace, who had fully healed from his injuries, built a fence for Mrs. Satterwhite. Now, Coco could run freely in the backyard without worries of her escaping.

Zephyr was doing well, and with Ryan, had assisted with unloading Grandma and Grandpa's possessions from the move. Zephyr, thanks to Ryan's tutoring, graduated and secured a job at the local detailing shop. He was considering potentially going into law enforcement. Even more importantly, last week, he'd surrendered his life to Christ and had made a public profession of his faith by being baptized. While his mom still wasn't open to the idea of attending church, Zephyr continued to invite her.

Kennedy secured the job at the Lake Radford Senior Citizen Center, a job perfect for someone who'd always appreciated the elderly population. Trace was back to work as a detective, partnering with Kade to solve the crimes that plagued the town.

Justice would be served on Jasper Cerutti. He'd authored both the note and the letter, had made the phone call to Harper, and had "hired" Mr. Motta to chase Harper, fire the shots at the Cox property, and assault Harper both in her neighborhood and in the parking lot by The Cottages. The man he'd killed had been missing for two years and was discovered in an area on the Cox property that likely would have been excavated had the Medills purchased it for their new home. Jeff and Vanna Cox's son's prognosis was good, and with the assistance of many, they were able to pay for his treatment. They removed the property listing and haven't yet decided what they'd do with the acreage.

Kade squeezed Harper's hand. "Let's stop into Dumaine's. I haven't been in there since the investigation."

Harper raised on tiptoe and kissed her boyfriend on the cheek. "You are acting so suspicious today."

Kade feigned surprise. "I am?"

"Oh, yes." After dating him for three months, Harper had come to realize that her handsome boyfriend struggled with keeping a stoic expression. At least with her. A man couldn't very well be a detective if his face gave everything away.

"Hmm. I hadn't noticed." He smirked and wrapped an arm around her.

They perused the specialty clothing items, the baseball cards, and some local gift items when Kade turned and pointed to a retro photo booth with its dark brown paneling exterior and a red curtain across the doorway. "We have to get a photo."

"Sure." That was one of the things she appreciated about Kade, how fun he was and how he wasn't afraid to do goofy things like cram into an iconic photo booth.

The black and white tiled floor added to the nostalgia, and Kade inserted the money. In the first photo, they did their best to smile normally. The second, they made a face, in the third, Harper's eyes were closed, and in the fourth, Kade was looking up instead of at the camera. "I think we need one more round," he suggested.

As they prepared for this round of photos, Kade fiddled with his shirt pocket and produced a ring. "Harper Amerson, will you marry me?"

"What? I...yes!"

That photo was the best as it had captured her complete surprise at his proposal. "We have one more picture."

He leaned toward her and captured her lips with his, sending her senses into spin mode with a kiss that deepened in passion until they heard the camera click.

"Perfect," Kade said, extracting the most recent strip. He placed the ring on her finger. "I know it's soon, and we haven't known each other for long..."

Was it possible for the first time in her life that she was speechless? So she merely nodded in agreement.

"But when you know, you just know."

Her pulse skittered as his lips claimed hers once more, sealing the promise of a wonderful future.

DEADLY SCHEMES

What happened last night hadn't really needed to happen. It certainly wasn't planned months or years in advance, like some things were.

But one had to be spontaneous if one was to succeed at lofty endeavors.

And, of course, people were often blind and had an idealistic view of always seeing the best in others—thinking he was all that and a bag of chips when it came to his "generous" personality.

He chuckled to himself. Their naivety was his gain.

He was patting himself on the back when he heard the screen door open. She stepped into the room, her long hair flowing around her face, and the immaculate, expensive clothing she wore only to work showing their success.

She was so beautiful. So smart.

His perfect partner.

Two steps and he was beside her. He wrapped his arms around her and nuzzled her ear. He had missed her when they went their separate ways this morning. He couldn't wait to see her and talk about the progress they'd made.

They shared most of their schemes.

Emphasis on *most*.

This latest development had been his little private se-cret—a small plan, a feather in his cap, as the saying went. Ah, the triumph when he'd succeeded.

Oh, he'd tell her later when the time was right. For now, she didn't need to know he had unexpectedly added murder to their list of crimes.

"I missed you."

She turned to face him. "I missed you, too."

Man, but she was attractive. Always had been, from the moment they met. Prettier than any Hollywood actress—and more cunning than anyone he knew.

Well, except for himself.

That's why they made such a great pair.

There was no acting when it came to his feelings for her. All the years they'd been together, all the plans they shared, and all they had accomplished. And now, they were living a life they'd never dreamed possible.

Together, they were unstoppable—invincible.

DON'T MISS THIS SNEAK PEEK

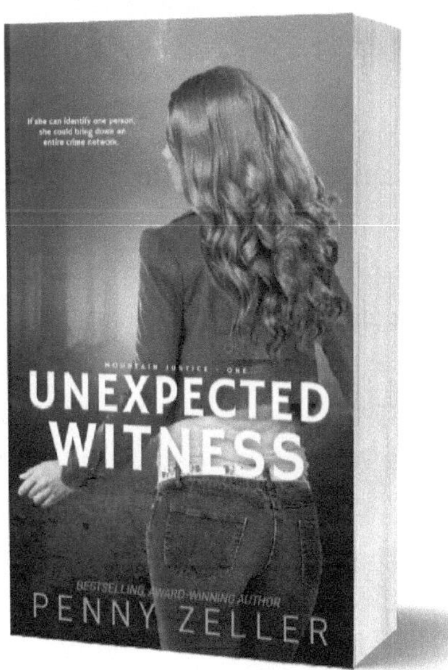

If she can identify one person, she could
bring down an entire crime network.

MOUNTAIN JUSTICE - BOOK ONE

Unexpected Witness

The day couldn't get any worse.

Mila charted the information from her last patient, relishing the silence after what had been a chaotic eight hours. Dr. Burch left fifteen minutes ago, and after she tended to a few more tasks, Mila would be on the road home as well. Her legs throbbed from little downtime, and a headache formed at her temples, courtesy of the challenging patients who collectively decided to make today their day for an appointment. Add to that the pungent stench of vomit still lingering in the air from an earlier patient, despite Mila's best attempts to sanitize the area several times. Thankfully, within the hour, she'd be on her way home where leftovers, a new book she'd borrowed from the library, and a hot bath awaited her.

She jumped as a loud banging on the front door interrupted the silence. The light above the door gave just enough of a clue as to the visitor's identity. That and his trademark worn-out red tennis shoes.

"What's he doing here again?" Brittaney Mead, the administrative assistant, stalked to the door she'd locked only moments before. "He's already been here once today." She cracked open the door and glared at the visitor. "You," she hissed.

"I gotta be seen."

"No, you don't. You were already seen today and besides, we closed twenty minutes ago. It's a Friday night. Go home."

"But..."

"No, go home. You got what you needed."

Mila started toward the door. "If he needs—"

"He doesn't." Brittaney shut the door and locked it again, waving away the man. "Besides, he can come back Monday."

Mila hated turning anyone away, even if the patient was a hypochondriac who stopped by nearly every day with a new ailment. She watched as Troy Pollard limped into the darkness. Mila finished charting, then emptied the trash cans while Brittaney resumed tending to a matter on her phone.

"There's Antonio," Brittaney said as car lights shone upon the outdoor steps. "Gotta go."

Antonio, Brittaney's boyfriend, pulled up alongside the clinic in his larger-than-life four-wheel drive truck with a massive lift kit. He honked the horn not once, but four times.

Brittaney grabbed her belongings and dashed out the door.

Leaving Mila alone in a building that was too quiet, too still, save the ticking of the wall clock with the second hand perpetually stuck on the number three.

Not much happened in Upton, population 1,498, even at seven at night, and especially not with a winter weather advisory in effect for a spring snowstorm. Who in their right mind would be out in that type of weather?

Besides, this wasn't the first time Mila had been the last one to leave.

Why then were her hands shaking as she completed her time card?

The furnace kicked on with a rumble. The noise startled her, and Mila took a few deep breaths to calm her already anxious mind.

Lights from a passerby illuminated the now nearly dark office, lingering longer than necessary toward where Mila stood.

She just wanted to get home.

Moments later, her clump of keys firmly in one hand and her purse on her arm, Mila stepped out of the clinic, locked the door, and grabbed the black railing as she made her way down the stairs and to the parking lot.

Streetlights overhead cast an eerie glow through the thickly falling snowflakes. A cup of tea and a bubble bath beckoned her before getting some much-needed sleep and repeating the process all over again tomorrow.

When Mila parked her car eight hours ago, it hadn't seemed so far away. But now, doing her best not to slip on the unshoveled parking lot, it could have been five miles to her vehicle.

The wind whipped around her, and she quickened her pace. Her car was just steps ahead.

It was then that she saw two figures to her left near a light-colored car. One person had his back to the car while the other stood facing him. She couldn't hear words being spoken, but she could see spasmodic movements.

Impending doom jolted her, but she shoved the fear aside. This wasn't the time for an overactive imagination.

Mila took a few steps back, debating whether to continue to her car, which was much closer than heading back to the clinic. Perhaps it was just two people in a spirited conversation.

But this late at night and in this weather?

She eyed her car, now only a few paces away, and squinted through the swirling wet snow that hampered her vision. She shuffled toward her car, attempting to hurry, but not slip.

And then Mila noticed something she could never erase from her memory.

She saw contact made from one person to the other. One withdrew his arm, knife in hand, the street light glinting off a dark substance coating the blade. The attacker braced the victim against the car, then launched into a series of rapid stabs. The victim slumped and crumpled to the ground.

Mila's legs locked and her body went numb. The attacker pivoted toward her.

Move, feet, move!

She willed her feet to obey.

He rushed toward her, knife in hand.

Mila's brain kicked into motion, and she fumbled with the key fob, furiously pushing the button to unlock the door. She reached for the door handle.

The fob had failed.

Again.

She pressed furiously on the button. *Unlock, unlock!*

Mila cleared a spot by wiping the snow with her hand, manually stuck the key into the lock, and flung open the door. She scrambled into the front seat and slammed the door.

Her heart constricted and her breath came in gasps.

Lock the car!

In her panic, Mila fumbled and accidentally hit the unlock button instead.

The man drew nearer, and finally, with a stutter, the lock clicked.

Her hand trembled and she twice missed the ignition before finally inserting the key. Someone—the man?—yelled, and everything moved as if in slow motion.

A hard fist pounded the driver's side window. The man yanked on the door handle, jerking the car. Did he have a gun?

The car refused to start. Mila turned the key to the crank position once again. *Lord, please!*

The man leaped on the hood of the car, his agile body apparently giving no care to the slippery conditions. He pressed his face against the snow-covered windshield. His hoodie covered most of his eyes and all of his forehead, but she could see his nostrils flaring. *Memorize his appearance, or what you can see of it, anyway.* The police would want a physical description.

If she made it to the police station.

The street light flickered, then blinked off completely. Mila attempted to start the car again as a mixture of fear and frustration overwhelmed her.

The engine finally roared to life. As quickly as he pounced on the hood, the man flung himself off and ran away. Begging her heart to return to a normal beating pattern, Mila didn't wait to see where he went. Instead, she shifted the car into reverse, but her tires spun on the ice as they sought traction. Completely backed out of the parking spot, she put the car into drive and cranked the wheel. The headlights illuminated the victim.

And his red shoes.

Mila fought the urge to retch.

She simultaneously turned on the windshield and rear defrosters and zipped out of the parking lot and toward the highway. At least the man had given up.

Should she pull to the side and call 911? Drive to the police station? She needed to share what she had witnessed.

Even in the dark and with a partially obscured windshield, Mila knew the road well. She traveled the ten miles from her home in Pronghorn Falls to the outlying town of Upton five days a week. The forty-five mile per hour sign reminded her curves lay ahead.

Bright lights appeared in her rearview mirror. An innocent person may be driving the car, but she wouldn't take that chance. Sure enough, the vehicle edged close, confirming her concerns. Mila pressed on the gas pedal and her car lurched ahead. Black ice was still a threat, even during this time of year, and she'd seen far too many victims of the elusive danger.

Nine more miles. Wait. She'd only traveled one mile?

The vehicle pulled up alongside her, then swerved back behind her again when an oncoming car appeared around the curve. Mila strained her eyes through the darkness, her already heightened anxiety levels soaring to nearly beyond manageable.

Her tires spun, causing her to slide and threatening to make her journey into the nearby borrow pit inevitable. She eased off the gas pedal to right herself and continued, ever mindful of the vehicle behind her.

Eight miles.

She gripped the steering wheel as a gust of wind nearly blew her to the shoulder.

Another car passed, coming from the opposite direction. If only there was some way to alert the driver she needed assistance.

She'd never be able to stop now and call for help.

The snow thickened, causing near-whiteout conditions. She'd have to slow down even more. The vehicle behind her nudged her bumper, causing her to almost skid out of control.

Seven miles to go.

Mila dared herself a peek at the dashboard clock: 7:35. She squinted through the darkness. The defroster struggled to do its job, and her heavy breaths weren't helping matters.

The dead battery alert on her phone sounded from within her purse. Why hadn't she remembered to charge it earlier?

The vehicle nudged her bumper again, this time causing her to fishtail.

Five more miles.

Her pursuer attempted to drive alongside her once again. What if he had a gun? Would he attempt to shoot her? Would anyone find her in the middle of a blizzard? Would she freeze to death or die from a gunshot wound?

She prayed again as what-ifs crowded her mind.

Three miles to go.

The car drove beside her for some time, periodically crashing into her. She swerved each time, fearing she'd overcorrect. Her valiant little car stayed its post as she fought to keep it on the road.

Finally, near the junction turnoff, an oncoming semi caused her pursuer to veer back behind her. And that was the last she saw of him.

Mila's hands trembled so badly as she finished the final distance to town that she was unsure she'd be able to keep her car on the road. Snow spattered against the windshield and her heart pounded. The parched cottonmouth sensation made swallowing difficult.

Several times, she checked, then rechecked her rearview mirror for any sign of the car. Would she be able to describe it to the police? A jumble of thoughts, fears, and worries competed for space in her distraught mind.

Had it even been a car? Maybe it was a pickup truck.

No, it was a car. The lights shining through Mila's back window were lower, not elevated as a truck's would be.

Mila barely shut off her car's engine before jetting from the seat and stumbling toward the steps of the police station. The cold air bit through her coat, but the shaking she experienced

from the moment she'd emerged from the clinic had nothing
to do with the cold.

If you want to be among the first to hear about Penny's
latest book projects, sign up for her newsletter
at www.pennyzeller.com. You will receive book and
writing updates, encouragement, notification of current
giveaways, occasional freebies, and special offers.

If you enjoyed this glimpse into the lives of Harper and Kade, please consider leaving a review on your social media, Amazon, Goodreads, Barnes and Noble, or BookBub. Reviews are critical to authors, and those stars you give us are such an encouragement.

Author's Note

Dear Reader,

Thank you for joining me on this suspenseful journey. When I first decided to write *Deadly Secrets*, I knew I wanted to create a strong female character who was just doing her job when she was blindsided by a crazed lunatic. Add in a handsome detective who takes his own job seriously and some faithful supporting characters, and I had the makings of a Christian romantic suspense. One thing I knew from the get-go was that I wanted to include a teen who was given a second chance to make something of his life after getting caught up in the wrong crowd. What better mentor than the godly Kade Lassiter?

As many of you know, I also write in the subgenres of Christian historical romance and Christian rom-coms. For my historicals, I embark on in-depth research, but such is also the case for my suspense novels. Not only do I spend time online researching, but I also bounce a multitude of questions off those currently or formerly in law enforcement. Evil behaviors and real-life crimes are another research topic. Such was the case with the robbery at Dumaine's, which was inspired by an actual event. People watching, including observing character traits, little quirks, and how random people respond to situations, has helped create characters. As always, fictional liberties are taken for plot purposes.

As one who has struggled with non-diabetic hypoglycemia of an unknown cause for years, writing Harper's symptoms came easily.

During the editing process, it was discovered that some plants are more unique than others. Case in point with this "minor" editing error that, thankfully, was caught before the book went to print: "You're in a rush. Special plants for tonight?" As one who loves flowers, might I suggest the special plants were daisies?

If you loved *Deadly Secrets*, please join me for *Deadly Schemes*, Kennedy and Trace's story. Also on the agenda is the third book in the series, which will feature Laurel and Griff.

As always, thank you for being a loyal reader. I appreciate you so much!

Until next time, happy reading!

Blessings,

Penny

Acknowledgments

Writing a book is never possible without the help of many. Thank you to my family for all of your encouragement. A special thank you to my oldest for acting out some of the scenes with me to make sure what I thought would happen in my mind would truly happen. And to my youngest, an avid suspense reader, who assisted me with some additional details.

To my Penny's Peeps Street Team. Thank you for spreading the word about my books, for always being so willing to read and review my stories, and for your steadfast encouragement and support.

To my beta readers. You are the ones who see my project at its beginning stages. Thank you for all of your wonderful suggestions.

To Gary Ellis, retired law enforcement, for ensuring my police procedures were accurate. I am so appreciative of all the time you spend poring over my manuscripts and providing me with detailed information. I couldn't have written this without your valuable insight.

To JJ and the others in my Crime Scene Writers group. I appreciate your patience in answering my numerous questions about laws, police procedure, and scenarios. JJ, you are a wealth of knowledge!

To my developmental editor at Mountain Peak Edits & Design. What would I do without your guidance on ensuring plots, characters, and settings are the very best they can be?

Thank you to Dodie for answering my questions about being a dispatcher for the police department. I appreciate your expertise and knowledge.

Thank you to Patti for being so willing to answer my question about proper subpoena protocol for pharmacies.

To my readers, may God bless you and guide you as you grow in your walk with Him.

And, most importantly, thank you to my Lord and Savior, Jesus Christ. It is my deepest desire to glorify You with my writing and help bring others to a knowledge of Your saving grace.

About the Author

Penny Zeller is known for her heartfelt stories of faith-filled happily ever afters and her passion to impact lives for Christ through fiction. Her books feature tender romance, steady doses of humor, and memorable characters that stay with you long after the last page.

While she has had a love for writing since childhood, Penny began her adult writing career penning articles for national and regional publications on a wide variety of topics. Today Penny is a multi-published author of over three dozen books and is also a fitness instructor, loves the outdoors, and is a flower gardening addict. In her spare time, she enjoys camping, hiking, kayaking, biking, birdwatching, reading, running, and playing volleyball.

Penny resides with her husband and two daughters in small-town America and loves to connect with her readers at her website at www.pennyzeller.com, her blog, www.pennyzeller.wordpress.com, and her Facebook page at www.facebook.com/pennyzellerbooks where she posts faith, funnies, writing updates, and encouragement. All of her socials can be found at https://linktr.ee/pennyzeller.

Christian Romantic Suspense

Close Proximity

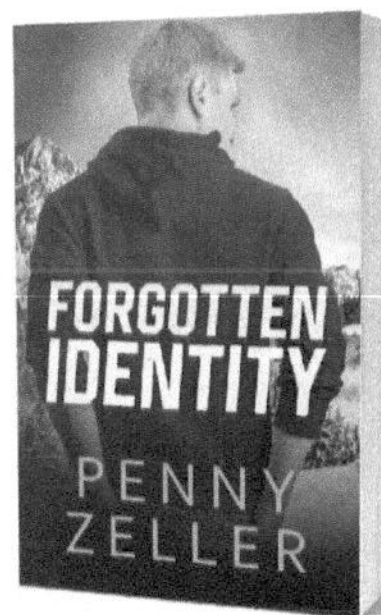  

Mountain Justice

WYOMING SUNRISE

HOLLOW CREEK

PENNY ZELLER
Over the HORIZON
HORIZON SERIES, BOOK ONE

PENNY ZELLER
Dreams on the HORIZON
HORIZON SERIES, BOOK TWO

PENNY ZELLER
Beyond the HORIZON
HORIZON SERIES, BOOK THREE

PENNY ZELLER
Love on the HORIZON
HORIZON SERIES, BOOK FOUR

LOVE LETTERS FROM ELLIS CREEK

Hilltop Series

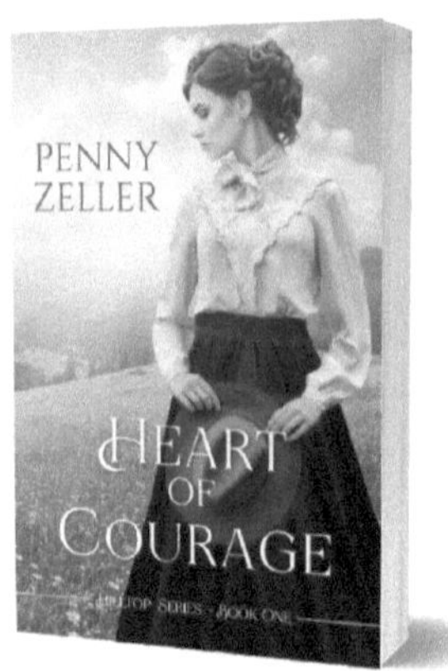

MONTANA HEARTS

small town shenanigans

christian rom-coms

CONTEMPORARY ROMANCES

STANDALONE

CHOKECHERRY HEIGHTS SERIES